STORM FALL

STORM FALL

REBEL WING

BOOK TWO

TRACY BANGHART

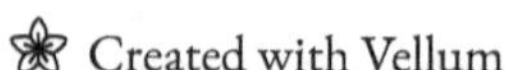 Created with Vellum

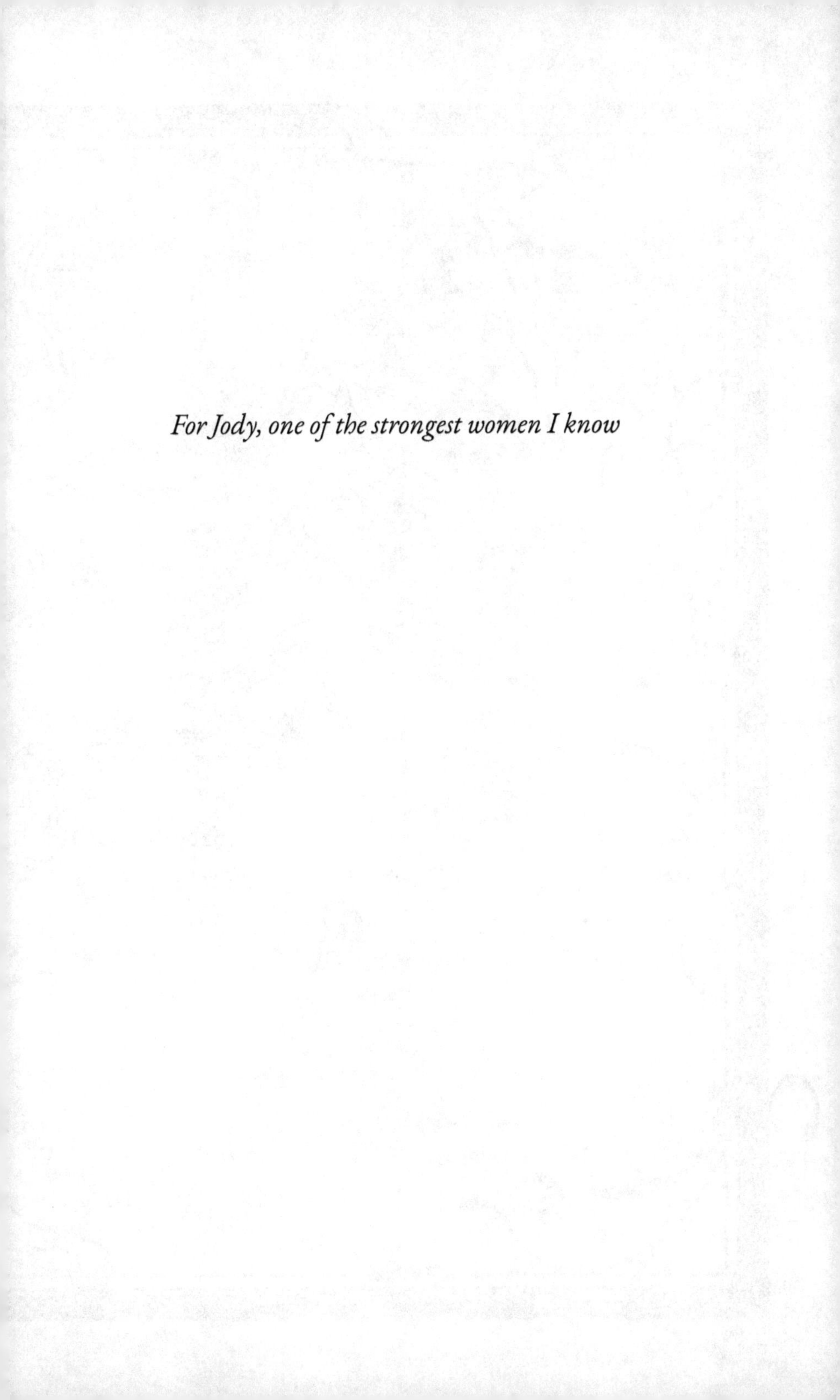

For Jody, one of the strongest women I know

RUSLANA
Pakan
Spiro
Feln
Revening
Tarik
Hevensack
SAFARA

olvik
Cress
PANTHEA
Pono
Lux
ATALANTA

ARIS

MILEK

DYSIS

CALIX

GALENA

PYRALIS

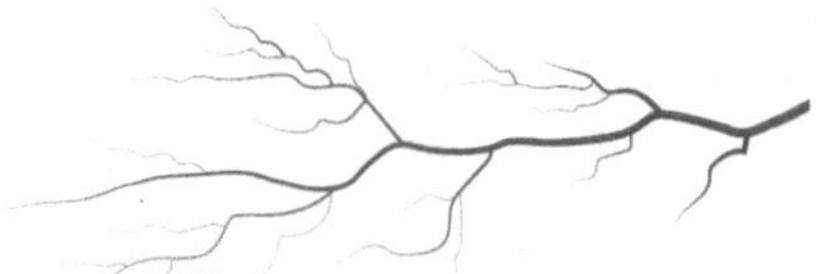

Chapter One

The swish of a wingjet, close overhead, sent Aris Haan to the shadows. She crept along the rough stone wall of her parents' home, her ears picking up a rush and then silence as the jet landed nearby. No doubt it was someone visiting the neighbors, or her mother returning early from work. But Aris needed to see for herself. It didn't matter that she was in the lazy seaside village of Lux; war had taught her that danger could find her anywhere.

Aris reached the arch that led to the landing pad and froze. A second wingjet perched next to hers. But unlike her mother's, this jet was needle nosed and a pale shimmering blue.

A Military wingjet.

She was caught between the desire to run away—away from the memories of her time as a soldier and the injustice that had sent her home—and the urge to fling herself toward the man she hoped would emerge.

With a hiss, the shield opened.

Short golden hair shone in the glare of the sun. Pale skin, with that knife-thin scar along his cheek. Two clear blue eyes locked onto hers.

"Milek." Her heart lurched. She'd almost resigned herself to never seeing him again. For a short moment, her life as Aristos didn't feel quite so far away.

It had been almost a year since Aris had been recruited to be a flyer in Atalanta's all-male Military, which was close to buckling under the Safaran invasion. Almost a year since she'd first met Dianthe, the terrifying, snake-tattooed woman who'd trained her and programmed the holographic diatous veil that had transformed Aris into Aristos, a "male" soldier.

And it had been two months since Aris had woken in the blank, white room of a mender clinic to find Milek Vadim, her commanding officer, gone, with no message or goodbye, and her place within her unit revoked. Worse, her part in the rescue of Ruslana's Ward Vadim, Milek's mother, had been erased. Because she'd done it as a woman, not as Aristos. Her diatous veil had broken, and her life along with it.

Even though it was *her* actions that spurred the new policy allowing women into Military, a confidentiality agreement and the threat of imprisonment kept her silent. She'd spent her time at home watching news vids discussing the change, but her name was never mentioned. She'd been determined to volunteer anyway, when she was ready. Aris was a soldier in every way that mattered, politics be damned.

But *ready* was proving elusive.

She could barely bring herself to fly, haunted by her final mission—by the dead faces of her fellow soldiers, the blank, dead eyes of the Safarans she'd killed. By the Safaran operative, Elom, who had kidnapped and tortured Ward Vadim.

Aris had spent less than ten minutes in that tiny cell with Elom, and yet he still stalked her nightmares. Every time she caught a glimpse of her own face in the mirror, she saw the red slash of scar he'd given her, and she could feel his fingers trying to rip out her throat. Every time she climbed into a wingjet, her stomach would cramp, and panic would close her throat.

Now Aris watched Milek close the distance between them. He wore his proper Ruslanan uniform, the sky blue complimenting his pale skin. Like Aris, he'd been in disguise, a Ruslanan soldier secretly embedded in Atalanta to aid the war effort.

Aris fought the urge to turn away from him, to hide the scar that swept from one side of her face to the other. Instead, she forced herself to meet his eyes squarely. With him, she shouldn't have to wear her old life like an ill-fitting jacket.

His gaze was filled with an intensity nearly matching the glare of the sun. "Hello, Aris. It's been too long."

She bit back the *who's fault is that* that rose in her throat. For the last two months, she'd felt like a dirty secret being kept hidden. "I'm surprised to see you here at all, sir."

"I . . ." Milek squinted into the sun for an instant. "Is there somewhere we can talk?"

With a nod, she led him to the courtyard, where a wooden pergola draped in ivy provided some shade. Her mind churned with questions and her hands trembled.

He stopped behind the nearest chair, his large hands clutching the delicate wrought iron.

There was so much tension in Aris's body, she felt in danger of shattering. She tried to keep her voice as professional as possible. "Please tell me why you're here, sir."

"Of course." Milek cleared his throat. "Specialist Aris Haan, I have been authorized by the dominion of Atalanta to offer you a place in Military sector as a flyer. I have also been tasked with giving you a field promotion to Lieutenant, if you choose to accept it."

"Excuse me?" Her heart gave a giant thump.

The lines of his face relaxed slightly. "I know the last couple of months have been difficult. It's taken longer to change the laws than my mother expected—she had to practically bully Ward Nekos into it—but they're finally starting to process the women who'd already been a part of the sector, hidden as men. I'm sure you've seen on the news."

Aris nodded, mouth dry. Just yesterday there'd been footage of two women rejoining their unit without their diatous veils. Their former comrades had jeered at them as they took their place within the ranks.

Milek added, "I wanted to tell you right away, so you'd know how important you are. How much we appreciate what you did." He cleared his throat again and glanced at his boots before continuing, his voice gruff. "But my mother wanted you to have time with your family, without reporters hounding you. She didn't want you to feel pressured. This offer is just that, an offer. A choice. You are welcome to decline it and stay, if you're happier here. No one ever has to know what you did, if that's what you want."

Aris sagged into a chair, her mind racing. All this time, they'd left her alone out of *respect*?

Milek sat too, leaning forward with his elbows on the table. "*Are* you happy here, Aris?"

No. The word didn't quite make it past her lips. How could she be happy, when her neighbors stared at her scar like it was the mark of some unknown shame? Their eyes slid away when she passed, the same way they had when she was a young, awkward, limping girl. Back then she'd had Calix Pavlos, her first love, to build her back up. Now she had endless questions from her friends about why she never spoke about him. Why she'd given up on him.

She couldn't tell them it was the other way around.

Aris had been in love with Calix for years. They'd planned their whole lives together, until he was selected for the Military sector and sent to war. That's why she'd joined Military in secret. But when she'd finally found him, when she'd asked him to accept who she'd become, he had turned his back on her. Her own response to his rejection haunted her; she hadn't cared nearly as much she should have.

"Has Calix forgiven you for helping to rescue my mother?" Milek's question, so closely mirroring her own thoughts, startled Aris.

"I don't know," she replied a little hoarsely. "We haven't spoken." It still surprised her how little that bothered her now.

"He shouldn't have asked you to choose." The conviction in Milek's voice sent a tremor through her.

"You're right," she agreed, her voice level, though her heart pounded. "He shouldn't have."

"Join me at Spiro as my flying expert." Milek slid his hands across the table, almost as if he wanted to reach for her hand.

"You're still at Spiro, then?"

"For now. All Ruslanans have remained at their posts. I'm still leading search and rescue missions, but we have another task as well."

"Which is?" she prompted, when he didn't continue.

"Finding Elom." The name fell from his mouth like a stone.

Aris fought down a shiver. "I wish your mother had let me kill him when I had the chance."

Milek's gaze clung to her face, to the scar that burned there. His voice fierce and protective and vengeful all at once, he said, "Elom will pay for what he did to both of you."

Aris's breath caught. The air between them thickened until she could hardly breathe. It was suddenly very difficult to forget their one, fleeting kiss. The single moment they'd shared just before they'd broken into the Safaran prison camp and rescued Ward Vadim.

She jerked to her feet and walked to the edge of the landing pad. He was offering her exactly what she wanted. To leave Lux and be a flyer again, as herself. To find Elom. And yet . . . .

She shook her head. "I don't fly anymore. I've been trying, but . . ." *But the nightmares won't let me.* The worst were the ones where she was flying with Galec and Talon and Wolfe, the men who'd died in that last mission. They would crash over and over into the side of the ravine, their faces twisted into rotting skeleton smiles as they'd scream for her to save them.

Milek's footsteps crossed the courtyard behind her. He stood beside her, staring out over Lux as she did, close enough that the back of their hands brushed.

"The first time you ever flew for me," Milek said, "you became a different person. Until then you'd skulked around point, jumping at every noise, looking over your shoulder as if you expected to be kicked. You stumbled. You fell. You didn't meet anyone's eyes." His voice strengthened. "Then you climbed into the wingjet, and you looked like you'd never been so happy or comfortable in your life."

Tears built behind Aris's eyes.

Without saying another word, he opened his arms to her. With a shudder, Aris stepped into the embrace. For a long time, Milek held her, even when she began to weep.

It dawned on her, slowly, that here, in the circle of his arms, she could safely remember all she had endured. And begin to forget. Because he, out of everyone, really *knew*. He understood.

Eventually, her breathing slowed and her fingers relaxed their death grip on his jacket. She opened her eyes, stared at the wet spot on his uniform made by her tears, and came back to herself. His embrace was a comfort, but he was still an officer. Her superior.

"Sir . . ." Aris pulled away, but Milek wouldn't let her go.

He squeezed her hands. "Look at me."

"I'm so sorry, sir." She met his eyes reluctantly.

"There is *nothing* you need apologize for," he said firmly. "I'm the one who's sorry. I'm sorry I wasn't there when you woke. And I'm sorry it's taken me so long to come here."

Aris tried to wave him off, but he wouldn't let go of her hands.

"Aris . . ." He paused, as if considering what to say. "I'd like you to come back. I hope you will, when you're ready."

"Thank you." She hoped he could see how much she

meant it. His warm hands engulfed hers, sending tingles along her skin.

"When you're ready," he repeated, as he released her, "we'll be waiting."

He was still standing very close. For an instant, she thought the space shrank, that he was leaning toward her. But by the time she'd lifted her head, he was through the archway, heading to his wingjet. He glanced back at her, once, with a grin. "It was good to see you, Lieutenant."

Lieutenant.

Aris took a deep breath as she watched his shimmering wingjet lift away. In seconds, he was a speck of silver in the distance. Above her, the clear blue arc of sky looked so close, so welcoming. Like it was waiting there just for her.

Without letting herself think, without letting herself breathe, she scrambled into the cabin of her own wingjet. Aris closed her eyes, feeling the hum of the machine in her bones. The pedals hung, perfectly balanced, under her feet, and the controls felt smooth and familiar in her hands. *Home. This is home.*

She ignored the nameless swirl of emotions that surfaced at the thought of Milek's smile, the warmth of his hands. She didn't want to identify, acknowledge, or explore them.

She just wanted to fly.

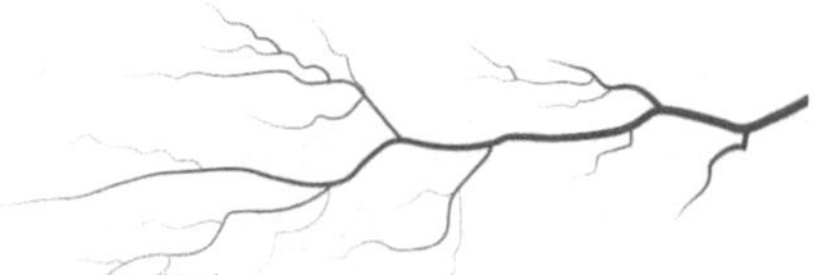

CHAPTER TWO

While she waited for the Ward of Atalanta to arrive, Galena Vadim stared through the glass at the wind-whipped trees outside his office. There was something so graceful about the curving tree limbs. The way they bent but did not break.

A shadowed reflection appeared next to her. She turned to face the man she'd once loved, his body trim beneath his pale-green tunic. "I understand why you spend so much time here, instead of at the capitol," she said. "Any small peace is welcome these days."

"I *am* fond of the quiet." Pyralis Nekos's warm brown eyes didn't waver as he looked at her, though most people still winced at the sight of her scarred face. The redness hadn't faded, though the edges of each slash had paled to a silvery pink. "It's a pleasure to see you again so soon," he added, the formal words sounding like a genuine welcome.

"How does the fighting look today?" She smoothed a hand over her blond hair, neatly collected in its knot at the nape of her neck. Usually they conducted these meetings over vids, but she'd been staying in Atalanta for longer and longer stretches recently, meeting with Atalantan and Ruslanan Military commanders.

And because Pyralis is here.

Her gaze shifted, taking in the warm wooden paneling, the ivory cushioned benches, the giant colorful painting of the Five Dominions that hung above Pyralis's desk. He rolled a projection table away from the wall and pressed a button to call up the map. The entire western half of Atalanta lifted into a glowing hologram above the table.

Galena crossed the room to get a better look. Current battles with Safaran troops were marked with red spirals. A black dotted line showed the forward positions of the Safaran enemy in Atalantan territory. The enemy line was farther away from the Fex River—and Panthea, Atalanta's capital city—than she had ever seen it.

"That's encouraging," she said, nodding toward the line. "The influx of Ruslanan troops seems to be helping."

Of the Five Dominions, Atalanta was the smallest, nestled between the golden deserts of Safara and snowfields of Ruslana. Little more than two years ago, Ward Balias, Safara's leader, had led an invasion into Atalanta, ostensibly to reach the rich resources of the Fex River.

Pyralis pointed to a spot in Atalanta's Mittaka region, where many red spirals hovered in a tight cluster. "We've made a lot of progress, but we can't seem to hold Mittaka. There aren't many villages here, but if Safaran troops breach this final stretch of forest, it's a straight shot to the river."

"What do your commanders say?" Galena asked,

studying the area more closely. "Do they want to send in more troops?"

Pyralis sighed. "They, like me, suspect this area of fighting is a diversion."

Galena glanced up at him. "For what?"

He ran his fingers through the streak of gray hair at his temple and shook his head. "We don't know."

She swept her hand across the region, distorting the image. "Not sending more forces to the area is a gamble."

"Oh, we'll deploy the soldiers." Pyralis turned off the table and rolled it back to its place against the wall. His mouth tightened as he looked at her face, not with pity but with determination. "I just wish I knew Ward Balias's next scheme."

Given the intricacy of Balias and Elom's plan to capture Galena, she had no doubt they'd try something else. Something equally treacherous.

Galena suppressed the shiver that ran through her. She still woke up in a sweat almost every morning, convinced she was trapped in that tiny cell with Elom looming over her. She could feel the restraints biting into her wrists, the fire of Elom's weapon cutting into her flesh. Even now, her heart raced just thinking about it.

With an effort, she steadied her nerves. "I've had more than enough of Safara's schemes. The war alone is quite enough to deal with."

Pyralis spared her a small smile.

So often these days, Galena found herself missing the simplicity of her shared history with him—their secret romance decades ago, when the only thing to worry about was his Promised back home. Now, Pyralis's wife, Bett, was in jail for selling the veiling tech to Safara and conspiring to abduct Galena. And Galena's husband, Josef, was dead, most likely murdered.

Galena and Pyralis stood shoulder to shoulder in a war that gave them no time to explore their history—or their future.

"If we could get Meridia or Castalia on board, it would help." Pyralis sounded about as confident at the prospect as Galena felt. The Wards of the western dominions would arrive in Panthea for an informal council in little more than a month, but neither was showing signs of support for Atalanta's war efforts.

"I do have some good news," she offered.

"Oh?" Pyralis leaned against his desk with his arms crossed. "That's a rare thing."

"I got word from the head of Ruslana's Tech sector before I came over. The prototype's finally done."

A wicked grin broke across his face, making him look much younger. "That *is* good news. When will it be fully operational?"

Galena tried not to let that smile derail her thoughts. It had a bad habit of doing so. "It's ready now. With your approval, I'll have it sent to Spiro, to aid Milek's efforts to find Elom. He's been back at the stationpoint for a few weeks now."

"You have my approval, and gladly," Pyralis replied. "If the tech proves as useful as we hope, Atalanta will begin large-scale production immediately."

Galena smiled. "That's not all. Milek visited the Haan girl a few days ago."

"And is she rejoining us?" He rubbed a hand along his chin.

"She's still adjusting, but Milek thinks she'll be back at Spiro soon." Truth be told, Milek hadn't been *as* certain as she made him sound. But Galena was hopeful anyway. Aris Haan, the girl who'd saved her life, was why she'd fought so hard to change Atalanta and Ruslana's policies toward women within Military sector. If a woman could lead a dominion, why shouldn't she be able to fight for one?

"We should alert the media," Pyralis said, turning toward his desk. "Perhaps you could hold a ceremony in her honor? A single face leading the 'women in Military' movement would do a lot to smooth the process and get the public on our side."

Galena stiffened. "We should wait until Aris has officially returned. And I'm not so sure announcing her name is smart either way. What if Ward Balias's men go after her?"

"If she rejoins her unit, she'll be in harm's way whether her identity is public knowledge or not." Pyralis's earnest gaze was as weighty as a physical touch. "We need this, Galena. Our female soldiers are being insulted, harassed, and worse. There've been protests in Panthea against allowing women to serve. We need to give the movement a hero."

"Don't you mean a target?" Galena argued. "And not just for Ward Balias. The dominion itself could easily turn on her, if the political climate remains this volatile."

Pyralis stopped short of reaching for her hand, though she could tell he wanted to. "*I* mean a hero."

If he'd had any other expression on his face, any *hint* that he relished the thought of using Aris for his own ends, Galena would have fought his plan. But the tension in his shoulders spoke of a man reluctantly putting the needs of his dominion above all else.

And she couldn't fault him for that.

"I want her consent before we splash her across the news." Galena bit the corner of her lip, thinking of the scared but resolute girl who'd braved so much to save her. "But when the time comes, I've no doubt she'll make a compelling champion for our cause."

Pyralis touched Galena then, the briefest brush of his fingers against her wrist. They didn't say anything, didn't move any closer, but the moment lingered in Galena's mind long afterward.

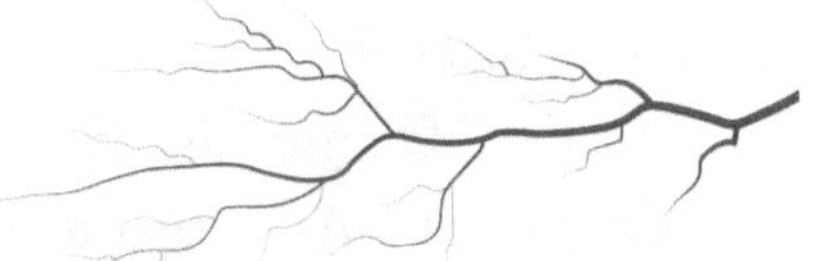

CHAPTER THREE

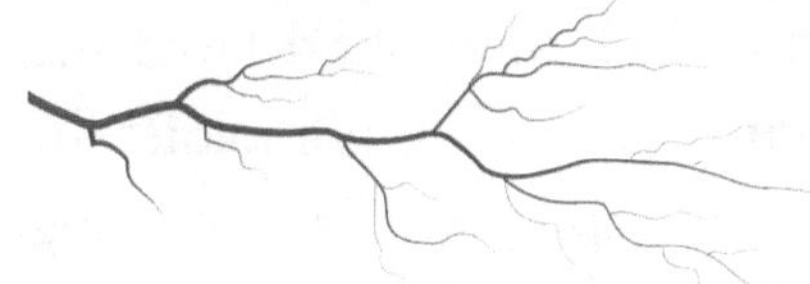

ARIS RUBBED THE TWISTED IVY OF THE Environment brand on her arm, a nervous tick she hadn't quite outgrown. Because she'd been selected for the Enviro sector first, and then volunteered for Military, she would always have two brands.

"You know it doesn't hurt." Dianthe's reminder cut through the antiseptic silence of the lab. The gleaming chrome chair and blinding white walls of the secret room in Dianthe's apartment were just as Aris remembered them, but now Dianthe didn't bother closing the false wall to hide the room away. With the new law, the diatous veil—and Dianthe's clandestine services—were no longer necessary. But she was still helping female soldiers find their way. She'd greased the wheels for Aris, procuring her uniforms, paperwork, and now stamping her with the Military brand. Aris's first had been removed when she'd been sent home after the mission to rescue Ward Vadim.

Dianthe grinned at Aris in the mirror. Aris wasn't used

to seeing Dianthe smile. It was almost as disconcerting as the crimson snake that curled across the woman's bald head, screaming black fire.

"Ready?" Dianthe asked.

"Of course." Aris tried to relax. The last time she'd felt the cool pressure of the branding tech, she'd had far more to worry about than she did now. Back then, she'd faced the prospect of hiding her true identity and living as a soldier for the first time. She'd been afraid of exposure, afraid of being sent to prison, afraid of not finding Calix.

Now, she didn't need to fear exposure or prison. She didn't need to find Calix or prove herself. She just needed to fly.

It's easier now. It'll keep getting easier.

After Milek had visited her, it had taken another month to get to this moment, here with Dianthe, the black rectangle of the Military brand once more emblazoned on the back of her neck.

Aris still hadn't been able to erase all of the effects of those last few missions. But blighting hell if she hadn't moved past them. The strongest people she knew—Milek, Dysis, Dianthe—believed in her. The least she could do was believe in herself.

Now, Dianthe accompanied her to the hub of the city. Their trip was an eerie echo of their first foray into Panthea together, when Aris had her first experience in the outside world as Aristos, and she'd showed Dianthe how she could fly. Only this time, neither of them hid who they were.

And people noticed.

Across from the nearest metroline stop, a group of men and women marched back and forth in front of the capitol.

They held signs and chanted, "Women should be moms, not dropping bombs!" over and over.

Aris nodded her head toward the commotion. "Are they here all the time?"

"More or less." Dianthe didn't glance in the protestors' direction. Her loose, ivory dress billowed as she walked, an interesting contrast to her tattooed, hard-edged face.

An older, gray-haired woman at the edge of the group caught Aris looking. Her eyes widened at Aris's uniform. She ran across the street, her IF THEY VOLUNTEER, OUR FUTURE WILL DISAPPEAR sign bobbing. Her soft face would have been grandmotherly if it weren't so twisted as she screamed, "Don't throw your life away! Don't throw our *future* away!"

Dianthe hustled Aris up the stairs to the metroline platform, leaving the woman yelling after them. Aris tried to ignore the stares of the other passengers as they boarded the train. Not all of them were hostile—a young girl and her mother even smiled openly at Aris—but she didn't like feeling on display.

The metroline train rocketed them through the city. Outside, blue sky battled with the tall, silvery buildings that glinted in the sun.

"Will you grow out your hair, now that you don't have to wear the veil?" Aris asked, casting a glance at Dianthe's tattoo, the red ropes of snake that encircled her skull.

Dianthe shot her a look. "I told you once that my tattoo served as a distraction—that if people were looking at it, they were less likely to notice the rest of me."

"Yeah, so—"

"So what makes you think I want them to notice the rest of me now?" Dianthe turned toward the panel of glass.

Aris watched her, wondering how Dianthe could possibly think she wouldn't be noticed, tattoo or no tattoo. The woman was a force.

When Aris boarded the military transjet, they didn't hug, but Dianthe flicked a little smile and winked. "Best of luck to you, Haan."

The machine shivered to life, its hum drowning out the voices of the other soldiers strapping themselves in, as Aris found a seat and pulled out her digitablet. The last time she'd boarded a transjet, she'd done it as Aristos: disguised, hoping to disappear within the ranks. Now, as herself, there was no hope of that.

Her eyes flitted around the echoing, thrumming jet; rows of soldiers lined its curving, windowless belly, surrounding the pile of bags and other cargo in the center. She was the only woman. Around her, the men laughed and talked with one another, occasionally shooting her sharp looks. No one sat next to her, but they didn't scream at her like that protestor had either, so she counted that a blessing.

With a swipe of her finger, she opened a comm from Dysis.

So you're really going back. It'll be odd, I bet, being your-self, no veil needed. I wonder who you'll room with, now that you're a big-time lieutenant. And a girl. I know you want me to come back too. But I can't. I'm sorry. Jax still needs me. Maybe… no. I won't make you empty promises. Be safe, Hummingbird. Show those men what you can do. ~ Dysis

She had hoped that when Dysis found out she was going back, Dysis would want to as well. Aris *knew* that her former sectormate couldn't be content to remain in her old life, away from the front lines, reading about enemy raids and female integration on her digitablet. She was too good a soldier. But Dysis's brother, Jax, had spent months as a prisoner of war, and when he'd finally escaped with the intel that led to Ward Vadim's rescue, he'd been severely injured. Until Jax returned to his own job as a spy for Atalanta, there was no way Dysis would leave him.

She just needed more time.

A couple hours later, the transjet landed at Spiro. Aris and a few of her fellow soldiers unstrapped themselves. One of them unclipped the netting that secured the cargo. As she reached for her bag, a strong hand shot out and grabbed it. "Here, let me get that for you."

She looked up at the soldier, ready to thank him. Until she saw the smirk on his handsome, angular face. "I've got it," she said warily, reaching for the strap.

He dangled it just out of her grasp, his face twisting with mock concern. "Don't worry yourself, doll. I wouldn't want you to break a nail."

Aris made a single, sudden swipe for the bag, but the man anticipated the move, yanking it above his head. He laughed.

Behind him, several other soldiers gathered.

"Give me my bag," she said, ashamed when her voice came out too soft to carry over the hydraulics of the ramp lowering onto Spiro's landing pad.

Her tormentor cocked his head. "Why on earth would

you need it?" The mirth fell from his face for an instant as he glared at her. "Bitches like you don't belong here."

The men snickered. A ginger-haired kid jostled her roughly as he headed down the ramp.

Aris's frustration, anger, and helplessness threatened to boil over. She kept her chin up with an effort. She suddenly felt like a limping, awkward child again, teased by a group of boys playing keep away with her lunch. Back then, Calix had stepped in to save her.

Now it was up to her. This was *her* fight. *Her* life.

She glared at the man still holding her bag, ignoring the others. This time, when she spoke, she made sure her voice came out loud and steady. "Your name, Specialist?"

"Why? Fancy a meet-up later?" The man's gaze dipped from her face to a slow sweep of her body. His grin cane back.

She kept her expression blank. "I asked you a question."

"Aero Contas." A flicker of doubt stole some of his arrogance, but only for an instant. "And *your* name, beautiful?"

She stared him down. "*Lieutenant* Haan. Give me my bag."

His eyes widened and the bag sagged lower in his hands. He sputtered as if she'd made a joke. The men behind him shifted.

She didn't crack even the smallest smile. "Now, Specialist. It'd be a shame to have to report you on your very first day at Spiro."

Without giving him time to recover, she yanked the bag out of his hand, whirled, and stomped down the ramp.

The sudden sunshine and swirl of bodies disoriented her. For a moment, while her eyes adjusted, all she could see were shadows moving through a glaring light. And then, like a mirage, a figure appeared before her. Tall, with short golden hair and a knife-thin scar that ran from eye to lip.

Milek.

"Welcome back, Lieutenant Haan." His gaze flicked to the other soldiers disembarking, all of whom gave him a wide berth.

"Thank you, sir. I'm sorry it took me so long." Out of the corner of her eye, she could see Lieutenant Daakon leading the others inside. He was stout and dark skinned, a gunner like Dysis had been. Aris had once walked in on the two of them about to kiss. Dysis had denied it, but Aris knew what she'd seen. The potential romance was complicated, of course. Same-sex relationships were forbidden by the same antiquated set of laws that had prevented women from joining Military, but even if the rule were to change, the simple fact remained: Dysis wasn't *actually* a man.

Aris wondered what Lieutenant Daakon's reaction had been when he found out the truth, and if they'd gotten a chance to talk about it. Dysis never mentioned him in her comms.

"Did you have any trouble with the reenlistment process?" Milek asked, interrupting her thoughts. He turned toward the collection of rounded buildings that made up Spiro stationpoint. In the bright sun, they glimmered a silver beige.

"It was no problem," she replied. Which was only true because Dianthe had taken care of the details.

Aris followed him toward the entrance. Behind her, the hum of the transjet intensified as it heaved back into the air, continuing to other stationpoints to deliver the rest of the soldiers.

"How are you doing?" Milek asked. "With the flying, I mean."

"I'm managing." With a swish, the thick glass doors opened. The two of them stepped into the quiet halls of Spiro. "I'm flying every day now, and there's been no nausea or flashes of panic in weeks. I . . . I feel mostly like myself again."

As he glanced over at her, his habitual gruffness slid into understanding. "War remakes us, teaches us lessons we'd rather not learn. Some of those scars remain for a long time, under the surface."

"It helped, knowing I could come back. That you—" He looked away and she panicked. "The unit, I mean—needed me. That made all the difference." Of course she didn't mean *he* needed her. It would be colossally stupid to have feelings for her superior officer, no matter what history or perceived closeness they might have.

"Good." Milek kept walking, unaware of her inner turmoil. "Commander Nyx would like to see you right away." His voice dipped a little. "And, uh, my mother as well."

Aris paused. "Ward Vadim is *here*?"

"Come on."

They walked down the corridor without saying more, the only sound the thud of their boots.

Despite herself, Aris tensed at the thought of facing Commander Nyx. He was even more intimidating than Dianthe, with ropes of scar that encircled his neck and a glare that could freeze a Safaran heat wave. The last time she'd seen him, he'd forced her to sign a confidentiality agreement and told her she faced imprisonment if she told anyone about Ward Vadim's rescue.

Milek led Aris to Commander Nyx's office. "I'll wait outside," he said, pausing at the door.

Aris couldn't hold back a gasp as she entered the room. It wasn't Ward Vadim's scarred face that shocked her. It was Commander Nyx. The person sitting at his white desk had his close-cropped hair, steely gray eyes, and determined jaw, but the heavy brows had thinned and the mouth, while still pulled into a tight line, was more delicately shaped than Aris remembered.

"You're . . . you're . . ." Aris stuttered.

"No one told you?" Nyx raised a brow.

"No, um, ma'am."

"It's *sir* still, Lieutenant," Nyx replied, her eyes flinty. "All officers, male and female, are to be referred to as such. A different label implies a different level of respect, which I will not tolerate."

"Yes, sir." Relief flickered through her. The *ma'am* hadn't fit.

"You remember Ward Vadim of Ruslana," Commander Nyx continued, without looking up.

Aris bowed to the Ward, who stood beside Nyx. "It's a pleasure to see you again, Ward Vadim."

"And you," she replied, stepping closer to shake Aris's hand. "I was thrilled when Milek told me you were considering joining us again."

Aris shrugged a little, biting back an awkward laugh. "Thank you."

"Sometime today or tomorrow," Commander Nyx said,

her no-nonsense voice little changed from its former, male iteration, "Ward Vadim would like to reveal you as the female soldier who was instrumental to her rescue."

Aris's mouth dropped open.

"But I will *not* do so without your permission," Ward Vadim interjected. "Whether or not to become a public figure is your choice."

A public figure? Aris's stomach churned. "I . . . I only thought about coming back here. Doing my job."

"If it were up to me, your role would stay classified," Commander Nyx said, her expression softening. Ward Vadim shot the Commander a look. "But I believe you coming forward would do some good. No doubt you've seen the reports."

Aris thought of Specialist Contas and the group of protestors shouting outside of the capitol. "I'm aware of the issues," she allowed.

"Women can be smarter than men, just as political," Ward Vadim said, an old frustration creeping into her voice. "We can lead Tech or Enviro sectors, become menders or business owners. Holy, we can even become Ward. But heavens forbid we prefer jobs requiring physical strength, weapons, or danger. Men have been taught that we're not capable, and they'll keep thinking that way until we prove them wrong."

Aris thought back to who she'd been before she'd first visited Dianthe. Before she'd become Aristos. Maybe it wasn't just men who thought that way. A year ago, she never would have dreamed she could become a soldier, fight a war.

"We need someone to be the face of the integration movement." Commander Nyx rubbed the back of her neck, maybe noting the lack of her diatous veil. How strange it must be to live without it after so many years. In the few short months Aris had worn hers, she'd grown so used to it that she hadn't even noticed when it shattered. "The question is, will that person be you?"

"If it is, what would that mean?" Aris wasn't sure whether to address her questions to the Commader or the Ward. Both women were staring at her too closely. "What about the hunt for Elom?"

"You're here to do a job, and we need you here to do it." Commander Nyx sat up straighter, her red ropes of scar bulging. "Your new Military photo may appear in news vids, and you'll surely be a point of discussion among reporters. But that should be the extent of it."

Ward Vadim added, "I'd also like to invite you to attend a ceremony in Ruslana. To honor all you've done for the war effort, and for me."

A ceremony? The conversation was turning surreal. Three months ago, she'd been threatened with prison time if she talked, and now they wanted to throw her a party?

Aris was from a small village, with small dreams. She wanted more now—or something different, anyway—but that didn't mean she'd suddenly developed a taste for life in the public eye. She cringed at the thought of standing in front of all those people at the ceremony, cameras flashing.

Aris tried to focus. "Will, um, reporters want to interview me?"

"Spiro is still in a war zone." Commander Nyx stood. "That means no reporters. Our gates are closed to anyone who doesn't have authorization. I will not let this disrupt our training or search and rescue missions. But they may approach your parents. You should make them aware of the possibility."

Her mother might not mind, but her father would be horrified.

Still, this wasn't about them. It was about her. And if Ward Vadim thought it was important, how could she refuse? With a steadying breath, Aris said, "If this is what you think Atalanta needs, I'm in."

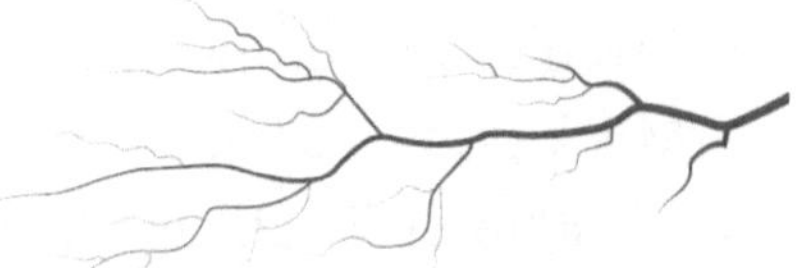

Chapter Four

Milek was pacing the hall when Aris emerged from Commander Nyx's office.

"All set?" he asked, pausing before her.

Aris nodded, still a little shell-shocked.

"I'll show you the Officer's Lounge first, while we're over here." Milek said. "And then we'll go to your room. You'll be sharing with Specialist Pallas."

Aris wasn't entirely surprised Pallas was a woman. Another flyer, Specialist Pallas had struggled with target practice even more than Aris had. "What about her sectormate?"

"Specialist Rozam is no longer here." Milek shot a quick glance at her. "When the ban was lifted, Pallas decided to continue on without her disguise. Rozam wasn't of the same mind. She chose to leave the Military." He turned down a corridor and stopped before a frosted door with "OL" etched into the glass. "Normally we wouldn't put an officer with a specialist, but I think you both will need the support."

"Aren't there any other women here at Spiro?"

Milek pressed a pad on the wall, and the door slid open. "No. Just Specialist Pallas, Commander Nyx, and you."

Aris glanced around as he ushered her into the Officer's Lounge. Like every other room on point, it had no windows, just blank white walls and a glowing ceiling. But a plush red rug covered the floor, and several comfortable, thick-cushioned chairs and sofas were arranged around a low table. Along the back wall, a long counter sported a jar of tea, a teapot, and a frother, along with a small foodsaver.

"It'll be different now," Aris said, thinking of the loud rec room with stained, sagging chairs where she, Dysis, Galec, and Otto had played splots and sent comms to their families. "But I think this kind of different will be good. Hard maybe, while we wait for you men to adjust. But good."

"I've adjusted," Milek said mildly.

She leaned against the arm of a chair, considering him. "You didn't adjust, though. It never bothered you. Even at the beginning, right after my veil broke. Why is that, do you think?"

He shrugged and took a seat. "I don't know. Honestly, if it had happened a different way, maybe it would have."

"What do you mean?" She sank into the chair, comfortable in this room—with him—in a way she hadn't been with her friends at home in Lux, who knew nothing of her life as a soldier.

After a moment, Milek replied, "If someone had told me women were going to join Military and that was all I had to go on, I might have asked the same questions other men are asking now. 'Can they really do it?' and 'Why would they want to?'"

"But?" She found herself admiring his broad shoulders and the hard line of his jaw. *Silly girl.*

He stood abruptly and walked to the counter. "But I was lucky enough to see you in action. You're an incredible flyer. And you worked harder than most of the other soldiers under my command. So many young men are chosen for Military and have no desire to fight. And here you were, fighting *for* this."

A blush swarmed up her cheeks. "Thank you, sir. I hope . . . I hope I don't let you down."

She'd made progress in the past month, but flying wasn't the easy-as-breathing activity it had been for her back then.

"You'll do fine." Milek busied himself with the teapot. A quiet hiss filled the room as he placed it beneath the frother. "But I understand that it might be difficult at first. We'll work through it."

"Do you think everyone has demons?" It was the closest she let herself come to acknowledging her own.

"I think we're all fighting something." He didn't look up. To her surprise he continued, his voice gruff. "Sometimes I wake up in a panic, convinced my mother is still captive. Or I dream that I'm too late, and Elom has killed her. It's almost worse when I wake up thinking my father is still alive."

"I'm sorry." Aris stared at the back of his head as he bent over the teapot, wishing she could comfort him somehow. She gulped down a breath and confessed, "I dream about Elom, too, and the men I killed. It's like they're waiting, just at the edges of my mind, ready to take their revenge."

Milek turned, leaned back against the counter, and met her gaze. "The men I've killed also haunt me."

"How do you make peace with it?" she asked. "What do you do to remind yourself that they deserved it?"

"That's the thing about war," he said after a pause. He handed her a teacup full of strong, milky tea. Its spicy scent stung her nose. "*No one* deserves to be killed. But sometimes it can't be helped. I find peace in the conviction that Ward Balias cannot be allowed to destroy Atalanta. Most of those we kill are not evil in and of themselves, but they *are* fighting as part of an evil."

Aris stared at the curl of steam rising from her cup, grateful for the warmth that seeped into her cold hands. "Do you think the Safaran soldiers see it that way?"

"Of course not. To them, *we* are the evil." The darkness in Milek's voice sent a chill along her spine.

Specialist Pallas was just leaving when Aris and Milek arrived at the room the two women would share.

With a brief, inscrutable glance at Aris and a nod to Pallas, Milek retreated.

"Hey, Aristos," Pallas said. "I mean . . ." Her voice petered out.

Like Aris, Pallas had abandoned the head shaving. Her short blond hair waved over thin brows and grayish-blue eyes. Without her veil, the girl was gawky and angular, with sharp cheekbones and a pointed chin.

"It's Aris, actually," Aris clarified, shifting her bag hand to hand.

"Right. My first name's Tia, but I prefer Pallas anyway." She cocked her head. "Nice scar."

Aris wasn't sure if a thank-you was appropriate.

"I'm heading to the mess for some food," Pallas said. "Want to join?"

Aris hadn't eaten anything since a small bowl of starberry-oat mash with Dianthe that morning, so she nodded, though the knots in her stomach grumbled uneasily at the thought of food. She dropped her bag in the room and followed Pallas down the hall.

The noise of clinking silverware and the low rumble of voices spilled out of the cafeteria before they arrived at the doorway. Pallas paused for a split second before entering, as if bracing herself.

When Aris crossed the threshold, faces snapped in her direction, like flags all caught by the same strong gust of wind. Her eyes automatically alighted on the long table just inside, where she'd always sat with Dysis, Galec, and Otto.

Otto was in his usual spot, his potbelly pressing against the edge of the table. Beside him sat an empty chair with a black ribbon strung along its back.

Galec's chair.

A lump rose in her throat. She could almost see him sitting there still, his close-cropped red hair standing at attention, mirth sparkling in his eyes. He'd be making fun of Otto's impressive belly, or giving them all an update on his daughter. Aris swallowed hard.

Across from Otto, facing away from the door, sat a muscular man with a shaved head. A tattoo of two skeletal hands reached up the back of his neck on either side of his Military brand, as if they meant to crush his skull.

"Who's that?" Aris asked, cocking her head toward the stranger.

"My gunner, Baksen," Pallas replied. "He's alright."

Aris nodded to Otto as they passed the table. His eyes widened, and then he smiled, looking genuinely pleased to see her.

The line for food was short; they'd missed the initial rush. As Aris grabbed a tray, a dish of pea-and-piggin pie, and a glass of water, a man came up behind her and reached for a bowl of fruit, his arm rubbing hard against the side of her breast.

"Watch it," Aris growled, moving out of reach. She sent a glare in his direction. It was the ginger-haired kid from the transjet.

"My apologies," he said, smirking. The guy standing behind him snickered.

Ahead of her, a tall, muscular soldier leaned over Pallas's shoulder. The girl's ears flushed bright red. ". . . wouldn't want you to ruin your figure. I have plans for that fine—"

Enough. Aris grabbed two sugar pastries and dropped them onto Pallas's tray, nudging her forward and away from whatever the feral-eyed soldier was about to suggest. Aris's sharp elbow found its way into his side as she pushed around him, but she didn't turn to gauge his reaction.

They wove back through the tables, whispers following them. Aris didn't meet anyone's eyes, but she could feel the weight of their stares. By the time she reached Otto's table, her chest was tight and anger pounded in her head.

"Mind if I join you?" Aris directed the question at Otto,

the first words she'd said to him since before the mission that had killed his sectormate. Galec's memory hung between them, along with an unacknowledged grief.

"Of course, Lieutenant." Otto grinned at her, but his face was tinged with sadness. "Back for more, I see?"

She wanted to tell him she was sorry. That she missed Galec, too. Instead, as she sat beside him in Dysis's old seat, she cocked her head at Baksen and Pallas, who'd taken the seat opposite her. "Have you got them playing splots yet?" Aris asked.

Otto's smile widened. "I have, and they're absolute *rubbish*."

"I wouldn't underestimate our skills," Pallas said with forced cheerfulness. She still looked a little shaken by the food line incident. Baksen was watching the muscled soldier who'd harassed her; he'd found a seat two tables over.

"Lieutenant Haan, please report to the landing pad," a tech voice announced over the intercom.

Milek had told Aris there'd be a briefing to explain her new duties as Lieutenant, but that wasn't for a few more hours. She shrugged apologetically to her dining companions, scooped two hurried bites of pie into her mouth, and dropped her tray onto the conveyor that shuttled the dirty dishes into the kitchen.

When Aris reached the landing pad, it was deserted save for the shining rows of wingjets along its edges. In the distance, a towering bank of cloud promised afternoon thunderstorms, and the air was sticky with humidity. She leaned against the warm, curved side of the building and waited, not sure who or what exactly she was waiting for. Her stomach rumbled, protesting the abbreviated meal.

A faint sound caught her attention. The whistle of a stiff breeze. She straightened. The forest that pressed along the edges of the dusty plain remained serene.

Out of nowhere, a spark of silver zipped along her peripheral vision.

What the—

The buzzing grew louder. In the middle of the empty landing pad, a tiny wingjet appeared, dropping gently from a hover to the ground.

Aris stared, open mouthed. Before she had time to process, the wingjet's shield slid back, revealing Milek. He hopped to the tarmac, an uncharacteristically large smile on his face.

"Where—where did you come from?" Aris stuttered. "I was watching—"

"That's the beautiful thing about an invisible wingjet." Excitement hummed in his voice. "You don't see it coming."

She couldn't seem to stop staring. "Pardon?"

"The tech's like the diatous veil," he explained. "But instead of changing how the jet looks, it just makes it disappear. Ruslanan techies have been working on it for years."

Aris's mind raced. She placed a tentative hand on the silver side of the wingjet, as she might on an unruly horse. *An invisible wingjet.*

"With it, we'll be able to scout over enemy lines and ferret out Elom without his spies catching on. We'll have the advantage." His face lit with an expression she'd never seen on it before. Like a child with a sparkly new toy.

"Why didn't you mention this before?" she asked. *As in, immediately after I landed?*

He laughed. "It's still classified. I had to get permission

from Commander Nyx first. She's authorized us to take it on a test flight. Are you up for it?"

"Absolutely." Energy sang through Aris's every nerve ending as she scrambled onto the wing. Inside, one narrow leather seat with thick black straps was wedged behind the curving nav panel. She glanced back at Milek. "There's only room for one person."

"I'll follow you in a recon," he said. "We'll be in touch via comms. If anything feels off, let me know. I'll watch to be sure the veiling tech works."

Aris dropped into the seat and strapped herself in. A control box, presumably for the cloaking tech, was affixed just under the nav panel. It had two switches, one green and one red.

"Try flipping the red switch," Milek called.

She did as he asked and with a low hum, the nose of the wingjet shimmered and then disappeared.

"Blighting incredible," she said in awe.

Milek whistled low in his throat. "Uncanny. It's as if your head is suspended in air."

"This is so crazy." Aris hit the lever for the dome, enclosing herself in the whirring heart of the wingjet. Below, Milek shook his head, a huge grin on his face, then jogged to the nearest recon.

Aris began the warm-up sequence. For the moment, her excitement outweighed the nervousness she'd felt on every flight for the past few weeks.

A minute later, she heard, "Ready to go, Lieutenant?" in her helmet.

She grinned. "How do you know I haven't already taken off?"

"Good point," he said, an answering smile in his voice. "There should be a small green switch below the cloaking switch. Do you see it?"

Her finger caught against it. "Yes."

"Flip that on. It makes your coordinates, altitude, and speed visible to all other wingjets in the Atalantan network within fifty miles."

Aris did as he asked.

A second later, "There. I see you on the nav."

Aris pulled gently on the controls. The tiny wingjet rose, its engine firing with a happy rumble. "What if Safara hacks into the network?"

"They haven't breached it yet," Milek replied. "But the jet can go completely undetectable if necessary."

At first it was disconcerting to stare out of the windshield only to see white tarmac below. No pointed wingjet nose, no sloping wings to her left and right. A silver shimmer clung along the edges of the glass, another sign the tech was doing its job.

Maybe the illusion would have bothered another flyer, but as Aris dipped and spun, her tension eased and her heart rate steadied.

She had never before felt so close to the wide, blue sky.

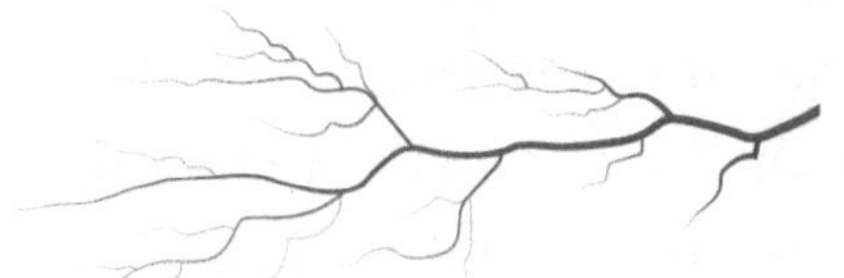

Chapter Five

Pyralis wasn't surprised when Galena shook her head at the glass of water an aide offered her. She kept her chin high, but he could see the pain in her eyes as she remembered her last experience in this room.

It was here in this bomb-resistant, high-security room below Atalanta's capitol building that Galena had unknowingly ingested dangerous meds and been spirited away by Safaran operatives disguised as menders. It still galled him that it had happened here, under *his* watch. He should have known, somehow. He should have made sure it never happened at all.

Galena sat across from him, beside Sera Rosum, Castalia's Ward. Sera's thick gray hair swung in a heavy braid down her back, and the two wings of her Health brand peeked out above her pale-pink dress's neckline. She drummed long golden fingernails against the smooth, white table.

"Surely you see the seriousness of this threat," Galena said, addressing Sera. Pyralis didn't blame her. There was no point in engaging Hal Wicton, Meridia's Ward; he'd already made it clear, in this meeting and others, that his dominion had no interest in joining the fight. Even now, his golden eyes wandered to the pretty aide offering refreshments.

Sera's hand paused, the *clack-clack-clack* of her fingernails ceasing. "You're right, Ward Vadim," she said. "I can't deny Safara's threat. And neither do I deny that you've suffered a terrible injustice." Her gaze drifted beyond Galena's shoulder. With a frown, Pyralis realized Sera couldn't bring herself to look at Galena's scarred face. "But Castalia is still dependent on trade with Safara, and there's no evidence that your kidnapping wasn't merely the action of a single extremist. Aided by Ward Nekos's wife, of course." At that, she shot him a narrow look.

"Do you honestly believe Ward Balias had no knowledge of Elom's plan?" he asked, his voice murderously quiet. They still couldn't prove that Ward Balias had known about Galena's capture. Even Bett had only ever spoken with Elom. But as far as Pyralis was concerned, Ward Balias had authorized the scheme. In his mind, there was no question.

"It doesn't matter what we believe," Hal broke in. "The Peace Accords clearly state that no dominion is required to financially or militarily support another unless the threat extends beyond a single dominion. We could *choose* to provide aid, as Ruslana has, but unless there is absolute proof that the government of Safara has targeted both Atalanta *and* Ruslana, we are not *required* to act."

"What of the Ruslanan soldiers killed in battle?" Galena

asked, obviously grasping at straws. "Surely that constitutes a threat to both dominions?"

Hal shook his head, his slicked hair retaining its precise wave. "Those soldiers have been deployed to a war zone; they are not being attacked on their own soil."

"And the people in Castalia and Meridia?" Pyralis clutched the edge of the table with white-knuckled hands to keep himself from punching the ass. "Do you mean to tell me your people care nothing for the plight of Atalanta? Are they *happy* to watch us fall?"

Sera leaned forward. "Ward Nekos, you must understand. Castalia's economy has lost ground in recent years, and Military sector doesn't have the resources to provide troops. If I were to back out of our trade agreements with Safara, my own people's livelihoods would be at stake." Pyralis caught a hint of genuine sorrow in her eyes. "I do understand the desperate nature of your situation, but there's nothing I can do."

Hal, on the other hand, offered no such sympathy. "Ward Nekos, you have the support of Ruslana, the wealthiest and most powerful of the Five Dominions. There's no damn reason you shouldn't be able to withstand Ward Balias's invasion. Meridia cannot be expected to offer you more handholding when you're not adequately using the resources you already have. And this ridiculous female Military-integration business? *Come on.*"

Pyralis opened his mouth to protest, but the odious man wasn't done. He stood from the table, his crimson robes standing out like blood against the white walls of the featureless room. "Unless you can provide some proof that Safara is a threat to more than one dominion, you'll receive no help from me. I've spoken with you on this matter several times now. I will not make the trip again. Good day."

With that, the Ward of Meridia swept from the room, his entourage of burgundy-uniformed bodyguards following him.

Sera stood, too. "I truly am sorry." She glanced at Galena, and then quickly away. "But I cannot sanction what would amount to a world war without more proof. You are protecting your dominions. I must protect mine."

As soon as the door shut behind the other Ward, Galena pounded her fist on the table. "Gods, the nerve of that man. How Meridia can keep electing him—I don't care if he's the most brilliant Commerce mind in their entire dominion, he's—"

"Hal's right," Pyralis said, to his own shock. He *hated* agreeing with that man, but in this case, he had a point.

She sputtered in protest. "How can you—"

"I mean, obviously, he's an ass," Pyralis said, shooting her a little smile. "But he *is* right that we can't *force* the other dominions to help us. And he's right, too, that Atalanta shouldn't be relying so much on outside aid. It's a defensive position, and it won't win us this war."

Galena sighed as she dropped into her seat again. "So what do we do?"

"We need to do what Ward Balias did," he replied, thoughts and plans beginning to swirl in his mind.

"What do you mean?" Galena asked. The brightness of the room pressed unforgivingly against her face, revealing her exhaustion.

A new energy coursed through him. "With your capture,

Balias found a way to hurt us beyond the fight on the ground. We need to do the same in return." Pyralis drummed his hand against the table as he looked at her ravaged, beautiful face. "We need to bring down Safara from within."

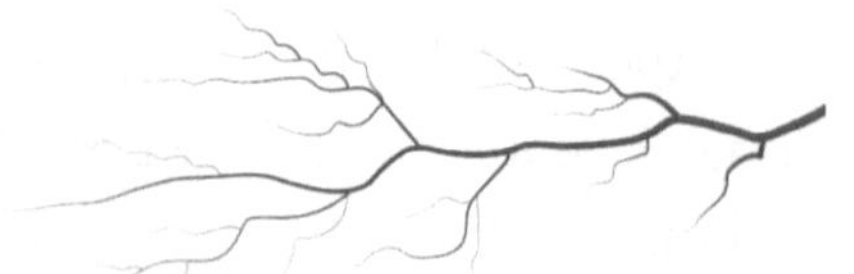

Chapter Six

Aris took her place with the other officers at morning formation, standing before the soldiers instead of among them. In the front row, Specialist Pallas stared straight ahead, eyes blank.

Beside Aris, the new retrieving expert, Lieutenant Cruz, mumbled something under his breath. With ruddy cheeks, heavy black eyebrows, and a nose that hitched markedly to the right, he had the air of a schoolyard bully. Aris already knew he vehemently opposed women in the Military; he'd told her so, point blank and with insufferable arrogance, during the briefing the night before.

As soon as the unit was in position, Milek addressed the assembled soldiers. "Good morning! Today, as you can see, we are joined by Lieutenant Haan, whom some of you may remember as Aristos."

A few murmurs wove through the crowd. Aris searched for familiar faces, landing on a transport flyer, Specialist Evander, she hadn't seen since she'd been back.

Brightly colored tattoos curled out from the edges of his uniform and along his face. When she met his eyes, he didn't crack a smile, but he didn't look disgusted either, like some of the other men. Maybe Evander remembered what she could do with a wingjet. It'd be nice if *some* of them did. The other flyers, at least, had once been impressed by her skills.

Milek continued. "After risking her life—and imprisonment—to save Ward Vadim's life, the Lieutenant was asked to rejoin the sector, here at Spiro, as our flying expert. I understand a few of you are still uncomfortable at the thought of fighting alongside female soldiers. Well, you better get over that fast. Because now you'll be trained by one."

The grumbles increased in volume. A single clear voice broke through the noise. "Personally, I enjoy a woman in charge!"

Laughter exploded across the field. Aris kept her face still.

"Silence!" Milek stared the men down, eyes hard. He flicked his head toward Lieutenant Daakon, who pulled the soldier who'd spoken from the line. It was the ginger-haired kid.

"Specialist Kyros, I'll be training with you today," Milek said, venom in his voice. "But first, give me three laps around the training grounds."

Kyros sighed, shoulders slumping, and jogged to the edge of the field. Milek turned his attention back to the unit. "I will not tolerate any disrespect to Lieutenant Haan, or to any other woman on this stationpoint. Your female comrades are risking their lives right along with you, just as they did before the ban was lifted. You will treat them with the courtesy they deserve. Is that understood?"

The collective "yes, sir" was not quite as decisive as it could have been, but Milek looked satisfied. To a point.

"Please remember that Lieutenant Haan now has authorization to discipline you," he added. "I don't imagine she'll shy from her duty."

He turned and nodded at Lieutenant Daakon, who stepped forward, saying, "Soldiers, pair off. Grab a mat. Time for combat training."

The pairs of fighters moved out of Milek's way quickly as he wove through them. Aris suspected their speed had more to do with the murderous look in his eyes than his rank.

Thuds and grunts soon filled the air. Aris hated hand-to-hand training—mostly because she was wretched at it—but the sight of soldiers circling one another had a strange effect on her. Remembering Dysis's swift kicks and graceful pivots when they sparred, the way the dust puffed up under their feet as they parried and jabbed, that single instance when Aris had caught Dysis in the shoulder and sent her tumbling to the ground . . . it all gave her a sense of fond nostalgia. And it made her miss Dysis even more.

A little island of stillness in the moving sea of bodies caught Aris's eye. In the corner of the training field Specialist Pallas stood by herself. Three men fought one another while she looked on, her lips pinched into a frown.

Lieutenants Daakon and Cruz were already mingling among the soldiers, offering pointers as necessary.

Aris made her way to Pallas's side. "What's going on?"

Pallas gestured to the whirlwind of the three fighting

men: Baksen, Specialiast Mann, a thick-necked, muscular transport flyer, and a soldier Aris didn't recognize. "They won't fight me. Not even Baksen. They say they can't hit a girl."

Aris shook her head. "That's ridiciulous. We had to go through the same training, collect the same bruises."

"But we trained with other women, our sectormates. We never really fought with the men, did we?" Pallas had a point. But the girl's expression didn't reflect her words. Dark shadows sat beneath her eyes, and her hands clenched in rhythm with Baksen's jabs and thrusts. She was obviously unhappy, trapped in a way the diatous veil had never confined her.

Aris took a deep breath and pulled against her elbows, stretching her back. It'd been months since she'd fought hand to hand, and she'd never been good. The men would watch and judge. But it didn't matter, even if it undermined her tenuous authority. Pallas deserved the chance to hone skills that might someday save her life.

"Alright, Specialist." Aris squared off with Pallas, who stared at her with wide eyes. "I've just given myself authorization to spar with you. Let's go."

Pallas shook her head but threw a halfhearted jab. Aris dodged, spinning to deliver a kick to the woman's lower back. "Come on," Aris urged as she lunged. "Don't go easy on me."

Pallas feinted and thrust upward, catching Aris's shoulder with her fist. The blow had enough force to send Aris back several paces.

"Nice." Aris shifted her feet, regrouping.

Pallas grinned. After that, she attacked without reservation. As Aris struggled to hold her own, it was obvious Pallas was burning off more than a little pent-up frustration. The woman's kicks and punches increased in intensity the longer they sparred, and Aris flashed back more than once to the beatdowns she'd taken at Dysis's hands.

As Aris picked herself up from the ground for the third time, a loud voice carried over the training ground. "Fall in!"

Aris nodded to Pallas—they were both panting and sweaty—and took her place in the line of officers.

"We've just received a report of a skirmish in southeastern Mittaka," Milek said. "Our troops are faring ill. Their air support's been shot down, and they need backup. We're the closest unit, so we'll be responding to their distress call. This is a different kind of mission for us, with an active combat scene. We'll provide fire support to the troops battling on the ground."

Aris resisted the urge to bounce nervously on the balls of her feet. She'd hoped her first couple of missions would be quick retrievals: easy, routine assignments to get her back into the swing of things.

"Once the threat is neutralized," Milek continued, "we'll proceed with our regular parameters, searching for survivors and transporting them to a field-mender clinic. Understood?"

A unified chorus of "yes, sir!"

"Liutenant Haan and I will lead this mission from the air," Milek announced. "Report to the airfield immediately. We leave in ten."

The soldiers filed back into the rounded building; they'd pick up their equipment from the armory before heading to the airfield. Lieutenants Daakon and Cruz followed them.

Milek turned to Aris. "Lieutenant, I'd like you to fly with Specialist Contas."

The name was a punch to the stomach. The *last* person she wanted to fly with was the jerk who'd taunted her on the transjet. "Sir? Are you sure? I mean—"

"In spite of their unfortunate attitudes, most of these soldiers know what you can do in the air. Contas is new to this point, and deserving of a lesson, I think." Milek's eyes gleamed. She'd caught a glimpse of him "sparring" with Specialist Kyros; it appeared he was in a teaching mood today.

Milek studied her closely. "This is your first mission. Do you think you're ready?"

His voice was official, but something in the way he looked at her suggested he was asking out of genuine concern, too.

Aris didn't want him to question her readiness for combat. She should be able to handle this. After all, what could Contas do beyond lob a few insults? And as for the flying, she was determined to keep her nerves in check.

You are strong enough for this, Aris. It was always Dianthe's voice that sprang into her mind when she needed reassurance or a kick into action.

Aris slapped a grin on her face, refusing to give her fear further purchase. "I would be *happy* to teach Specialist Contas a lesson, sir."

Milek's answering smile sent warmth flooding through her. And somehow, despite the danger, her heart soared at the knowledge that she'd soon be in the air.

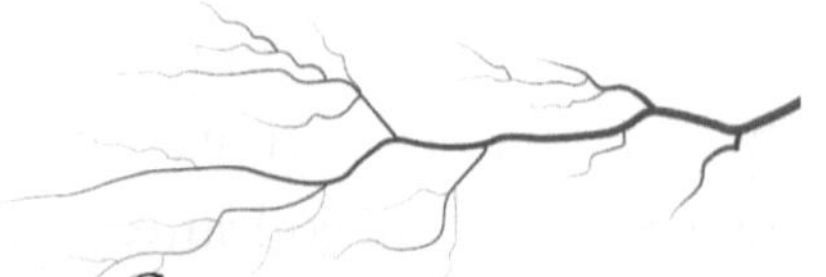

CHAPTER SEVEN

OH HOLY, I'M GOING TO DIE. ARIS TIGHTENED HER hands on the wingjet controls until her knuckles went white. *Just a little farther. You can do this.* She dove closer to the tree line, every nerve twisting.

"This is donkeyshit. I should have been paired with Mann. A girl has no business flying into city traffic, let alone a war zone." Specialist Contas sucked his teeth again, the disgusting sound filling the tight confines of the cockpit.

Aris focused on his words instead of the shadows eating at the edge of her vision. "Believe me, I would have preferred any other gunner to you."

He jerked a little, as if her voice had startled him.

"You came back because of that scar, didn't you?" He asked, poison in his voice. "When you were at home, what happened? Did the little kids laugh and call you a freak? Or maybe, you couldn't find a man willing to spread your legs?"

She swallowed back her first response, which was to scream and eject him from the wingjet, and instead measured her words carefully. "You will address me as Lieutenant or sir, as befits my rank as your *superior*," she stated flatly. "Your behavior since you arrived at Spiro has been a disgrace, and you can be sure there will be consequences."

Contas snorted.

Aris wanted to threaten him, demean him the way he had her. But they were getting close to the battlefield, and she needed to concentrate. She'd deal with him properly once they were on the ground, when there weren't people counting on her.

"Recon One, still on schedule?" Milek's deep voice crackled over their comms.

Aris glanced at the nav. "ETA four minutes, sir. Stand by for visual confirmation of target." She didn't spare her companion another glance. But she couldn't entirely erase his words from her head.

Here, near the Safaran border, the trees were short and scrubby, a faded yellow rather than the rich green she was used to farther south. The remains of a village came into view, its raised pathways black and broken, still smoking in places. The homes were ravaged by firebombs, their white roofs tumbled to burning coal and gray-tinged ash. Aris's heat-seeking tech showed hot spots all over the place.

Safaran soldiers clung to the shadows at the edge of the village, but their black uniforms still stood out. From this height they looked like an army of beetles scrabbling along the ground.

"Recon One has visual. Recon Two?" she said.

Over the comms, Specialist Pallas replied, "Recon Two confirmed."

Without warning, several Safaran wingjets zipped

around a copse of larger trees. In a flash, Recon Four was hit. Aris swerved and dodged, instinct guiding her. She couldn't watch to see if her comrades ejected in time; one of the enemy jets was right on her tail, spraying the air with gunfire. Blasts of fiery red exploded from beneath its wings.

"We've got enemy engagement! Return fire!" she shouted. Adrenaline spilled through her in a clarifying wave. She spun underneath the Safaran jets, setting up for a clear shot. Her gunner didn't fire.

"What the hell are you doing? Take the shot!" But it was too late. She righted them and yanked on the controls, sending them straight into the hazy, smoke-choked sky.

Beside her, Specialist Contas dry heaved. It was his first firefight, but hell if he deserved her sympathy now. "Get it together, Specialist. I will not let you get us killed."

In the jet beneath her, Pallas was engaging the enemy. Fireballs filled the space between the wingjets as each craft evaded fire. The transports stayed out of the main fray because they didn't have the maneuverability of the smaller recons Aris and Pallas flew. But their guns were bigger.

Aris dove again and this time Contas managed to get off a shot. A line of trees below the enemy exploded into flame.

Seconds later, one of the Sarafan wingjets flipped, jerked off its flight path by a well-aimed missile from one of the transports. When it crashed to earth, a huge explosion filled the air with oily smoke. Hopefully it had landed on the enemy encampment, not on the Atalantan troops battling on the ground.

"Let's go, let's go," Aris mumbled, as another Atalantan jet burst into flame. Aris dropped one hundred feet with teeth-clenching speed and then spun to give Contas a clear shot of a Safaran wingjet, but he was too busy trying not to vomit.

The enemy jet veered away. "Damn!" Aris flipped and dove again, opening a lane for Specialist Mann to move in and engage. His transport fired off two missiles in quick succession, turning the Safaran wingjet to burning scrap in midair.

She spared a split-second glance at Contas, yelling, "Step the hell up!"

As Aris skated over the enemy foot soldiers' line, Contas did his job at last, letting loose a barrage of fire that drove the men back from the Atalantan line.

Aris listened more closely to the frenzied chatter over the comms. "Recon One to Transport One, status?" Aris asked, waiting impatiently for the reply. Milek, Daakon, and Otto were flying Transport One. *Please please please . . .*

"Transport One to Recon One. We've got the final wingjet engaged. Stand by," Milek responded, sounding as cool and in control as ever.

Fire burst crimson and gold along the black wing of the final Safaran wingjet. So much destruction everywhere.

Aris let out a breath.

"Recon One, do a sweep." Milek ordered.

While the rest of the fleet turned their attention to the battle waging on the ground, Aris circled wide, scanning the skies for other threats. Beside her, Specialist Contas coughed loudly and wetly, as if choking back bile. She couldn't bring herself to say something reassuring. All she managed was, "Think of water, like the ocean. Should help."

He turned to look at her, his helmet banging against the headrest. "You're insane. Why do you choose to do this?"

"You mean 'Why do you do this, *Lieutenant,*'" she replied automatically. The question didn't surprise her, but his tone did. He was asking like he actually wanted an answer. "Why do *you* do it?"

He swallowed thickly. "If I hadn't been selected for Military, I sure as holy hell wouldn't be here risking my blighting life."

"Well, someone has to. It's not an easy job, but it's a worthy one." Without the risk—the sacrifice—the whole dominion would be under Ward Balias's thumb. And Aris knew, better than most, how abhorrent that would be. "I'd rather die fighting for my dominion than sit at home watching it burn."

He scoffed. "Like I said, you're insane."

A few minutes later, she gave the *all clear* and Milek echoed it. "Enemy threat neutralized." He added, "There's a lot of ground to cover in searching for survivors. I need everyone down there. This is still an active scene, so keep your solaguns up and your eyes open."

One by one, the wingjets landed, fanning across the scarred countryside. Aris landed less gracefully than usual, enjoying Contas's groan of discomfort as they bounced along the ground. Maybe saving someone today would make him feel differently. Then again . . . she wasn't counting on it.

The sun was near setting, but when Aris opened the cabin's glass hood, suffocating heat still pressed in on her. By the time they'd jumped to the ground, their solaguns held at the ready, their eyes streamed and skin stung from the thick smoke and smell of burning oil.

"Gods, I can barely breathe," Contas said, his voice already hoarse.

Aris took out the utility knife strapped into the leg of her pants and cut away a strip of the shirt underneath her uniform jacket. She slid the fabric up under her helmet to cover her nose and mouth. It helped her breathing a little. Slowly, she and Contas picked their way over the uneven ground, flanked by the other flyers, gunners, and retrievers of their unit. Several hundred yards to their right, Milek calmly bent to check a prone body for a pulse. Aris's heart lurched when he stood, shook his head, and moved on.

Through their helmet comms, the soldiers took stock of the dead. "Transport Three, Specialists Evander and Severn, deceased," someone reported.

Not Evander. Aris hadn't known him well, but she'd known him. Covered in colorful tattoos, he'd often filled the rec room with his booming voice, singing bawdy love songs and pretending to drink vutzo from an imaginary shot glass.

"Four Atalantan infantry soldiers, deceased," said Lieutenant Daakon.

"Two Safaran soldiers, deceased," came another voice.

It took some time to reach the wounded, but Aris could hear them, their groans, screams of pain, and prayers coaxed from desperate throats. She held her breath as she passed silent, solagun-burned bodies.

The hulking carcass of a Safaran winget belched clouds of stinking smoke across her path. A bloody arm reached from beneath the rubble, its lifeless hand curled into a claw of agony.

Contas shuffled over a torn-up ridge of dirt. "I can't. . . . I wasn't expecting . . ."

Aris's gaze was still drawn to that bloody hand. "I always expect this. Only way I can handle it is to prepare for it." The tears streaking her ash-covered cheeks were only partly caused by the venomous air.

"But how can you prepare for *this*?"

The hand clenched suddenly into a fist. Aris gasped. "I think we've got a live one." She scrambled across the torn-up ground, sending a message over her comm requesting the closest retriever. All S and R soldiers were trained in combat mending, but retrievers were usually the best, as it was their job to stabilize victims for transport.

It wasn't until Aris reached the crumpled wingjet that she realized the arm was clad in Safaran black. It didn't stop her from dropping to her knees beside the soldier. Now she could see he was caught beneath the wreckage. Not the flyer, then. He was a foot soldier. She bent closer to take a pulse and got her first look at his face.

Wide, dark-brown eyes stared back at her, blinking once, twice. Dirty, blood-streaked cheeks. Thin lips drawn back in terror or pain. Gods he looked young. And so scared. Even though he was the enemy, Aris's heart clenched for him.

"What is it?" Contas asked, coming up behind her.

"Just a kid." Aris brushed some dirt off the boy's shoulder, knocking his solagun away as a precaution. Not that he was in any state to use it.

Contas hunched closer and then reeled back. "Oh holy."

The boy coughed weakly, bringing up a splatter of blood. "Help me. Please," he whispered.

"Hold on, now. We'll get you out." Aris cast panicked eyes over the kid's small frame. What she could see of it, anyway. His legs were caught beneath the still-burning wingjet. She stood up and grabbed a bent edge of wing, heaving with all her strength, but it didn't move.

"Help me, Specialist," she growled. Contas stood a few feet away, bent over his knees and breathing heavily. "Specialist, *now.* Or he'll die."

After a moment, Contas stood and positioned himself on the other side of the boy and grabbed the wing. Over the black, broken wingjet, he met Aris's eyes. "He's Safaran. Why—"

"Shut up." Aris braced herself. "We're search and rescue. This is what we do."

A skittering of stones and loose dirt announced the arrival of Otto and several of the other retrievers, who scrambled down to where Aris and Contas stood. With the extra manpower, they were able to shift the jet slightly, just enough to free the boy's legs.

But by that time, his wide stare had turned inward and the agony had left his face. With the sense of something precious wasted, Aris bent over him and gently closed his eyes.

She moved on to help those still struggling to survive, but she knew she'd be haunted by the memory of that young Safaran soldier for a long time.

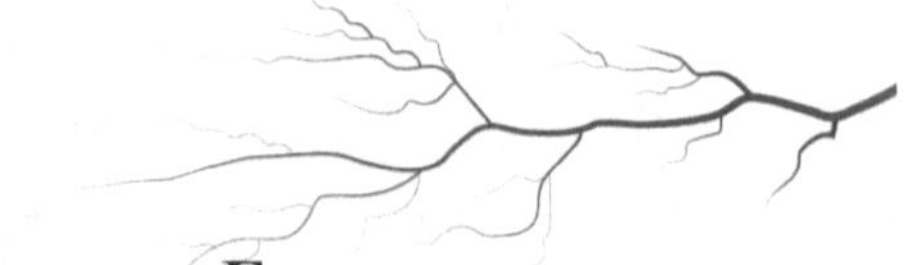

CHAPTER EIGHT

WHEN THEY ARRIVED BACK AT SPIRO, ARIS couldn't get out of the wingjet fast enough. As soon as the soldiers were dismissed and the other officers had filed back into the building, she hooked a finger at Contas. "Specialist, follow me."

Once inside the building, she stalked straight to Milek's office, ignoring the grumbles and dragging footsteps behind her. Milek and Lieutenant Daakon turned when she tapped on the open doorway. Behind them, the faces of the soldiers killed in today's battle stared at her from the monitor on the wall.

Milek raised a brow, which hitched up the thin scar along his pale cheek. "Is there a problem, Lieutenant?"

"Indeed, sir," Aris replied. "Specialist Contas here. He's a problem." She wanted to punch the guy. He didn't even bother to stand at attention.

Lieutenant Daakon gathered his digitablet and left the office with a small nod.

"Go on." Milek's striking blue eyes hardened into a glare as he stared at Contas. The kid wasn't smart enough to cower.

"It's my opinion that Specialist Contas is not a suitable fit for this unit," Aris said. "His poor attitude and less-than-ideal response to high-pressure situations do not befit a soldier in such a specialized field. In addition, he sexually harassed me during the mission."

Milek's face tightened, but he kept his voice steady. "Your recommendation?"

"Wait, you're going to listen to her?" Contas stared incredulously at Milek. "But she's—"

Thunder broke over Milek's face. Aris almost felt sorry for the soldier. Almost. "Lieutenant Haan is your superior officer. You will address her as such and treat her with the respect befitting her rank."

"But—" Contas sputtered.

Milek snapped his gaze to Aris. "Your recommendation?"

"Reassignment to a support unit on a bigger, more central stationpoint. Preferably one that has a good handle on integration. No one should have to depend on Specialist Contas for their safety." In the end, he'd get what he wanted: a relatively safe job away from the front lines. But that was fine. She wouldn't risk someone else's life just to teach him a lesson. Still . . . "Punishment for disrespecting an officer would be appropriate as well."

"Noted," Milek replied. "Until your new orders come through, Specialist, you're on waste-removal duty. If you say a single disrespectful word to Lieutenant Haan or Specialist Pallas, I'll have Lieutenant Daakon run you until your legs fall off. And *then* I'll let Commander Nyx discipline you. Understood?"

Specialist Contas stood a little straighter, though he looked like he'd swallowed glass. He nodded and spit out a "yes, sir."

"Dismissed." Milek turned his attention to the digitablet on his desk.

The soldier stomped out, shooting a hateful glare at Aris. She started to leave the room herself, but Milek spoke from behind her. "Lieutenant, a moment more of your time, please. Close the door."

She did as she was told, her pulse picking a quicker, slightly unsteady beat. She turned back to face Milek. "Sir?"

He leaned back against his desk and looked at her thoughtfully. The edges of his mouth softened. "I'm sorry about Specialist Contas. I didn't think he would be brazen enough to actually harass you. We'll need to find you another gunner."

"I need Dysis," Aris said, the familiar ache returning. "It'd be so much easier if she were here."

"She's welcome to return." Milek leaned forward and Aris took a step closer, drawn to him despite herself. The remnants of adrenaline still flooded her system, electrifying every nerve.

Aris smiled a little. "Oh, she knows. I tell her often enough in my comms. I think she *wants* to come back, but she won't admit it. She's determined to stay with her brother."

He rubbed his chin, considering her words. His "hmm" told her nothing of his thoughts, but the way his strong finger ran along his bottom lip sent inappropriate fantasies rocketing through her mind. Just that small, casual gesture, an entirely innocent, unconscious brush of skin against skin, and she was a yearning, angsty mess.

It was the adrenaline. She remembered the dreams she had after difficult missions when she was still living as Aristos, the way she'd imagine Milek's hands on her in the dark. The electricity under her skin when they sparred. The one kiss they shared.

It was just the pressure getting to her. Best to ignore it. That's what she'd always told herself before.

"Lieutenant Haan, are you okay?"

Blight it. She was staring.

She was about to turn, to wave a hand with a "sure, fine, just need to get something to eat," when she noticed the intensity in Milek's gaze. It was almost as if...almost as if he guessed at the thoughts running through her mind. Guessed at the heat that tingled under her skin.

And felt it too.

A blush flared across her cheeks.

"There's another problem I can't quite figure out," she said, clearing her throat. It was as if she no longer had control of her tongue, or her gaze, raking across his face. Lingering on his mouth.

Milek straightened, which brought him closer to her. She could almost feel the heat of his body. "And what is that?"

She gripped her courage tightly and forced herself to meet his eyes. "You're so respectful, so supportive. I knew you would have my back with Contas. And yet..." She drifted the slightest bit closer. "You kissed me before our last mission. And now, the way you look at me...I don't think it's the way you look at your other soldiers. Your female soldiers. Is it?"

Aris couldn't believe the words out of her mouth, couldn't believe how close she was standing, how much she wanted him to answer.

How terrified she was of his answer.

"I'm so sorry for putting you in this position," he said. "You don't know how hard I've tried to forget that kiss. How hard I've tried to see you as any other soldier."

The heat under her skin burned hotter. She could see so clearly, now, how she haunted him.

Just as he haunted her.

Tentatively, she reached out and brushed her palm against his arm, no longer able to resist the urge to touch him.

Slowly, slowly enough that she could see clearly what he was doing and stop him if she wanted, Milek put his hands on her waist. With a sigh that sounded like a confession, he said, "Aris, I don't look at *anyone* the way I look at you."

The words cut the last frayed cord of Aris's self-restraint. She tipped up on her toes, grabbed his face with both hands, and kissed him. The way she'd dreamed of kissing him, the way she'd wanted to ever since he showed up in Lux, squinting into the sun.

In the next instant, they were pressed together, hands and lips and heat everywhere.

Aris knew her own heart must be pounding, but she was only aware of Milek's pulse racing under the hand she pressed against his chest. Her other hand curled around the nape of his neck, coaxing him even closer.

Her body ached at the hunger in his kiss, the desperation

with which his lips clung to hers. He lifted her and set her on the desk, their mouths still locked together. Her legs snaked around his waist, as her hands slipped down the hard muscles of his back.

It didn't seem possible that he could want her with such ferocity, with a force and need that matched her own. As she slid her hands up under his shirt, he pushed her jacket off her shoulders, down her arms, until the stiff fabric released her. Underneath, the shirt she'd sliced apart during the mission let a cool breath of air caress her skin.

Against his lips, against her better judgment, she whispered, "Is this allowed?"

"I don't care," Milek growled. He stroked her cheek with his thumb and kissed her harder.

What might have been a moment or an hour later, Commander Nyx's voice came over the intercom. The announcement had nothing to do with them, but it was enough to bring them back to the harsh lights of Milek's office. To the small space, now heated by their breath.

Aris's legs were linked around his waist. She had never seen so much color in Milek's cheeks, nor his eyes so dark with desire.

The room throbbed with the sound of their quickened breathing as they stared at each other. Neither of them looked away, neither could bear to let go, and yet . . .

Reality swirled between them, threatening to tear the fragile moment apart.

"What do we do now?" Her voice was rough and quiet. Inside, her heart hung poised in the balance. One word from him, and it would fall.

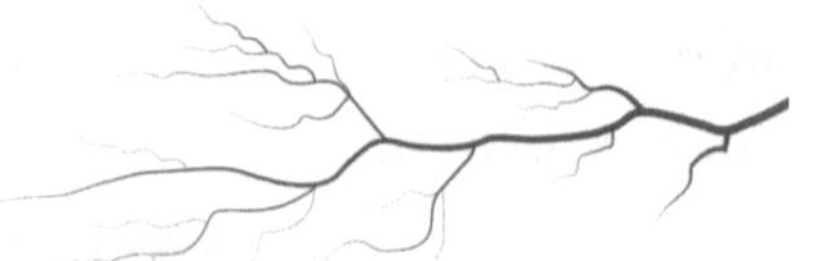

CHAPTER NINE

GALENA PACED HER OFFICE IN SIBETZA, RUSLANA'S capital city. Thick, gray carpet silenced her footfalls as she circled the large wooden desk, chrome benches, and low black table that filled the center of the room. One wall was hidden behind thick burgundy curtains, another covered by an enormous vid monitor.

She paused at her desk and tapped the screen of her digitablet again. Why wasn't Milek picking up? He'd never before missed one of their weekly calls. If he had a mission, he always left her a message so she'd know not to worry.

Suddenly, the screen on the wall blinked on. Milek dropped into his office chair and into view. He was breathing heavily, as if he'd been running down the hall.

"Are you alright?" Galena perched on the edge of her own chair. His rush set her on edge. "Do you need some time? I can call back."

Milek shook his head as he smoothed the front of his jacket. "I'm fine, Mother. Sorry. I'm just running late."

Galena looked closely at his image. "You're never late. What's happened? Is there news on Elom?"

"Aris—Lieutenant Haan—returned from her first reconnaissance mission in the invisible wingjet, and I wanted to debrief her before I spoke with you," he replied. "We hacked the comms of a few men from Elom's security detail. Thought we had a credible lead."

"And?" Even as Galena's pulse raced at the news of Elom, her mother's sense tingled. *Since when was Milek on first-name terms with Aris Haan?*

Milek shook his head. "She didn't see anything definitive in the search area. But the coordinates were on the outskirts of a city, so there was a lot of activity. She thought one building looked suspicious. . . . Several black terrans surrounding it, more heat signatures than would suggest a family."

"That sounds promising," Galena said. She hadn't expected to have actionable intel so soon.

Milek shrugged. "I'll pass the details up the chain so more investigation can be done. Commander Nyx and I agreed that sending in our own team wouldn't be wise. The location requires a covert touch. Too many civilians for an airstrike."

Galena couldn't stand to sit still any longer. She stood up and paced before the large monitor on the wall.

"I'm sorry I don't have more for you," Milek said. He looked down at her from the vid, his cool blue eyes the exact same color they'd been when he was born. He would hate knowing this, but every time she looked at him, she still saw his round baby cheeks peeking through the hardened soldier he'd become.

"Don't be sorry," she said. "You've already made more progress than I expected. I'm surprised you and Lieutenant Haan have the invisible wingjet out on missions already."

"Aris was ready," he said.

Hmm. "I'm glad she's reacclimating so well. How is she handling the promotion? And all the media scrutiny?"

Milek sat back a little. "She hasn't watched the news, and Commander Nyx has been able to keep reporters from coming on point to interview her. I think she's smart to stay out of it as much as she can."

"She'll have to make a statement at the ceremony next week, maybe grant an interview. Is she prepared for that?" Galena was actually looking forward to the event. It wasn't often they could justify celebrations these days.

"She'll do fine," Milek replied, smiling a little.

Galena watched him closely. "And are the male soldiers respecting her new position?"

There was a certain twitch he got at the corner of his mouth . . . there.

"We've been making progress. It will take time." He saw her expression before she had time to settle her features. "What?"

"You and Lieutenant Haan . . ."

He ducked his head, but she could still see the wash of pink warm his cheeks.

"Milek!"

"What, Mother?" The innocence in his eyes was a complete sham.

"You *like* her, Milek," she said sternly. If he thought he could lie to his own mother . . .

Milek stood so quickly his desk rattled. The screen filled with the pale-blue sheen of his jacket. She wanted to see his face. "I know it's completely inappropriate. I've . . . we understand that a relationship isn't feasible right now—"

"*No*, Milek," Galena said, a sudden, unexpected wave of emotion slamming through her. "Don't do that to yourself."

He sat back down. Shock widened his eyes. And no wonder; she never spoke to him like that. "What do you mean?" he asked.

She wouldn't let him make her mistakes. "I know what it's like to deny yourself happiness because you think it's the right thing to do. But it's *not* right. If you and Aris care for each other, don't let anything stand in your way."

Milek stared at the surface of his desk. She could tell her intensity was making him uncomfortable, but she didn't care. It didn't matter if it was a fling, a fleeting moment between them. She didn't want him to have regrets. She and Pyralis had carried theirs for nearly twenty-five years.

"I keep trying to convince myself I don't have feelings for her." He looked up at Galena, a wry smile flitting across his lips. "But the truth is, ever since I found out she was a girl . . . ever since I saw her stand up to the boy she'd been seeing, declaring herself a flyer—a fighter—to save you, I've been lost."

With unexpected tears clogging her throat, Galena confessed, "Aris is the only woman I've met with even a *hope* of being worthy of you, dear."

"The Military will make it forbidden sooner or later," Milek said, his voice dragging. "I can't be with her if it means she'll lose her job. I refuse to make her choose."

Galena wished, more than anything, she could be in that room with him. He might be twenty-two years old, nearly twenty-three, but he was still her little boy. "You don't know what the future holds, Milek. All you have is now. Steal your happiness while you can."

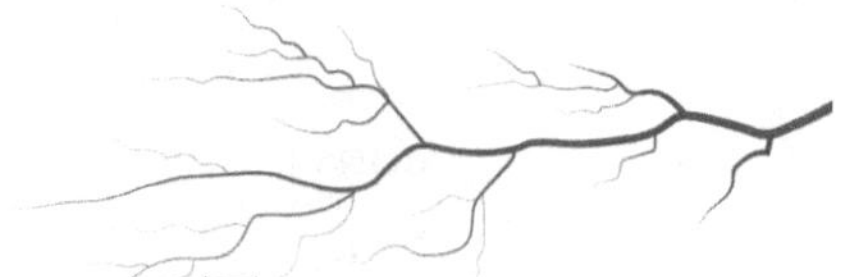

Chapter Ten

The day was hot—sundress weather—and Dysis Latza could appreciate not having to confine herself within the stifling layers of a uniform. But as she walked home from the sprawling glass school building where she taught mechanics, her dress swinging loose around her, she still found herself stretching her legs, squaring her shoulders, just as she'd done when she was disguised as a man. As her hands swept against her thighs, she could almost feel the smooth fabric of her Military-issued pants instead of the rumpled cotton of her dress.

Which was stupid.

She had everything she wanted: her brother Jax, a spy who'd been injured escaping the same Safaran prison camp where Ward Vadim was held, was home and safe. She had her old job back and an honorable discharge from Military sector. She'd cut all ties to that part of her life, except for an occasional comm from Aris, begging her to come back.

Dysis was moving forward, taking care of her brother, falling back into the comfortable, familiar routines of her life.

It was blighting boring, and more nights than not, she dreamed of missions past and future. A future she had absolutely no interest in.

She told that lie so often and so well, she almost believed it herself.

As she rounded the last bend in the trail before the edge of her street, she rubbed her hand along a pockmarked, misshapen chunk of concrete rising out of the ground, an ancient monument to the vast city that had once stood on this ground. There were slabs of broken wall throughout the town, piercing the sky in an array of sizes, an eerie collection of standing stones that tourists had once visited before the war. Now the only visitors were refugees.

It was considered good luck to rub the bumpy, weather-stained surface. Dysis didn't believe in luck, but she liked the feel of the rough stone against her fingertips.

She turned onto the street, which sparkled a little. At night, the pavement would glow a pale blue, making it easy for terrans and pedestrians to navigate after dark. At the corner, the house she'd lived in all her life leaned back against the forest, its steep, solar-paneled roof angled up toward the trees. Jax's terran, a little two-seater, sat out front.

Inside, Dysis slipped her hardpack off her shoulders and dropped it next to the door. "Hey, Jax! I'm home!"

She kicked her sandals off next to a myriad assortment of flying boots, sandals, and a single pair of needle-thin heels that she never wore and couldn't believe she even owned. She was too tall for shoes like that. But when she'd come home from

Spiro, after months in uniform, she couldn't help herself. She'd worn them the day she bought them, and they'd sat by the door since, tipped on their sides like abandoned toys.

The shoes that caught her eye now rested next to the silly silver heels. They were large, tan boots, so familiar she almost ignored them, until she realized why they were so blighting familiar. They were Military issue.

"Jax!" she called again, a new edge to her voice. The hallway opened to the large living space where they spent most of their time. The white walls and furniture hid nothing. Jax wasn't there.

Dysis fled to the back of the house, where the glass wall exposed a view of the forest. Outside, in the shade of the tall trees, her brother stood talking to a man in full Military uniform.

Dysis slammed her hand against the panel beside the glass wall. As soon as it slid open, she slipped out. "Jax!"

She jogged the few steps to them. *He can't be leaving so soon. He's not ready.* Panic clogged her throat. "Jax, you can't go yet. You're still limping. The mender said you have another month of recovery—"

The visiting soldier turned and the words froze in her throat, blocked by a lump so big she couldn't breathe.

Lieutenant Daakon's brown eyes held an expression that made her want to turn around and run the other way. "Specialist Latza," he said in his quiet voice. "I'm not here for your brother. I'm here for you."

Jax cleared his throat. "Ah. I'll be inside. Dysis, you let me know if you need anything." He leaned on his stick as he crossed the stone patio, but his straight shoulders told her what she'd been denying for weeks. Jax was almost there—almost ready to be a spy again.

But this wasn't about him.

With a deep breath, she met Daakon's eyes again. "What are you doing here?" Her voice came out as strong as she'd hoped it would.

His sturdy dark body blended with the shadows beneath the trees. He was so solid, so strong. But she knew the softness he hid beneath those corded muscles and that steady gaze. Gods, she was going to throw up.

"How could you not tell me?" he asked, eyes narrowed, not answering her question.

Her breath hitched. "Tell you what?" It was stupid, feigning ignorance. But she was nothing if not bluster and fire. No one knew that she was soft inside, too. No one knew how much she wanted to throw herself into his arms.

"*You know what*." Harder, angrily, he said, "You let me believe . . . you let me get close to you."

Dysis closed her eyes for a split second, pulling all her defenses tightly around her. She didn't want to hurt Daakon. But she didn't want to explain herself either, explain why she'd let him think she was male, even after it was obvious he had feelings for her. She couldn't tell him how she felt; it wouldn't do a blighting bit of good. She wasn't—couldn't be—what Daakon wanted, and nothing would ever change that.

So she raised her chin. "I wanted information on Jax. I used you to get it. End of story."

She expected him to yell. Instead, his face broke. He covered it with his hands for a second, then rubbed his cheeks briskly, as if trying to scour away her words.

"It wouldn't have mattered anyway," she said, hating herself. "I'm not what you want, am I? If you'd known I was a woman . . ."

He didn't finish her thought for her. He didn't say anything else for a minute, just stared at the ground and scuffed his foot against the smooth, pale patio stones. It was all she could do to keep from grabbing his hands, from pulling him to her. She wanted to feel his arms around her; she wanted to kiss him until the rest of the world disappeared. They'd only shared moments . . . a look here, a short conversation there. An almost-kiss that had haunted her for months.

She forced her gaze to the dappled shadows beneath the trees. She and Jax had played in this forest as children, pretending to shoot each other with solaguns and making forts that fell to ruin each winter under the weight of snow. They'd found all sorts of artifacts among the leaves and rocks that littered the forest floor: broken glass bottles, plastic balls, an armless doll, handfuls of tarnished, twisted silverware. Somewhere out there a treasure trove of lost civilization waited, their hoard abandoned to the years they spent mourning their parents, leaving the forest to its own secrets. Dysis wondered if she could find the cave that hid all those treasures, all the beauty and wonder of her childhood.

Not likely, after so many years.

Her voice gruff, Dysis added under her breath, "Sorry."

"Specialist," Daakon said softly, his voice rougher and deeper than she'd ever heard it. "Major Vadim sent me here to bring you back to Spiro. You're needed."

She tried to switch gears. "I'm needed?"

"Lieutenant Haan wants you back as her gunner. I think

she's been having trouble with the others." He scuffed his foot on the ground again.

"Because she's a woman, you mean." Dysis glared at their long, thin shadows on the tile. Aris didn't talk much about her missions—she couldn't, in case comms were intercepted—but there'd been an edge to her writing since she'd returned to Spiro. And it was impossible to miss the news vids.

Just that morning Dysis had seen an interview with Aris's parents. The pretty blond reporter who'd done so much of the reporting on Ward Vadim's husband's death had sat down with them to talk about their "famous" daughter.

The reporter had started gently, asking if they were proud of Aris, if they'd been surprised to find out about her secret life. Aris's mother had preened for the camera, just as her father shied away from it. But they'd both clammed up when the woman had leaned in with a predatory gleam and said, "Many people in Atalanta feel that your daughter should be punished rather than praised for impersonating a member of Military sector. What do you say to those who feel women have no place on the front lines of the war with Safara?"

Dysis had wanted to teach that smug woman a few very important lessons about life on the front lines.

Daakon shifted his weight, drawing her attention. "We need to get going. Major Vadim wants us back by nightfall."

Dysis took a breath, steadying herself. "I'm sorry you came so far. But I'm not going anywhere. Jax needs me." The words came out brusque, even though the voice in her head sounded young and terribly afraid.

Through the windows, her brother met her gaze. Even from the distance, she could tell he saw the scared little sister beneath her overbearing exterior; it was written in lines of sympathy on his face. She tore her gaze from his.

Daakon took her hands, shocking the ever-living hell out of her. "Your brother will be returning to duty soon, and you'll be here alone. Aris needs you. Your dominion needs you. But Jax . . . Jax doesn't need you. Not here, anyway."

All the breath left her lungs. It wasn't fair, how well he knew her.

"That isn't my life anymore," she said, the words sounding weak even to her own ears.

Daakon dropped her hands. "Liar."

Dysis glanced at Jax again. Already, he felt so far away.

But Daakon was right. She'd been lying to herself for months, about Jax *and* herself. It was time to face the truth.

Chapter Eleven

Aris sighed as the tiny wingjet shimmered back into visibility around her. Twilight sent golden streaks across the landing pad as she touched down. It was her second solo mission in as many days, and she was no closer to finding Elom than she had been back in Lux. Both leads had gone nowhere; this one had been even more frustrating than the first. She'd flown practically to Safara's capital, holding her breath as she dodged one Military wingjet after another. Invisibility had its drawbacks; she had to be vigilant every second to avoid an in-air collision . . . and it was impossible to forget the land she flew over was enemy territory.

She hit the lever and the windshield slid back. All she wanted was a hot meal, a hot shower, and her bed.

"Lieutenant Haan." Milek waited for her on the tarmac, squinting into the last rays of the setting sun. "Welcome back."

"Thank you, sir." A new wave of adrenaline coursed through her as she jumped down beside him. But she kept her voice steady. "Another dead end. Maybe Elom is sending false information out to mess with us."

"I've no doubt he is," Milek replied. "But we need to chase down every lead. It's the only way to distinguish which sources of intel are legitimate."

"If you say so." She didn't have the energy to be optimistic. Or, frankly, to be around Milek. They'd agreed they should minimize contact; there was no denying there was something between them, but it didn't seem professional to pursue it.

And right now, frustrated by the failed mission, she didn't feel confident in her ability to remain professional. It was all she could do to keep from slipping her arm around his waist. Leaning into him. Letting her head rest on his chest...

Yeah. She needed to go.

Milek kept pace with her as she headed for the door.

"Listen, Major," she said, trying to head off his concern. "I'm tired. I need to—"

"Aris." His hand snuck to the inside of her elbow, drawing her into the shadows made by two wingjets at the edge of the tarmac.

Just that small connection was enough to undermine every smart, responsible thought in her head. When he stopped moving, she didn't, not until her body was pressed fully against his.

Whatever self-control she'd been clinging to over the past week crumbled. Milek was probably trying to tell her something really important, but her mouth got in the way.

For an instant, he paused against her lips, humming like he was still trying to talk, and her stomach twisted. It would be just like it was with Calix...Milek was going to tell her they had to follow the rules. He was going to stop her, remind her how unprofessional this was.

She couldn't even control herself for one week.

Disgusted with herself, Aris started to pull away, but Milek's mouth followed, deepening the kiss. Telling her with his body and his hot hands cupping her cheeks not to stop, not to let any distance come between them. Abandoning all rational thought right along with her.

Her breath caught, forgotten, as she arched against him, flames leaping under her skin.

"This is a bad idea," she breathed into the space between their bodies.

"Or a beautiful one," he murmured against her lips. "You're all I can think about, Aris. Staying away is killing me."

"We shouldn't kill ourselves over this," Aris whispered, almost laughing, gasping as Milek kissed her neck. "We can't give Balias what he wants."

Milek laughed against her skin, drawing her even closer. "So this is self-preservation?"

Aris drew his head up to kiss him deeply, her fingers sliding along his short hair. "Something like—"

The screech of the loudspeaker tore them apart. "Lieutenant Haan, report to Commander Nyx's office immediately. Lieutenant Haan."

They both looked around. No one else was on the tarmac. Aris's heart pounded, even as relief poured through her. They were lucky. They hadn't been caught.

But they hadn't been careful either.

She smoothed her hair. "I guess I'm late to my debriefing."

Milek grinned as he gave her a little push toward the door. "This is one debriefing you're going to enjoy. You rudely interrupted me trying to tell you about it, so you're just going to have to be surprised."

She slanted a skeptical look back at him. "What's that supposed to mean?"

He pushed her again, lightly. "Go see. And tell Daakon to meet me in my office after dinner."

Before she could ask him to clarify, the door slid open.

She hurried to Commander Nyx's office, running Milek's cryptic words through her head, resisting the urge to touch her lips, which still pulsed with the echo of his.

The empty corridor smelled of lamb and roasted potatoes; as soon as she was finished, her first stop would be the mess hall.

Commander Nyx's door was open. And there, in the doorway—

"Dysis!" Aris slammed to a halt and stared slack-jawed at her friend.

The tall girl's olive skin had darkened in the summer months they'd spent apart. Her short black hair stood up in spikes, and the small key-shaped Tech brand on her temple offset her dark-brown eyes. Aris remembered the very first time she'd seen Dysis, in the room they shared. Dysis had stabbed at her temple, bemoaning the fact that their original brands weren't removed when they'd volunteered. Aris had just nodded, struck dumb by the intimidating, angry man standing before her.

Dysis had always been good at playing her part.

"Oh hey, Hummingbird," she said now, as casually as if they'd seen each other minutes ago, not months. Trust her to use Calix's old nickname for her; Dysis had always enjoyed teasing her about it.

Aris was not deterred. She launched herself forward and the two girls embraced, a combination of laughter and back slapping, awkward and exuberant all at once.

Commander Nyx's sardonic voice cut through their reunion. "Lieutenant Haan, if you would join us inside, please?"

Aris filed into the room behind Dysis, a huge smile still plastered to her face. Milek was right. She was definitely going to enjoy this briefing. Good surprise.

Lieutenant Daakon stood in the corner of the office, his face unreadable. She wondered how *his* reunion with Dysis had gone.

"Lieutenant Haan, Specialist Latza will be bunking with you and Specialist Pallas for the time being. I've sent someone to move a third cot into the room. I trust this is acceptable?"

"Yes, sir," Aris replied.

"Please escort Latza to dinner. We'll debrief on your recent mission tomorrow morning after formation. Oh, and I understand you're both going to the ceremony in Ruslana. You leave in two days' time. Find some dresses to wear." Nyx's attention was drawn to her digitablet.

Dysis straightened. "Why can't we wear our uniforms?"

Nyx didn't bother looking up. "Ward Nekos requested dresses." Dysis opened her mouth, but Nyx raised a hand. "I don't care if you disagree. It's not your decision. Get going."

As soon as they reached the hall, Aris turned on her

former sectormate. "I'm so glad you're back. I can't even tell you."

Dysis made an exasperated noise. "I couldn't exactly refuse when Daakon showed up at my door."

"Yes, you could have." Aris shot her a look. "But I'm glad you didn't."

"Jax is going back to work soon. After the ceremony, I think. So . . ." She shrugged, focusing her attention on the blank white walls.

Just before they reached the main hallway—and the cafeteria—Aris paused, ignoring the insistent growling of her stomach. "I told Mile—Major Vadim that I wished you'd come back, but I had no idea he would send Lieutenant Daakon for you."

"Yeah, well. He did." Dysis glanced at her knowingly. "How *are* things with Major Vadim?"

Aris ignored her, though a traitorous blush climbed her cheeks. "How are things with Daakon?" she countered.

Dysis looked away, her face tightening. "Awkward. Messy. Just as you'd expect."

"I'm sorry." Aris squeezed her arm, knowing the words were nothing, wishing she could do something to ease her friend's pain.

"It is what it is," Dysis huffed. "Let's go eat. I'm starving."

"Ugh, Otto. Being a porkpie doesn't give you permission to be gross. Close your mouth." Aris rolled her eyes when Otto ripped another bite of lamb off the bone with his teeth.

"Liked it better when you pretended not to care," he mumbled around the giant mouthful.

"So much of this I missed—" Dysis stabbed a shriveled olive with her fork— "and yet, somehow, the food didn't make the list."

"It grows on you," Otto returned.

"It certainly has on you," Dysis said, eyeing his belly.

All around them, the cafeteria was filled with the rumble of voices and the clink of silverware. Pallas and Baksen sat with them but didn't say anything. Pallas had been subdued for days, ever since the mission that had killed Evander. Tonight, she slumped over her plate, picking at the greasy lamb, and didn't grin at Otto's jokes. Her eyes kept flitting to the empty seat at the table across the aisle, where Evander used to sit. Like Galec's chair, it was tied with a black ribbon and left alone out of respect.

Evander hadn't been particularly welcoming of their new female "status," but he hadn't been a complete idiot about it either. And, before the integration, he and Pallas had been friends.

"My fat is my camoflauge," Otto continued. "Works better than whatever contraption you females were using." He waved his fork toward Aris, Dysis, and Pallas.

Aris snorted. "You didn't have a clue."

Otto wiped his mouth with the back of his hand. "My dear Lieutenant, you are wrong. We all knew there was something off about you three. Too much . . . feeling."

He shuddered.

"Surely you mean the feeling of humiliation when we did better than you at, well, everything?" Dysis said, smirking. "If you'd really known you'd have reported us."

Otto shook his head and popped a small, round potato in his mouth. "Nah. Then I'd have lost my favorite splots players. At least you made winning a *bit* of a challenge."

Aris cracked a smile, but Otto's words were more than an awkward joke. Maybe, somehow, he had known, or suspected. And still he fought at their sides with no complaint, then and now, despite the derision of the others.

"When do you leave for Ruslana, Lieutenant?" Pallas asked, filling the sudden void of conversation.

"In two days." Aris was already anxious about it. Milek had said she'd have to sit on the dais, in front of everyone. It would also be the first time reporters would have access to her. Commander Nyx had already warned her that she might have to speak to them.

Her parents had sent her a comm after their interview, furious at the leading questions and the reporter's obvious disapproval of Aris's choices. Aris hadn't brought herself to watch it yet. She tried to stay away from all news vids these days, but the other soldiers loved to turn them up whenever she dropped by the rec room looking for Pallas or Otto. She couldn't miss the dismissal and derision with which the more conservative reporters spoke of her, or the footage of angry protestors like the ones she and Dianthe had run into.

"Commander Nyx said we have to wear *dresses*," Dysis groused. "I don't understand why we can't wear our uniforms for the ceremony. All the men will be in theirs."

"You're going, too?" Pallas raised her brows.

Dysis nodded. "Jax invited me. He couldn't decide on an *actual* date. Too many women to choose from, apparently."

"Where does one find a ball gown in two days, anyway?" Aris glared at her plate. "It's not as if I've got a heap of the stupid things lying around. I guess I'll have to ask my mother to bring a dress to Sibetza."

A dark shadow loomed at Aris's elbow. "I see you in a sequined number. Short and tight." Specialist Contas's eyes wandered along her body, his hands clenched at his sides. "The kind of dress you can rip right off."

Aris stood, drawing herself to her full height, aware of Dysis moving behind her. "You need to walk away. Now, Specialist."

"Or what? I'm on a transjet out of here tomorrow, thanks to you." His handsome face twisted. "You can't touch me, bitch."

Dysis stepped forward. "You're right. She's too polite." She grinned, adding, "But I'm not" as she punched him in the face.

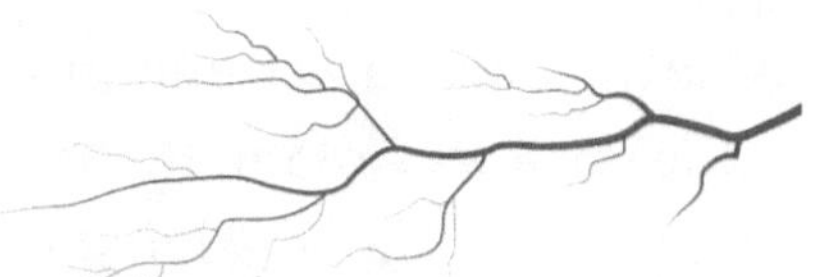

Chapter Twelve

Long before dawn the next morning, a soft knock woke Aris. Dysis and Pallas moved sleepily, but she waved them off, slipping out of bed on silent feet.

When she pressed the panel, the door slid open to reveal Milek. Her heart did an automatic cartwheel.

"What is it?" she whispered. The bright hall lights made her squint.

His short hair was spiked up on one side, his own eyes still heavy with sleep. But his voice was urgent when he replied, "A transjet flying troops to Bieza picked up chatter from a Safaran unit just over the border. They're protecting an 'asset' that needs to have direct comms to Ward Balias."

"Elom?"

"We think so." His gaze flicked behind her, into the dark room. "We've got a forty-eight-hour window. That's it."

"I can be ready in ten minutes," she said. "Meet you at the landing pad?"

He nodded and with a quick, private smile, he strode down the hall.

Aris collected her uniform and body armor and dressed in the small washroom. In the dim glow from the emergency lights, her scar shone a dull silver. She said a fast, silent prayer that *this* mission wouldn't be a waste of time. Elom needed to answer for his crimes, and she wanted to be the person who dug him out and exposed him to the world.

"Meeting Major Vadim for a morning . . . workout?" Dysis leaned against the wall by the washroom door as Aris returned to the bedroom.

Aris nearly jumped out of her armor. "Blighting hell, Dysis," she whispered. "You scared me."

"Imagine *my* surprise to find you and Major Vadim sneaking around before 'lights on.' What's happened?" She shifted; in the faint light from the washroom, Aris could see she'd crossed her arms.

She didn't want to lie to Dysis, but Milek hadn't authorized her to tell anyone about the missions with the invisible wingjet. With a shrug, she said, "Just a quick recon run. I'll be back by lunch."

"You and Major Vadim like your secrets, don't you?" From her tone, it sounded like Dysis thought Aris's covert activities were of a more personal nature. Which wasn't exactly untrue. But was also not something she could talk about.

"I've got to go." Aris escaped quickly, but she was pretty sure Dysis noticed the bright red blush that lit her cheeks as she hustled past her and out of the room.

Fog cloaked the landing pad, giving the lights that lined it golden halos. A faint glow to the East hinted at dawn. The air held a heaviness, a volatility that sent Aris's gaze to the sky, looking for lightning.

Milek waited for her near the invisible wingjet with a red secure-tech digitablet. "Sorry for the early wake-up." His voice sounded strangely muffled by the fog. "But I didn't want to waste any time."

"I'm glad you got me. I wouldn't have wanted to wait either." Aris brushed her hand against his hip as she leaned in to look at the digitablet. "Where am I going?"

He brought up the map. They stood a little too close as they huddled over the tablet, but there was no one to see. "Our intel suggests Elom is holed up in this hilly region at the base of the mountains," he said, pointing to an area just over the Safaran border. "We need you to do a flyover to look for any troop buildups or suspicious activities."

"No problem." At least this mission was along the border and not as far into Safara as the last one.

Aris took the digitablet and hopped into the wingjet, powering up the nav so she could input the coordinates. When that was done, she climbed back down and handed him the secure-tech device.

As he reclaimed it, Milek let his fingers linger against hers. She drifted closer, his body pulling her like a string. It was dangerous to stand this close.

Milek cast a quick glance around the landing pad. They were alone, cocooned in the mist and the quiet. He pressed a fast, hard kiss to her lips. When he might have pulled away, she clung to him, coaxing him to kiss her longer, deeper. She knew they were taking a risk, that there was a chance they could get caught. She promised herself she'd stop, move away, be professional, even as she drew him against her, their breath and heat and lips mingling until she was wild with it.

Somehow she ended up with her back against the wing-jet's cool side, her hands tangled in Milek's hair. She wanted to curl her leg around his thigh, slide her fingers under his shirt to feel the smooth muscles of his stomach. Instead, with a regretful sigh, she forced a small distance between them.

They looked at each other for a moment, eyes wide, their quickened breaths beating against the fog like birds' wings.

Reluctantly, Aris scrambled into the wingjet. Milek winked at her as she yanked on the lever to close the dome. She tried to erase the big dumb grin off her face. It was time to concentrate. She flipped the switch to engage the veiling tech and pulled gently on the controls, bringing the machine up to a hover over the airfield.

"Comms up?" she asked as she cut through the fog to a clear patch of sky above.

"Coming in loud and clear." A smile in his voice, Milek added, "Take care of yourself, alright? I'd like to have another . . . er, debrief . . . as soon you as you get back."

"A debrief, huh?" Aris's pulse still fluttered through her, igniting every nerve ending.

"I felt like we were communicating quite well." She could practically see the mischievous glint in his eyes.

She laughed.

As she flew toward Safara's border, the fog burned off with the sun, but a thick bank of clouds marched toward her from the horizon. The summer storms were rolling in early today. Aris stayed below the cloud line, afraid the featureless mass of gray would be disorienting without visible wings and a nose to ground her.

She glanced at the nav panel and noticed a large pixilated patch obscuring part of the map. She toggled a few things; it wasn't until she'd flipped off the heat-seeking tech that the map returned to its former clarity.

"There's a glitch in the heat-seeking tech," she shared with Milek over comms.

"Has that happened before?" He sounded more annoyed than concerned.

"No. But it might be the weather. Heavy cloud cover here. Everything else is working just fine."

"Keep me updated. You notice any other issues, you get out of there immediately. Don't take any risks."

"Yes, sir." Aris smiled at his protectiveness.

She kept to a steady, northwesterly track, moving ever closer to the border with Safara.

In the distance, a jagged bolt of electricity pierced downward through the darkening clouds. "Blighting fantastic," she muttered. Disorienting or not, she needed to make it through the clouds to the clear sky above, at least until she passed the storm cell. She checked her progress; only a few minutes from the outside edge of the search area. She had to dodge the storm quickly; her best chance at finding Elom's camp was to stay low to the ground so she could get a visual confirmation.

With an inner sigh, she pulled up on the controls, spiraling through the thickening storm clouds. Immediately, her vision contracted to a swirling mass of gray and silver white. Rain spattered against the glass dome with the sound of thrown pebbles. She caught herself flinching.

Just a little dance. Nothing you can't handle.

Aris pushed through the mess at an angle, gaining altitude. Wind buffeted the small jet, throwing her off course. She clenched her hands around the controls so they wouldn't shake. Ahead, a wedge of blue sky muscled through the clouds.

Almost there.

Aris pointed her wingjet's invisible nose toward the widening gap. Lightning flashed uncomfortably close, blinding her for an instant.

"Status?" Milek's voice filled her helmet, drowning out the crack of thunder.

She glanced quickly at the nav panel before returning her eyes to the chaos outside. "Just reaching the search area. Stuck in some weather, but I'm coming out of it."

At that moment she burst from the clouds into a fall of sunlight . . . and saw a shimmering patch of the wingjet's nose flicker before her.

"Blighting hell!" She swore. "The veiling tech's been damaged. I have to—"

"Aris, get out of—"

A loud hiss of static garbled their words.

"Damn." Aris spun and dove, desperate to change course. She didn't like the signal interference. That meant more than one system was affected. As soon as she crossed back into Atalanta, she needed to assess—

A piercing whine clashed with an urgent beeping from the nav panel. Incoming fire.

How is that possible?

Aris pulled straight out of the dive, shifting direction as fast as she could to outrun the missile. She needed to disappear into those storm clouds. She flipped belly up and began a steep climb.

The wingjet jerked sideways off its trajectory, its left wing bursting into visibility as it was engulfed in flame.

"Milek!" Aris shouted, her voice as urgent as the nav's beeping. "I'm hit." Oh Gods. She was too high. Without a wing, there was no way—"I'm going to have to punch out!"

"No! It's too dangerous! Just take her down easy. You can do it."

Aris pulled the chute straps tighter across her chest. Punching out was always a last resort; it was usually safer to try to land a malfunctioning wingjet. But sometimes it was necessary if there was too much damage—or if you were too high. And sometimes it didn't matter. Sometimes you were dead either way.

"I'm sorry, Milek." Static crackled, interrupting her again. "I'm too high. There's too much—"

Another blast shook her. She tried to keep the jet level, but the controls did nothing to stop its sudden descent. Punching out would probably kill her.

But an uncontrolled fall would definitely do the job.

She jerked on the dome lever with all her strength, letting in the screaming wind.

She drew in a last, desperate breath as she was sucked from the burning jet and flung into the deadly freedom of the naked sky.

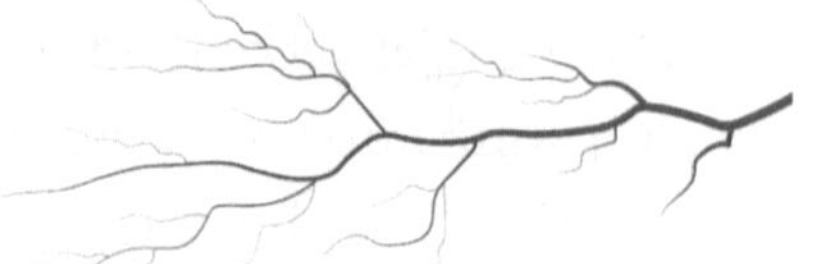

CHAPTER THIRTEEN

IF PYRALIS WERE THE TYPE TO SUFFER TENSION headaches, this meeting would have produced a crushing one. Atalanta's top Military commanders had already informed him that Safara's troop levels were increasing—and no one knew how. They'd also insulted Galena's planned security measures for the ceremony, which was just a day away, and complained about the weather in Sibetza. And now . . .

Galena stared incredulously at the sat-projection on the table. "So you're saying all those red dots are Ward Balias sightings?" There were dozens of them, hovering above a three-dimensional map of Safara. Many regions of the dominion were black, empty swatches that cut through the map, where Atalantan surveillance didn't yet reach. Too much dark space.

Commander Freni, a grizzled soldier with short graying hair and pockmarked cheeks, shook his head. "No. Those are the Balias sightings *this week*. And that's just within the areas where we've been able to access news feeds and hack into surveillance."

Pyralis shook his head. "But that's impossible. These locations are too far-flung. There's no chance he could have traveled that far so quickly."

"And he's been silent for weeks," Galena added. "No statements to the press, no sightings by our surveillance tech before now. This type of behavior, even if it were physically possible, is entirely unprecedented."

Pyralis paced the length of the room, a wood-paneled, secure-tech office in Ruslana's capitol. Galena chose a different room each time Atalanta's Military commanders met here, and kept guards stationed inside and outside the only entrance. She was probably being overly cautious, but he didn't blame her. Her abduction had made it clear that Ward Balias's reach was frightening in scope.

"We're looking into it," Commander Freni said. "On the tech side, it *could* be possible they've wised to our hacks and are feeding us faulty intel." The other two commanders let Freni do the talking, as usual.

Pyralis turned his attention to the youngest of his advisors, Commander Quin. Scrawny and bespectacled, he always looked like he *wanted* to say something, but he didn't often speak up.

"Commander Quin, in your experience, do you think it probable they're sending us these sightings to derail our efforts?" Pyralis asked.

Quin glanced up from the sat-table in surprise. But it only took him a moment to recover. "If Ward Balias suspects our plans to infiltrate his inner circle, he might flaunt his obvious well-being and safety as evidence he's untouchable.

But most leaders tend to lie low when they're aware of a threat. He *could* be sabotaging our surveillance access points to feed false sightings, but that would require a considerable amount of skill and effort."

Pyralis stared at the splatter of red dots hovering over the map. So many for one man, but if you looked at them as the movements of multiple men . . .

A sudden conviction filled him. "He's not sending us faulty sightings. He's got the blighting veil tech." Pyralis seethed. "He's made decoys of *himself*."

Galena studied the map more closely. "Gods, you're right."

She looked like she wanted to kiss him. Pyralis wished she would.

"Ward Nekos, you have an auditory comm on line ten," a tech voice echoed through the room. "A Commander Nyx."

"Excuse me, gentlemen." Pyralis headed for the desk Galena indicated. Embedded in its surface were ear buds for auditory comms. As soon as the bud settled into his ear, the comm fizzled on.

"Commander Nyx? This is Ward Nekos," he said.

As she spoke, his face drained of color. "You can't be serious."

Galena hurried over as he ended the call. "What is it? Is my son okay?"

His voice hoarse, he murmured, "Lieutenant Haan has been shot down over Safara."

Galena's eyes widened with shock. "No," she breathed.

Behind the desk, they linked hands, a silent, secret support.

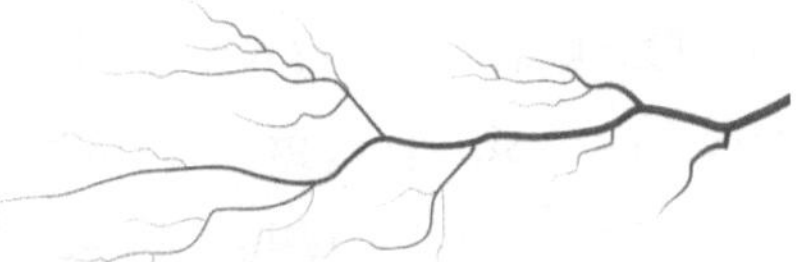

Chapter Fourteen

Dysis shoveled a bite of olive salad into her mouth, wincing at the saltiness that overpowered it.

"Specialist Latza, I'd like a word, please." Daakon stood just over her shoulder, appearing out of nowhere. His quiet voice cut through the laughter and conversation like a knife. Heads turned toward her. She glanced up at him, then away. Quickly.

None of the officers had said anything about the punch she'd thrown the night before, even though it had started a cafeteria-wide brawl, but she'd known a reckoning was coming.

She slanted Otto a look as she stood. His face was mottled with bruises, but he still grinned at her as she followed Daakon from the room. Unfortunately, Aris was still out on her special secret mission and would be of no help.

As soon as they were in the hall, Dysis turned on

Daakon. "You know it wasn't my fault. That guy was insulting an officer."

Daakon kept walking. His frown transformed his boyish face into a sharp-edged mask.

Dysis's steps faltered. *Oh Gods.* She must really be in trouble.

He turned then and waited for her to catch up. The bright lights of the white hallway caught against his dark skin and for an instant she saw something . . . something *else* in his face. Not anger or frustration.

Sorrow.

Her heart plummeted.

He led her to a hallway she'd never been down, to a room she'd never entered. It was full of comfortable furniture—a couple chairs, a couch with a worn blanket thrown across it. Two standing lamps at either end of the couch provided a dim amber glow.

"What are we doing here?" Dysis asked.

Daakon didn't answer. He withdrew two cups and a bottle from a cupboard along the wall. Dysis stood in the middle of the room, shoulders hunched, aching with tension. What the blighting hell was going on?

"Sit." He held out a cup full of rosy liquid.

Pushing the blanket out of the way, Dysis sank onto the couch. She sipped the liquid suspiciously. Her gaze flew to his face. "Vutzo? No thank you." She'd only tried it once before. She still remembered the pounding headache she'd woken up with the next morning.

"Drink it." He sat beside her, hands tight around his own cup. With a swift movement, he knocked the liquid down his throat, hissing after he swallowed.

Dysis took another sip and tried not to gag. She stared at the bright red carpet. "You're kicking me out, aren't—"

"Lieutenant Haan was shot down this morning." His words fell against hers with the force of a firebomb.

Dysis became a statue. No breath, no beating heart, no brain to process what that meant.

"I'm sorry, Dysis. I thought I should be the one to tell you."

Aris had said it was just a quick recon trip. Surely a mistake had been made. Surely—

"Did she survive?" The words grated against her throat.

His silence said it all.

She gasped in a breath, then sucked the rest of the liquor down her burning throat. She stood on shaking legs and grabbed the bottle Daakon had left on the counter. The liquid sloshed onto the floor as she poured another cup. Strong hands reached out to steady hers.

She yanked herself away, the cup crashing to the floor between them. The room filled with the sharp scent of apricot and ginger.

"I'm fine," she snapped. "You don't need to hover. Or comfort me. Or whatever you're doing."

He just stood there, too close, a dark shadow eating up every bit of light.

"Why did you even tell me? Why didn't you wait for the briefing?" She pulled herself up to her full height, meeting his gaze head on.

"I knew you'd be upset. I thought I could—"

"You thought you could what?" Every bit of herself was threatening to explode into agony, but she couldn't let it. She would *not* break in front of him.

"Help," he said, sighing. "I thought I could help."

Energy buzzed under her skin, like she was going to split apart. "I've got to go."

She whirled, but he grabbed her wrist, pulling her back to face him.

"Dysis, *stop it*. It's *me*. Please let me help." He grabbed her other hand. Drew her closer. Too close. They hadn't been this close since that day, nearly a year ago, when they'd almost kissed.

She yanked against his grip once, twice, the pain and the panic building inside her. And then it happened.

She broke.

With a hoarse cry, Dysis buried her head against Daakon's chest and sobbed.

He held her tightly, his arms heavy and secure around her. They were almost the same height, her face wedged into the space at the base of his throat. His scent, lemon and spice, assaulted her. She curled her arms around his neck.

Aris is gone. Aris is gone. Aris is gone.

Dysis strained closer, deeper into Daakon's arms, trying to hide from the truth. Eyes closed, buried in his skin, his scent, she could almost forget.

Daakon ran a hand over her head, smoothing her short hair, sending shivers down her back.

The vutzo was warming her, inside out, loosening her joints and her heart. Hardly aware of what she was doing, she pulled his head down to meet hers. She'd already lost her best friend, why not lose herself this last, little hope?

When her lips touched his, Daakon froze, his whole body rigid against her. Her tears fell faster.

But instead of pulling away, telling her he was sorry but he didn't *see* her that way anymore, he kissed her back. His lips tasted of her tears and the apricot ginger vutzo. She melted into him, her heart breaking open with sorrow and joy.

<hr>

Eyes closed, Dysis stretched until her hands brushed the edge of the carpet, until her shoulders popped, and the tension in her lower back eased.

Carpet?

She sat up, heart pounding. A soft, worn blanket fell to her waist.

On the floor next to her, Daakon still slept soundly. The blanket had fallen off his shoulder, exposing his well-muscled chest and the large tattoo of a Ruslanan ice dragon that snaked along his torso. Its wickedly sharp claws stabbed toward his heart.

As she stared at the grim tattoo, flashes of memory overwhelmed her. The spicy vutzo burning her throat. Daakon holding her, so tightly, as she cried.

And then . . . and then . . .

At the memories, her cheeks warmed, along with all the places that he'd touched. She pulled the blanket up to cover her body.

Daakon opened his eyes.

"Hi," she whispered. "I think we fell asleep." The thin blanket and a whisper of air was all that separated them.

"Hi, Dysis." For a long moment, he stared into her eyes, searching her face. She almost leaned closer, almost pressed her lips to his. But then he rolled onto his back with a sigh. Not the good kind.

An edge crept into her voice. "So, was that the *official* protocol for comforting a subordinate? Or did you decide to improvise?"

"It wasn't like that. You know that." He got up, yanking his pants off the edge of a chair and his shirt from where it dangled over one of the lamps.

Dysis swallowed hard, but when she spoke her voice was strong. "What *was* it like then? Were you taking advantage of me or leading me on?" She swore with every fiber of her being that she would not cry.

The words made him wince, as if they'd been physical blows. He finished dressing and slumped onto the couch.

The couch where we—

"I didn't take advantage of you," he said, rubbing his temple as if he had a headache. "I wouldn't. If anything—"

"Don't you *dare* say I took advantage of *you*," she growled. Her stomach churned.

He leaned forward, his face hardening into uncharacteristically rigid lines. "It wouldn't be the first time, would it? You know who I am. You knew when you were first here at Spiro, playing with me to get information on your brother."

Tears filled her eyes. She raised her chin and turned away, her naked spine as straight and stiff as an iron rod. She couldn't deny his accusation. "You should go."

"Look, I'm sorry," he said, his voice softening. "I really am. I care about you, Dysis. You were so sad, and the vutzo. . . . But I made a mistake. I can't be what you want me to be." Daakon's voice cracked.

Her heart broke in a thousand new ways, pain slicing

through her like shattered glass. "I get it," she said, not looking at him. She couldn't let him see how his words tore her apart. "You are who you are."

"I could wish to be different, I could wish . . . but . . ."

"But wishing is what children do," she mumbled, agony lining her words. "And we know better."

"I'm sorry," he said again. "I didn't mean to hurt you."

She raised her chin, though she still couldn't bring herself to look at him. "You didn't." *Liar.* "But I need to leave now. I told Pallas I'd meet her for dinner." *Liar.*

He didn't move, and she couldn't bear to wait for him to go. She wrapped the blanket around her and stood up, searching for her discarded clothes with as much dignity as she could muster. Her hands shook as she pulled on her uniform.

It was so much worse getting what she wanted once, knowing it would never happen again. And there'd be no talking about it with Aris, the only one who could possibly understand how she felt. Aris, her best friend.

Aris, who was dead.

Dysis's heart pumped sluggishly, pounding in her temples, as if it, too, were about to forsake her. She was zipping up her jacket when the door slid open. Daakon jumped to his feet. She didn't have time to react.

Milek stared at them with red-rimmed eyes, a flash of shock flitting across his face. After a beat, he cleared his throat. "Both of you, in my office. Now."

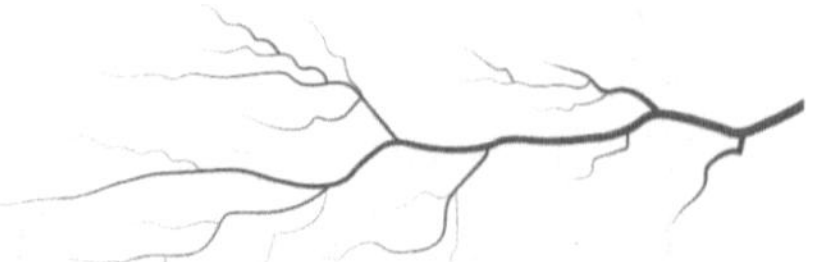

Chapter Fifteen

The funeral pyre clung to the edge of the cliff, high above a golden crescent of beach and the vast blue of the ocean. Surrounding the platform, tall wooden columns were draped with black streamers that snapped in the wind.

Dysis stood at the edge of the crowd, close to the line of trees. She couldn't bear to watch Aris's parents weep as they placed handfuls of yellow pixypots on the still, silk-swathed body. She couldn't handle the sound of the wild-haired girl up front sobbing. She couldn't stand the sick pounding of her own heart.

Major Vadim had made her come, as part of the official contingent from the Atalantan Military. Other soldiers from other stationpoints were there as guards, circling the mourners as a protection against would-be protestors, callous reporters, or Safaran attackers.

Dysis had wanted to stay in Spiro. She'd wanted to *do* something. But Major Vadim had insisted.

She could see him, barely, through a gap in the crowd. He stood near the pyre with a handful of flowers. His face was pale and still as chiseled stone. He hadn't spoken a word the entire flight to Lux. Even from this distance, Dysis could see the tension in his clenched fists, the stiffness of his shoulders. Beside him, Dianthe's head was bowed, the blood-red snake tattoo that circled it drooping, as if mourned too.

The bracing ocean wind brought a soft voice to Dysis's ears: Aris's mother saying goodbye. It was almost time.

A man entered the clearing not far from where Dysis stood. "No . . . I don't believe . . . oh Gods." His voice cracked and stuttered.

Like Dysis, he wore an Atalantan Military uniform. His dark-green eyes and warm, tanned skin sent a shock of recognition through her.

Calix. Of course he would come.

He didn't notice her. When his eyes widened, Dysis followed his gaze to the pyre; the platform had disappeared beneath a blanket of flame.

Calix crumpled to his knees, head in hands.

"This is all my fault." His hoarse whisper carried on the sharp, smoke–scented breeze.

Something twisted deep in Dysis's gut. "Oh. You're a Safaran gunner then?"

Calix's head shot up as he tried to identify who'd spoken. It didn't take him long; Dysis was the only one near him.

"Were you talking to me?" he asked, his voice still rough with emotion.

"It's not your fault Aris died," Dysis said quickly,

looking back toward the pyre. She should have let him have his moment to grieve.

He cleared his throat. "It *is* my fault. Aris and I . . . If I had asked her to Promise on Selection night, like we'd planned, she would have stayed in Lux. She would have been safe."

Dysis moved closer, holding her hands at her sides with an effort. She suddenly wanted to throttle him. "Safe? Aris didn't need to be safe. She needed to live. You didn't understand her at all. You didn't even try."

"Excuse me?" Calix stood up, advancing closer himself. "Who the hell *are* you?"

"I was Aris's sectormate. And I know exactly what you did to her, Calix." Dysis tried to keep her voice down, but the anger spilled out anyway. A few of the other mourners glanced in her direction.

Calix glared at her, eyes burning. "I've been trying to figure out how to tell her that I made a mistake. That I *am* trying to understand. That I . . . that I still . . ."

Love her.

The unspoken words hung in the air.

"Well, it's too late." What else could she say?

"Yes. Clearly. Thank you." His face crumpled as he looked back toward the fire. He swallowed reflexively, as if his regret might actually choke him.

Dysis snapped. She was so *sick* of too little, too late. "Oh for Gods' sakes. Get it together. You're mourning a girl you *abandoned*, don't forget."

"I didn't abandon her." He kept his eyes on the pyre. "She'll never know it, but I gave up everything to be here today, with her. I wasn't strong enough before, but I sure as hell am now."

Dysis glared at him. "What could you have possibly given up to be here?"

Calix looked at her with a strange resignation. "I lied. I broke the rules. The law, actually."

Dysis laughed outright, earning horrified looks from the two women standing closest to her. She yanked Calix closer to the trees. More quietly, she murmured, "*You* don't break the rules. Aris has always been very clear on that point."

He shrugged. "When I heard about her death, I couldn't get permission to come here today. Not being Promised, I had no claim. So I just . . . left."

Dysis's mouth dropped open. "You *left*? Like, left your stationpoint? But that means—"

"I'm a deserter." Calix glanced toward the crowd, which was now singing a slow, mournful lullaby. The music eddied around them, hiding their conversation within its eerie melody.

He'd *deserted*, risked jail, just to say goodbye. To bear witness to a corpse. Dysis shook her head. "That is the most ridiculous thing I've ever heard."

"And it is none of your business," he said stiffly. "Now, if you'll excuse me, it's time I pay my respects."

"Listen," Dysis said more gently, as she reached for his arm again. "You need to get back to your unit. Tell them you're sorry. If you go back now, you'll hardly be punished."

"I can't." The sadness in his eyes was excruciating. "Aris's parents are devastated. They've been getting hate mail. There are reporters and protestors *stalking them.* I need to stay here in Lux and help them through this. I wrote them a comm this morning saying that I'd received a fortnight's leave. I'll go back to my unit and face the consequences when I know Aris's family and friends are okay."

To Dysis's horror, tears pricked her eyes. It was the last thing she had expected him to say. But she couldn't let him do it. "You're not Aris's Promised, Calix. That's not your job. It isn't worth jail time, believe me."

He pulled from her grip as his face flushed an angry red. "Stay out of it. You don't know a damned thing about who Aris was or how her family is suffering. I've known her parents since I was born. That history didn't just disappear when Aris chose to become a soldier and risk her life. *I* know how to help them."

He turned his back on her and wove into the singing mourners.

"Blighting hell," Dysis swore under her breath as she dashed after him. Of all the idiotically noble reasons to break the law. She couldn't let him go to jail. Not for this, anyway.

She caught up to Calix and slipped in front of him, forcing him back a few steps. His hands twitched with his obvious desire to move her forcibly out of his way.

"You have to go back," she hissed into his ear. "Whatever you think is going on, whatever gesture you're trying to make . . . it's not the right move."

He glared at her, surrounded by the tapestry of people that made up Aris's life.

Major Vadim is going to kill me.

With a resigned sigh and a roiling stomach, Dysis did what she knew Aris would want her to do. "That's not Aris, up there on the pyre," she whispered, so only Calix could hear. "We think she's still alive."

"*What?*" Calix froze, his gaze still fixed on the edge of the cliff, where the flames blackened the white shroud. They were close enough here that the wind blew the fire's heat against Dysis's cheeks. The body on the pyre—a Safaran soldier who'd been left to rot on the battlefield—could so easily be the lie.

The diatous veil, hastily configured by Dianthe, had been enough to convince Aris's parents and friends. It wouldn't have withstood more than a passing glance, but it didn't have to, now that the body was shrouded and the fire was doing its work.

Dysis pulled Calix out of the crowd, back to their place near the trees. He came willingly, his face shifting through emotions so fast she couldn't identify them. Dianthe slanted a look their way, but no one else seemed to notice them.

As soon as this last song faded into silence, the funeral would be over and everyone would move toward Aris's parents' house. Dysis had maybe a minute to convince Calix to keep his fool mouth shut.

"You can't say anything." She forced him to focus on her. "I only told you so you'd go back to your unit and not risk jail time. If all goes well, Aris's family and friends won't be mourning for long. You shouldn't stay here, okay?"

Calix's cheeks flushed and his lips tightened to a straight line. "Are you telling me Aris's parents don't know she could still be alive? Are you telling me they think this is *real*?"

Dysis wanted to shake him. "They *have* to think it's real. The world has to believe Aris is dead," she said, willing him to understand. "Major Vadim's plan to rescue her relies on Safara believing we collected her body with the wreckage of her downed wingjet. Anyone here could be a spy."

"Why? And if Aris isn't dead, who the hell is that?" He nodded toward the pyre.

Already, Dysis regretted what she'd done. So what if Calix was thrown in jail? If her big mouth endangered Aris, she'd never forgive herself. "Because she was shot down over the border. She's in enemy territory alone, maybe injured. If the Safarans know she's there, if they search for her, they could capture or kill her before we have time to get her back. And because of her new fame, as it were . . . they'll *want* her."

The charade would buy them time. But Aris was still in grave danger. And if she'd been injured in the crash . . .

When Major Vadim had called Dysis and Daakon into his office the day before, she'd assumed it was to reprimand them for . . . well, for having sex in the Officer's Lounge. But Major Vadim had told them that he was certain Aris had survived punching out of the wingjet. He'd heard her scream over the rush of wind when the dome opened, followed by the thud and whoosh of her chute opening. Then her breathing: heavy, fast. Comms had cut out after that, but he'd heard her breathe.

The retrieval team had searched around the wreckage of Aris's wingjet, briefly, before Safaran forces fired on them and they'd been forced to retreat. They hadn't found evidence of her body, her chute, or the ejected seat, so they'd announced over comms that she was dead, which is how Daakon had received his intel. But Major Vadim didn't believe it. He was convinced she was still alive. And needed to be found.

Dysis *wanted* to believe Aris had survived, but it felt

safer to reserve judgment. Major Vadim, on the other hand, looked like he *had* to believe it, or he might die himself.

Calix grabbed her arm. "If Aris is in danger, why the hell isn't someone looking for her now?"

Dysis wrenched free, as people started slowly walking down the path, away from the pyre and the ashes of the body they thought was Aris. "I've already told you too much. Just trust that you're not the only one who wants her back. So get your ass to Mekia before they notice you're gone. And keep your mouth *shut*. If you tell a single person, you might as well be ordering her death yourself."

"It's time." Major Vadim's gruff voice made her jump. She hadn't noticed him approaching. Beside him, Dianthe eyed her with an unreadable expression, the black eyes of her snake tattoo glaring. Truth be told, the woman gave Dysis the creeps. Her mentor, a woman named Theo, had been far less intimidating.

Calix was in Major Vadim's face in an instant, hissing, "How could you leave her there on her own?"

Dysis could tell the precise moment Major Vadim realized who he was looking at. And what Calix meant. She cleared her throat. Chin up, she said, "I'm sorry, sir. He knows."

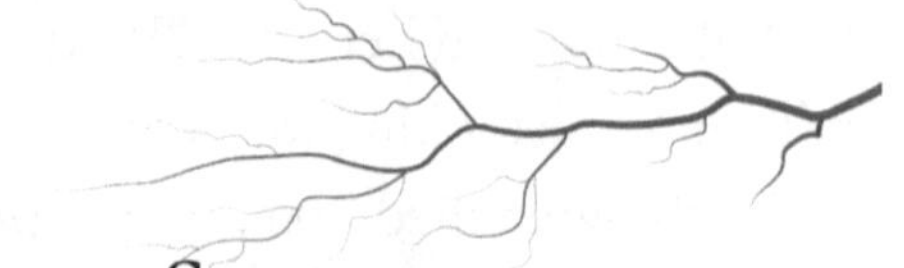

Chapter Sixteen

With a grimace and a groan, Aris woke. Pain lanced through her injured arm, threatening to yank her into darkness again. She fixed her gaze on the rough bark of a nearby tree until her head stopped spinning. Above her, she'd twisted the dun-colored chute through some tree branches, providing shade from the slanting afternoon sun.

She slipped the last nutrigel from her emergency pack. She'd meant to save it another few hours, but her hands were shaking.

When the small pouch was gone, leaving the oily memory of starberry in her mouth, she pushed her emergency beacon. Again. And again. She glanced toward the sky. No sign of wingjets, Atalantan or Safaran.

When she'd fallen from the sky the day before, she'd landed hard in a copse of scrubby trees several miles from where the wingjet went down. The seat had ejected with her and partially cushioned her landing, but she'd still scraped the side of her head along the ground. And her arm screamed with pain. Her collision with the glass dome as she'd punched out had slashed the skin, and she was pretty sure her wrist was broken. Once she could stand without feeling like throwing up, she'd taken stock of her injuries and assets: the chute, which could be used for shelter; and a small emergency pack encased within the chute straps, which included three nutrigel packets, disinfectant spray, two bandages, a solar torch, a compass, and water purifying gel. She also had her utility knife, solagun, and body armor. It wasn't much.

She'd begun her awkward, pain-filled hike toward the gray plume of smoke marking the wingjet's remains. It would make it easier for S and R to find her if she could make it to the wreckage. More importantly, she couldn't let the veiling tech fall into Safaran hands.

Sure enough, she'd gotten within a mile when an Atalantan recon and transport had descended on the location. From atop a mountainous ridge, she watched tiny figures emerge from the transport and search the wreckage. She couldn't tell who they were from this distance, but she hoped Milek was one of them. She scrambled along the rocky terrain as fast as she could, but before she could reach them, three Safaran jets screamed overhead. One of the Atalantans used a flare to set fire to what remained of her wingjet. The recon still in the air held off the Safaran jets until the soldiers on the ground made it back to their transport. She watched in an agony of worry as the Atalantan jets fought their way to the cover of a heavy bank of storm clouds, shooting down one of the Safaran wingjets.

Aris had sunk to the ground, tears flooding her eyes as her chance of rescue disappeared. The other two Safaran wingjets didn't follow. Instead, they floated in the air, circling like giant black buzzards before finally landing, presumably searching for survivors or tech they could use. She had to hope the fire had destroyed the veiling-tech box; she'd lost her chance to do it.

Since then, she'd been traveling in the opposite direction, praying the Safarans would assume she'd died in the crash. The terrain was hilly and treacherous as it approached the mountain range at the border with Atalanta, and she'd made slow progress.

Now it was midday and scorching. Even the shade provided by her chute barely cut the heat. She couldn't afford to rest any longer.

What she'd give to be up in the air, speeding back to Spiro and into Milek's arms.

He must think I'm dead.

The realization sent a bolt of pain through her. Would he tell her parents? Were they mourning her already?

Am I already a ghost?

As the nutrients from the gel steadied her, she risked a look at the gash on her arm. Still oozing blood, puffy around the jagged edges. She'd found no water to clean the wound, though she'd sprayed some disinfectant from her tiny medpack. It needed cleaning, stitches, a fresh bandage. All things she didn't have. And there was the broken bone to address as well. Her wrist had swollen to double its size, encircled with purple-black bruising. She couldn't bend it or put weight on it. In a way, though, she was lucky. If her leg had broken, she'd be slowly starving to death where she'd landed . . . or attempting to drag herself across this forsaken dominion on one leg.

She gathered the chute with her good hand, trying not to jostle her other arm. Time to get moving again.

It was nearly impossible to run with a broken arm. Every step sent blinding pain from her wrist to her shoulder, and it was all Aris could do not to cry out. But if she made a sound, they might find her.

The gash along her forearm started bleeding again. Aris buried it in the yards of her chute so as not to leave a blood trail. She pressed her injured arm tightly against her chest and kept going, working her way farther and farther from her downed wingjet. *Toward* the border with Atalanta, she hoped.

Every time she paused to catch her breath, she pushed the emergency transponder affixed to the front of her body armor. The movement had become a kind of tic, a physical, invisible prayer she sent into the world. Part of her acknowledged it must be broken—if Milek knew where she was, he'd have rescued her already—but she couldn't stop pressing the button.

Panting and shaky, she sank to the ground at the base of a scraggly tree for another short break.

The sound of a breaking twig echoed as loudly as a crack of thunder.

Aris untangled her arms from the heavy fabric of the chute and reached for her solagun. She didn't bother to stand. The tree she leaned against provided a small pool of shadow; if she moved, she'd expose herself.

Another snap. Shuffling.

Aris held her breath, her heart aching for Milek, her parents. Dysis. This couldn't be it. She wasn't ready to leave them.

Please Gods, protect me.

The noises moved closer, the trees swaying in response, as if moved by a tiny breeze. Aris squinted, trying to catch a glimpse of the black Safaran uniforms.

With a snort, a small splotchy brown piggin came into view, its knobby tusks bobbing. Aris let out her breath in a silent rush. It ignored her, skimming the rocky ground along the edge of the trees in search of food.

Food.

Without giving herself time to think, Aris sent a bolt of solagun fire straight at the creature. It squealed once, loudly, and fell to its side.

Aris took a shaky breath. For a long time, she sat frozen, muscles tense, scouring the woods for signs of movement.

No one came.

At last, she swept the chute off her lap and struggled to her feet. Nausea-inducing pain flared through her wrist.

Weakness dragged at her, the effects of the nutrigel gone already. Unless she wanted to end her own misery now with the solagun, she had to find a way to eat that blighting piggin.

One-handed, Aris gathered some twigs and small sticks into a pile next to the animal. She slipped her utility knife from the sheath built into her Military pants. In the center of the hilt, a tiny magnifying glass glowed. She held it over the collection of tinder, angling it so the sun hit the clear circle directly.

A few moments later, a wisp of smoke curled into the air.

The fire was a risk. She glanced up frequently to study

the shadows around her makeshift camp. Evening was falling quickly; soon the smoke would be hidden in the darkness.

Once the flames burned steadily, Aris shifted her attention to the piggin. Every soldier had some survival training, but it was vastly different from actually killing, cooking, and eating an animal in the wild. Still, she'd seen her father slaughter chickens before, and her mother often cut and dressed meat.

Using a knee to steady the carcass, she drew the knife firmly along the leathered skin of its belly. Her vision blurred. She blinked rapidly, willing the world to come back into focus. No passing out. Not now, when she was so close.

With shaking fingers, her wrist in agony, she hacked out two crude chunks of meat. Warm blood ran across her hands, slicking the knife and making her stomach roil.

But later, when piggin fat dripped down her chin as she bit into the crispy, half-burnt meat, she thought it was the most delicious thing she'd ever tasted. Better than her mother's peshka. Better than frothed cream with fresh starberries and mangoes.

It tasted like salvation.

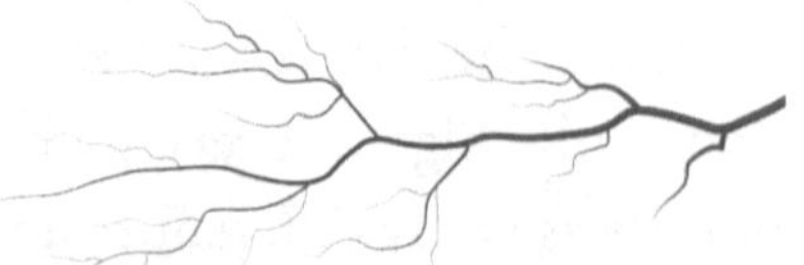

CHAPTER SEVENTEEN

MILEK PACED THE CARGO BAY OF THE TRANSPORT jet. Dysis watched from a corner, her whole body thrumming with tension. This was her fault.

Calix stood in the middle, where the Safaran's disguised body had rested during the trip to Lux. Dianthe leaned against the transport's curved wall a few feet away, glaring at him.

"You need me," Calix said again. His hands were clenched at his hips and his eyes never left Major Vadim's face. "However you're planning to retrieve Aris, I should be there."

Milek paused to glare at Calix. Again. "I *told* you—"

"What if she's injured?" Calix interjected. "I'm a mender. I can help."

Dysis almost groaned out loud. It was bad enough she'd be with Daakon, alone, for the retrieval mission. Adding Aris's former flame would be absolute torture.

"You need to stay out of this, Pavlos," Dianthe growled. "You have no idea what's really going on here."

"I know Aris isn't dead!" Calix raised a fist, as if he wanted to pound on the wall. "I know you're letting her family mourn her for nothing!"

"Not for nothing!" Dysis shouted, stepping forward to put herself inches from him. "This is the only way to protect her! You shouldn't even know—"

"That's right. He shouldn't know," Milek interrupted, his voice deadly quiet. His glare was so sharp it should have made her bleed. "But he does."

"Look, I'm sorry, alright? I didn't . . ."

Major Vadim's focus shifted to Calix. Dysis shut up. "Aris's whereabouts and condition are unknown," he said. "Her life depends on the Safarans believing she's dead, so we have time to find her before they realize they should be look-ing." He resumed his pacing, his entire body strung so tightly she expected to see him bow from the tension.

"But—" Calix started.

"Even if we did want you on the mission, Specialist," Major Vadim continued, "there would be no time to procure orders from your superior officer. If you truly care about Lieutenant Haan, you will return to your stationpoint and tell no one what you've learned."

"I don't need orders." Calix straightened his shoulders. "I've been granted a fortnight's leave for the burning. My time is my own. Or, rather, yours. Please." His gaze shifted to Dysis, as if he was asking *her* permission. "Let me do this for Aris. I've failed her in so many other ways."

Dysis tried to ignore his words. She opened her mouth to tell them he was lying about having leave, that he had deserted. Major Vadim would send him back to Mekia immediately.

Except . . .

Calix kept looking at her, silently begging her to keep his secret.

Damn damn damn.

Dianthe stepped closer to Dysis, towering over her. Her black eyes glittered. "What possessed you to tell him, Latza? Surely you knew how disastrous it would be."

Dysis kicked one of the metal ribs that ran the length of the cargo hold. All of this, in the end, was about Aris. Calix wanted to help Aris, and Aris wouldn't want him to suffer. Dysis couldn't out him. Huffing, she said, "I know. It was a mistake."

"Look, I'm a good mender," Calix said. "And I know the particulars of Aris's medical history. I would be an asset to this mission. But it's more than that. I . . . I would gladly give my life to save hers."

He met Major Vadim's glare head-on, and something like understanding passed between them.

For a moment, no one spoke. Dysis shifted her weight. Calix had been such an idiot to Aris. But . . . but at least he was trying.

Dianthe stood with her arms crossed, storm clouds in her eyes.

"Alright, Specialist. You're in." Major Vadim said the words grudgingly. "It will be your responsibility to ensure Lieutenant Haan receives whatever medical care she needs. But if you jeopardize this mission in any way—"

"I'm dead. Got it." Calix's determination lined every word.

It took too long to get back to Spiro. Too long to unload, too long for Dysis to grab a shower and a tasteless plate of food. And still Major Vadim didn't call her for the briefing on how they would retrieve Aris. To make the waiting even more agonizing, she somehow got stuck shuttling Calix around.

He looked nearly as impatient as she felt.

The cafeteria was empty; a distress call had come in shortly after they'd returned and most of the unit was on their way to the rescue point. "We should have left by now. What's taking so long?" Calix grumbled as he pushed the oily fish stew around his bowl.

Dysis glared at him. "You shouldn't even be here."

He met her glare and raised it a scowl. "I think this whole scheme is pointless and cruel. It shouldn't have even *been* a secret—"

"And when we find her, what are you going to do?" Dysis sat back and considered him. "Profess your undying love? Tell her you're so very *very* sorry you tore her heart out and stomped on it? How do you think she's going to react when she sees you?"

Calix gave her a twisted smile. "Tore out her heart? Stomped on it? And yet it healed awfully quickly, didn't it, seeing as she's already moved on?"

Dysis shot back, "That happened long after—"

"Oh no it didn't." His eyes narrowed. "I saw it months ago in Mekia, before the mission to save Ward Vadim. Aris said she was there for me, but she couldn't keep her eyes off Major Vadim. And he was the same damn way!"

"So what, you're jealous now? Is that it? You don't approve of her choices, but as soon as someone else comes along who does, you change your mind?"

"It was never about controlling her." Calix growled. "It was about keeping her safe."

"You don't get to *keep* her, safe or otherwise. Not anymore." Dysis stood. She was done with this conversation. And she was done with waiting. She stomped to the kitchen to clean her dish, ignoring him.

Daakon was waiting in the doorway when she turned around. "We're ready for you."

"Good." She swept by him without meeting his eyes.

As she followed Daakon down the hall, Calix tagging behind like a lost puppy, she fantasized about pushing them both out of a moving terran. The thought calmed her.

In the Equipment Room, they filled packs with nutrigels and water-treatment gel, ready-to-eat meals and mender gear. From the armory, they collected solaguns, utility knives, and sythins—the narrow rods would incapacitate but not kill, which could be useful if they needed to capture a Safaran for interrogation. Dysis refused to speak to Daakon or even look his way. She couldn't. If she did, she'd remember his ice-dragon tattoo, the warmth of his skin under her fingers.

Gods, she still wanted him. And she hated herself for it.

After they'd collected their supplies, they suited up in body armor and met Major Vadim on the landing pad. The wind whipped around them as they walked out into the night, sending a chill down Dysis's spine.

"We can't risk flying into enemy territory to search for Lieutenant Haan by traditional means," Major Vadim said.

"I'll get you as close as I can to the border, then you're on your own." He nodded to Daakon. "The Lieutenant has the coordinates of your search area. We were able to narrow it down some, based on wind currents at the time of the crash."

Wind currents? They'd be searching for weeks if that was all they had to go on. "What about her emergency transponder? Shouldn't that give you a precise location?"

Major Vadim cleared his throat. His hand pounded against his thigh, over and over. She wondered if he'd have a bruise. "She hasn't activated hers yet."

Dysis's stomach sank. That wasn't a good sign. "Why aren't you going with us, sir?"

His mouth tightened. "I have to run operations here. As much as I'd like to be on the ground, it's more important that I make sure you can get back out. Nothing can go wrong on this mission. You understand? Nothing. We *have* to find her."

Dysis nodded. The look in his eyes told her everything. She had no idea if Aris was in love with Major Vadim, but Major Vadim was definitely in love with Aris.

"Do not contact me until you find Lieutenant Haan," Major Vadim continued. "We'll have only one shot at a retrieval after your signal—we can't be sure our comm lines are safe right now. It is *imperative* they don't know she's alive until we get her to safety. As soon as you find her, hit your emergency transmitters immediately. We'll get you all out of there, whatever it takes."

"So we'll have no way to communicate, except with our emergency beacons?" Dysis asked, touching hers gingerly.

"What if you get more intel or a better location after we leave?"

Beside her, Calix and Daakon said nothing. She glanced at Calix; he, at least, looked equally unhappy with the plan.

Major Vadim bent to grab a bag and tossed it into the transport. "I've assessed the risk. Until we've verified that our comm security is safe, we have to assume all of our transmissions will be intercepted. We suspect Elom and his men were actively targeting the Lieutenant. If they know she's alive, they'll go after her. And with their resources and knowledge of the region, they'll find her first. Got it, Specialist?"

Dysis nodded, even though she'd rather go in, guns flaming, and leave destruction in her wake.

You better be out there, Aris. Dysis heaved her bag onto her shoulder and stepped into the transport. Calix did the same, his expression filled with determination. Such a shame he hadn't shown that kind of commitment four months ago.

In silence, everyone took their seats and strapped themselves in. With Daakon up front as Major Vadim's gunner, Dysis sat in the open cargo area on an uncomfortable chair that unfolded from the jet's wall. Facing Calix.

She kept her gaze locked on the ridged metal flooring between them. She couldn't help bouncing her knees. Energy coursed through her. The trip took just under an hour, and she spent the time clearing her mind, focusing on the mission. It didn't matter than she'd be alone with Daakon and Calix for days, maybe weeks. It didn't matter that Aris hadn't hit her transponder.

Dysis was going to find her. She was going to bring Aris home.

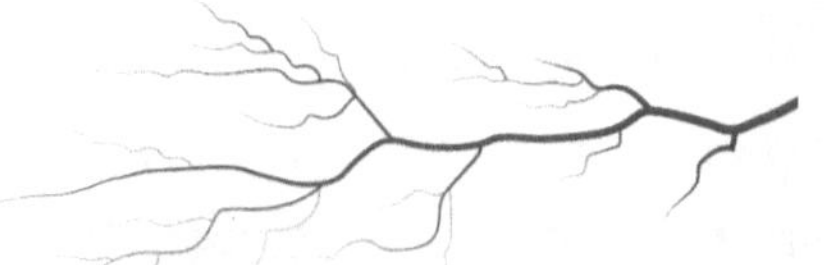

Chapter Eighteen

With her meal eaten and the fire put out, Aris stuffed a couple small chunks of piggin into her emergency pack. She was still weak, even with the food. Her swollen wrist and the oozing cut on her forearm sent heat rushing through her whole system. Even her toes felt too warm.

But she had to keep moving. She needed to find water and get closer to the border, in case her transponder wasn't working because it was out of range. At the very least, she needed to put some distance between her and the campsite. If the Safarans sent out search parties, it would be obvious someone had been here.

As night fell, she set off into the trees, her medpack cinched to her waist, torch in hand, and the chute under her arm. She walked as steadily and quietly as she could. Every few minutes, she risked shining the torch ahead to check for ravines and looking down at the compass to be sure she was still heading east.

The dark and the forest pressed close, and every noise sounded loud as thunder. The rustle of an animal became the stomping footfalls of an army. The chirp of a bird became a scream in her ears. The isolation tore at her resolve, fear and doubt niggling at her to stop, convincing her that this strange, black forest would be where she died.

Aris had never been one for hiking or camping. In Lux, she'd taken slow, careful walks on the beach with Calix, or twilight flights in her wingjet to watch the moon rise. Her nights were illuminated by the cool glow of Lux's raised pathways and peopled by the familiar faces of her friends and family. Her world had never been as black and featureless as this desolate, uninhabited tract of land.

The harsh beat of wings echoed above her. She ducked, heart racing. A few seconds later, a creature screeched as the bird moved in for the kill. Aris pushed herself forward. She didn't shine her light toward the sound; she had no desire to see the monsters that walked with her.

Her mind clung to the memory of Milek's arms. Milek's kiss. The way he looked at her, as if the world began and ended in her eyes. She would make it over those blighted mountains because she had finally found the life she wanted. A calling, a job she loved, friends she respected, and a man who appreciated her strength. She refused to let this nightmare tear her life away.

Meanwhile, the questions surrounding her present circumstances dogged her. She should never have been shot down. No one had any idea she was even there. She was in an invisible wingjet, for Gods' sakes. Following covert orders. Everything had happened so fast—the storm, the cloaking tech failing, the attack—there was no way a Safaran jet or emplacement could have caught sight of her at that exact moment. They had to have been looking for her.

How would they have known?

And where was Elom?

She'd seen no evidence of his camp, beyond the attack itself. Still, if the intel was correct, Elom and his men were out here somewhere.

Aris clenched the torch tighter, fear feathering along every nerve at the thought.

Night brought a chill to the air, but the dry heat of the desert still lived under her skin. Her arm pulsed in time with her heartbeat, and a haze further confused the strange forms of trees and boulders that rose in front of her as she walked.

Suddenly, the dry, graveled dirt slid out from under Aris's boots. She went down hard on one knee. Her panting breath filled the darkness, excruciatingly loud. A muffled thud behind her sent ice down her spine. Was it a footstep? Was someone out here with her?

Her vision warped and wavered. She licked her cracked lips, dying for a sip of water.

Maybe she *was* dying.

Behind her, another thud and a rustle. Something was chasing her. She didn't have the courage to turn on the torch and find out what. Instead, she staggered to her feet and ran.

Somehow, in the heat of her fever dream, every noise took on the weight of running feet. The wind became Elom's breath on the back of her neck. He was after her, he'd found her, and he wanted to make her pay.

Aris whimpered as she slid awkwardly down another incline, jarring her already bruised body. Trees loomed at her, yanking the chute from her arms, cracking against her injured wrist. She cried out but kept running, chased by a demon with Elom's face. The torch disappeared, torn from her hand by a claw of branch.

For hours, or maybe it was days, she ran. Her chest burned. Her arm went numb.

And then she saw it. A tiny light flickering through the trees.

In that moment, Aris forgot she was in enemy territory. Forgot that a light, in Safara, almost certainly meant her death. She tripped, righted herself, and took off toward the small break in the sinister dark.

A few minutes later she stumbled out of the trees, into a clearing lit by several dim lights. Aris pulled out her solagun, her blurred eyes searching for movement. The world undulated before her. Shadows formed and dissipated like giant snakes slithering across the ground. In the sky above, a strange crimson and orange light echoed the swirling chaos of her mind. How had she gotten here? Where was she?

She rocked on unsteady legs. And that was it, her undoing.

When she stopped running, the demon caught her.

Elom reached out, his bald, brown head lit by the glowing sky, and wrenched her bad arm. Pain exploded through her, so fast and fierce she couldn't possibly stay conscious, however desperately she wanted to save herself. She screamed as she collapsed, the sound chasing her into the black.

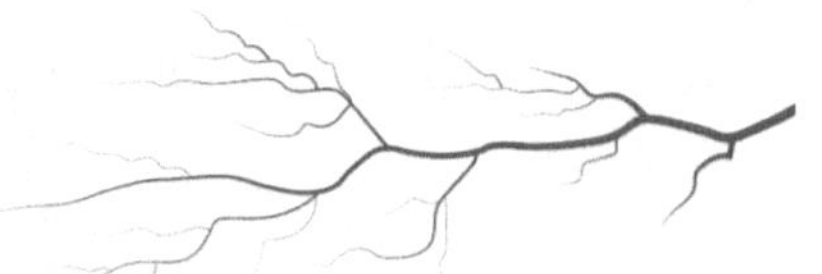

Chapter Nineteen

"What exactly are you saying?" Pyralis gave Lieutenant Jax Latza a hard look. The spy sat across from Pyralis at the conference table, flanked by Commanders Freni and Quin, two of Atalanta's senior Military officials. Latza had recently been reactivated, and this meeting had been organized at his request.

"I'm saying that we have no idea where the resources are going. Ward Balias has been diverting funds and supplies for months, but despite all of my digging, I can't figure out what the hell he's doing with them."

Pyralis drummed his fingers on the table. "Are Meridia and Castalia sending him more resources?"

Commander Freni shook his head. "If they are, we haven't found evidence of it."

"And your sources have given you nothing?" Pyralis asked.

"There have been disappearances, more than usual." Latza's brows drew together, creating deep furrows along his forehead. "Some unexplained deaths. I've lost two of my best contacts within the last month, and the others aren't willing to talk. I know the money has to be going somewhere."

"Thank you for the information, Lieutenant." Pyralis stood. There wasn't much he could do with the intel, but it was certainly troubling. "I'll ask my tech specialists to try to run down what they can on their end."

Lieutenant Latza bowed. He left quietly, his steps still a little jerky. The man had been through hell; Pyralis would always be grateful for the part he'd played in Galena's rescue.

After Commander Freni updated him on the mission to recover Aris Haan, the latest troop positions, and other pressing intelligence, Pyralis dismissed his commanders. With a sigh, he sat back in the stiff chair. Outside the wall of windows, the lights of Panthea glittered.

He'd been staying at the capitol the past few days and was already tired of the city. It was all so frenetic: Metroline trains streaked across the landscape in too-bright sweeps of light, while shopkeepers' voices created a cacophony as they hawked their wares. The war hadn't yet touched the gleaming skyscrapers and busy streets, but his nightmares were haunted by the day it would.

And somewhere deep within the high-security prison that huddled at the edge of the city, his wife wrote him endless letters he wouldn't read. They arrived almost every day, sometimes several at a time. At first, he'd read them, poring over Bett's large, sloppy handwriting as he tried to decipher her rantings. He hoped she might offer some bit of information that could help them fight Ward Balias. But it was all accusation and demand and persuasion. Begging him to visit her, swearing that she still loved him, ranting at him when he didn't answer.

Now, whenever a new letter arrived, Pyralis let it sit on his desk for hours before throwing it away, unopened. He'd almost asked his assistant, Kellan, to stop delivering them, but he hadn't quite brought himself to do so yet. Galena understood why he couldn't. Without that last, tiny connection, it would be like Bett had died. And as angry as he was, as little as he cared for her, he didn't wish her dead.

He pressed a button in the recessed control panel of the conference table. "Kellan, could you come here, please?"

The door slid open immediately to admit his russet-haired, whip-thin assistant. "Yes, Ward Nekos?"

"Any word from Ward Vadim yet?" Pyralis asked. Outside, darkness had settled fully over Panthea.

"She's expecting you in Sibetza tomorrow morning." Kellan's neutral voice betrayed nothing, but he had to know Pyralis and Galena's relationship was more than the politely professional one they cultivated for news vids.

Pyralis appreciated his discretion. "Perfect. Please arrange a terran to the airfield for first light."

"Certainly, Ward," Kellan said.

"Thank you." With a sigh, Pyralis stood and stretched his stiff legs. He looked out over the city for another few minutes before heading several floors down to his suite. All the while, Lieutenant Latza's words echoed in his mind. Missing resources, mysterious disappearances. Add that to the too-frequent sightings of Ward Balias throughout Safara, and Lieutenant Haan's attack. . . . He shook his head wearily as he sank onto his bed.

It'd be a miracle if sleep found him tonight.

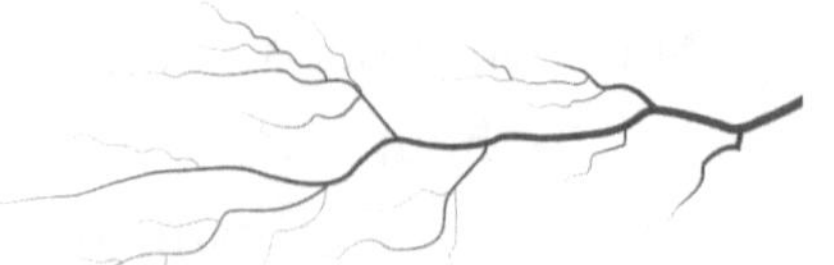

CHAPTER TWENTY

"So," Dysis said, hauling herself over another pile of boulders. "Just so I'm clear. If we're hurt or attacked by Safaran soldiers before we find Aris, we don't hit our emergency beacons. We just . . . deal?"

Her pack wrenched her shoulders as she jumped from the last rock to the ground. Major Vadim had dropped them just over the Safaran border at the foot of the mountains the night before. They'd been up with the dawn and had been hiking for hours.

Daakon and Calix didn't answer her. Just like they hadn't answered her last five questions. And the silence was getting to her.

There wasn't a chance in hell she'd hit her transmitter before she found Aris. But she had to say *something*. All this macho, stoic business wouldn't cut it. They had to work together. Communicate.

Daakon paused to consult the map on his digitablet. The morning light gave his skin a grayish cast. She hurried to his side and peered at the digitab. "Have we reached the search zone yet?"

He started to pull the device away, but at the anger building in her face, he thought better of it.

Smart man.

Instead, he pointed to a black circle on the map that looked to be several miles north of them. "That's where the wreckage of Lieutenant Haan's wingjet was found," he said grudgingly. "We're only a few miles away from the edge of the search area."

Highlighted in pale blue, the search area was not as vast as she'd originally feared, but it was still plenty big. It arced east from the wreckage toward the mountain, and south toward the blinking red dot that indicated their location.

"Is it all just empty land, like it is here?" Calix stepped up next to Daakon's other side so he could look at the map, too.

Daakon ran a fingertip across the blue, zooming into the map. "There's a single village to the east, at the base of the mountains. Here." He pointed. "Otherwise, yes. It's just more of this."

Dysis looked around. Scrubby, gnarled trees. Sandy dirt. Rock falls every few yards, like the mountains had started to crumble. "Let's keep going," she said, trying to ignore the sense that eyes were watching them from the shadows that climbed the hills.

As they crossed into the search area, they headed farther west, skirting the village.

Dysis studied the terrain, the twisted branches of the trees, searching for signs of Aris or her chute. "It's been three days," she said, more to herself than the others. "What's she eating? Drinking? There's nothing here."

Worry ate at her as they made their way, slowly and methodically, toward the crash site.

"She's likely in rough shape, whether she was injured or not," Calix said, deigning to reply at last. "But she's clever. She'll find a way to collect enough water to stave off her thirst. And we've passed a few plants that could be eaten, if necessary. She's surviving."

Dysis scoffed. "You have quite a lot of faith in the skills of a girl you think should be sheltered away, boxed up like a doll."

Calix whirled toward her and barked, "Aris is not a doll."

Dysis didn't back down. "Did you ever tell her that? *Treat* her like that? I don't for one second think that *you* actually believe—"

"You don't know anything about what I believe," he growled. "You don't know anything about me at all."

"I know *everything* about you!" Dysis hissed, mindful that they were in enemy territory. She stepped up to him, invading his space. "Who do you think listened to her cry in the dark, worrying over you? Say what you want about her moving on quickly. You totally rejected everything she became. You made it easy."

His face went red. "I know! Don't you get it? I *know*. I messed up. I . . ." Suddenly, all the fight left him. His shoulders slumped. "I know it's too late for us. I'm not trying to win Aris back. I just . . . I want to apologize."

Dysis's mouth fell open. "*What*?"

"Is it really so hard to believe?" Calix glanced at her, an odd arrogance filling his expression. "You think you know

Aris . . . after what, a few months? She and I have known each other since we were children. We were friends first, before we loved each other." He cocked his head. "Do you even know what that kind of love is like?"

Dysis didn't say anything. Let him believe what he wanted.

Calix straightened, and she realized how close they were standing. So close she could see tiny golden flecks in his green eyes and the shadow of stubble along his jaw. She took a step back.

He continued. "Aris should know I'm proud of her, because I am. Even if I couldn't say it before."

Before Dysis could think of a reply, Daakon yelled.

Dysis took off at a sprint toward the flash of blue uniform far ahead, half-hidden by a copse of trees. Her boots slipped before finding purchase on the rocky ground.

"What is it? Did you find her?" Dysis slid down a slight incline, dislodging a cascade of gravel. When she reached him, Daakon pointed to a black lump on the ground.

Aris's empty wingjet seat. It would have ejected with her. That meant this was where she'd landed. Dysis scanned the surroundings, frantically searching for some sign of her friend. Calix ran up beside her and sank to his knees. He ran his hand over the chair, either in reverence or relief.

"I don't see her," Dysis panted, moving to examine more of the small clearing. She stood and shouted into the trees, "Aris!"

Daakon made his way over and put a hand on her shoulder. She shook it off automatically. "Look," he said. "This is a good thing. We have a starting point. But we can't just wander through the woods yelling her name."

"She's got to be close." Dysis stepped farther into the trees, ignoring the branches that reached toward her face.

"There's blood." Calix's voice cut through her concentration like a knife.

Dysis rushed back to him. His face was pressed up close to the seat as he examined it. With Dysis and Daakon looming over him, he pointed to several rusty streaks along the gray material. "See?" he said. "She's hurt."

Dysis leaned closer and noticed a splatter of dried blood on the ground, too. She swept a hand toward the stain. "Is that a lot of blood? Is she badly injured?"

Calix rocked back on his haunches and glanced around the clearing. She was surprised he was so calm. "It's not a lot, no. Certainly not enough to suggest a mortal wound." He stood and made his way slowly toward the trees, his gaze firmly fixed to the ground. "And it might actually help us. See? There's a blood trail."

Dysis followed him, noting the brown splotches that marked the dusty yellow dirt. Calix shot a grim smile back at Daakon. "We have our starting point."

"Let's make sure no one else does." Daakon kicked dirt over the splashes of blood, smoothing the ground with his foot so the trail disappeared.

They hiked until midday, while the sun beat down on them with merciless intensity. Eventually the blood trail faded and then disappeared completely. By that point, it took little guesswork to assume Aris had been heading for the crashed wingjet.

"She was trying to make it to the retrieval team," Dysis said. She sat in the shade of a small tree. Here the land was torn open by deep ravines and winding riverbeds, all dry.

They had crossed a single dirt road, the only sign of civilization.

"She was injured, so she would have been moving more slowly than we are. She probably arrived too late." Daakon handed her a ready-to-eat meal in a silver pouch and a chrome flask of water.

"Or she changed course," Calix said, taking the food Daakon offered him. "Maybe she saw the Safaran troops that engaged the S and R team."

Dysis snatched Daakon's digitablet from the ground beside him so she could study the map. They were close to the crash site, less than a mile. "Maybe she's hiding out by the wingjet, waiting for another rescue attempt."

"We can only hope." Daakon tried to catch her eye, but she concentrated on the too-salty, acidic flavor of the food pouch. It was meant to be citrus beef. Not her favorite. But the water helped with the heat.

They rested until the sun began its downward slant. Not long afterward, they climbed a narrow ridge that would take them directly to the broken wingjet, if their map was correct.

They never made it.

A high-pitched whine broke through the silence. Dysis glanced at Calix, who looked just as confused. Daakon led them closer, clinging to the shadows. It turned out the wingjet wasn't on the ridge but below it, in a tree-swathed ravine that still smoked and sent the bitter smell of burning metal into the air.

A flock of black-clad figures swarmed around the wingjet. The mysterious whine was an electric saw. They were cutting apart the charred remains and loading them into a transjet.

Dysis shivered, despite the heat. It was like watching them dismember a body.

"Any sign of Aris?" Calix whispered.

They crept farther along the ridge, seeking a better vantage point. Dysis scoured the makeshift Safaran camp. There were two large tecons with their fabric flaps pulled back, allowing free access. Not the best place for a prisoner. They might be holding Aris on one of the wingjets. There were three: the transjet and two smaller recons. She strained her ears for the sound of screams over the squeal of the saw.

"I don't see anything, but there are only five or six soldiers milling around." Dysis put a hand on the solagun at her side. "We can take them down and conduct a search."

"No," Daakon said firmly.

"We can't miss this chance," she said. "Stop being—"

"I'm being practical," he interrupted. "We don't have the manpower or weapons to take on those soldiers." His eyes flicked to the bustle down below. "And I counted at least eight."

Dysis restrained herself from slapping him across the face, even though it was very, very tempting.

"But we're not going to let this chance go either," he said. "Get comfortable. We're staying here until dawn tomorrow. We'll take shifts watching those soldiers. If there's even a *hint* of Aris down there, we'll hit our beacons immediately. Got it?"

Dysis nodded grudgingly. "Fine. I'll take first watch."

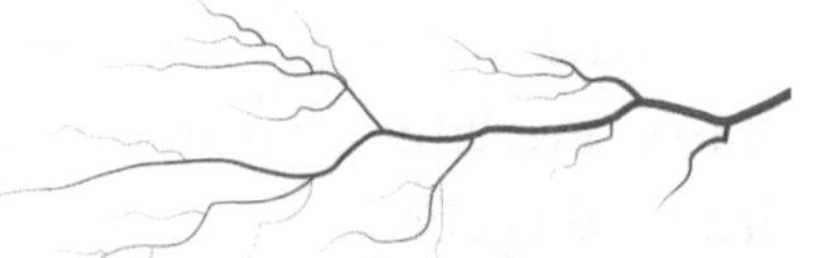

CHAPTER TWENTY-ONE

ARIS WOKE UP SCREAMING.

Her nightmare had come to life. She was in a white room, restrained in a med-bed with bone-white sheets. Elom bent over her with a medigun, his dark eyes boring into her soul. And she knew, with every frantic breath she took, that he was about to kill her.

She thrashed, straining as far from him as she could get, still screaming. She refused to look him in the face; she didn't want to see his joy in this moment. His satisfaction.

"I could do without the noise." He pressed a button on the side of the bed and the back rose. She heaved herself forward, trying to leap off the bed, but her arms were tied down and her legs tangled in the sheets. Elom pushed a hand against her collarbone to hold her still as he pressed the medigun tight to her skin. "This should help."

A sharp, quick pain pricked her arm. Aris fought against his grip, lashing out like a wild animal. With a frustrated grimace, he let go. But it didn't matter; she was still restrained. And whatever he'd injected still ran in her veins. How long would it take to kill her?

"What did you do to me?" she howled. Her vision was blurry, everything lined with a smoky edge. Was that the drug taking effect?

Elom just crossed his arms. Waiting.

Aris braced for paralysis to sneak through her limbs. She shouted obscenities at him as she waited for the oblivion to come.

But it didn't. In fact, nothing happened at all.

"What was that?" she asked more calmly, though she still strained against her bonds.

"Something to help reduce the inflammation in your wrist."

"My wrist?" Why did he care about her wrist? The realization took longer to process. Her arm. It didn't hurt. She looked down. The gash was neatly bandaged, her wrist constrained in a splint.

"It was broken in two places. I set the bone. The cut was infected, too. You wouldn't have survived much longer on your own," Elom said.

For the first time, Aris found the courage to look him in the eye. Only, now that she was calmer, the haze fading, she could see . . .

He isn't Elom.

She stared hard at the man, her heart ricocheting in the cage of her ribs like a wild bird trying to break free. The likeness was eerie. In height and build, the two men could be twins. But this man's nose was different: thinner, straight, where Elom's was battered, a fighter's nose. The stranger's face was also thinner, almost gaunt. And he was younger, maybe thirty, where Elom was probably in his forties.

"Who are you?" Aris asked, not particularly comforted. She was still at a stranger's mercy, still tied to a bed.

"Don't tell her anything," a female voice pierced the silence.

Aris turned toward the sound. A woman stood by a strip of cloth hanging over a doorway. Beyond her, the golden-plum haze of twilight.

The woman was of average height, probably a little taller than Aris, her smooth brown skin a shade darker than the man who stood beside the bed. As she came closer, Aris could make out wide chestnut eyes, wiry arms, and thick black hair that fell in braids down her back. Her expression reminded Aris of that of Commander Nyx. This woman was in charge. And she was not happy.

"It doesn't matter who we are," she said, coming closer. "Who are *you*?"

Aris kept her mouth shut.

The man made an impatient noise. When he turned to look at the woman, Aris caught sight of the black rectangular Military brand on his neck. Her stomach clenched. *Safaran Military.*

"You aren't helping," he said. "Why would she talk to us now?"

The woman glared at him. "We'll make her."

"Why fix my arm if you're just going to torture me?" Aris's eyes dropped to her own chest. No emergency transponder. She tried to steady her racing heart. If they wanted information, they should have left her in agony. She would have told them anything.

"You're from Atalanta." The man said it as if he knew for certain, but his eyes held a question.

Aris said nothing, her body tense. "Where's my body armor?"

"We removed it when we cleaned your wounds." The man gestured to a stack of clothing on a chair against the wall. Aris glanced around, taking in her prison for the first time. The room was little more than a shack, with paint peeling from the walls in strips, revealing dirty stone beneath. The light came from an old-fashioned lamp, not solar ceiling tiles.

"I told you not to answer her questions!" the woman hissed.

He threw up his hands. "Why? We want her to answer ours!"

She leaned over Aris, her eyes flashing. "How did you get here? Are there more of you coming?"

Aris met her gaze squarely and kept her mouth firmly, purposefully closed.

The man leaned back against the low counter that ran the length of the room. It might have been a casual pose, if his hands hadn't been clenched at his sides. "We don't have to trust her, but we do have to tell her. There's no way she'll answer our questions otherwise."

"What if she's a spy?" the woman argued. "She could be working for Balias. If we tell—"

"You think I'm a spy for *Balias*?" Shock tore down Aris's spine. Maybe she was still delirious.

The man studied her closely. "We hope not."

"I don't understand," Aris said. "Why would Balias even send a spy here?"

The man's face went still.

"Do you have any idea what this war is doing to us?" the woman asked, as if she couldn't help herself.

Aris's mouth dropped open. "My dominion is under siege. This isn't about what it's doing to *you*."

The woman's shoulders bent as if from a heavy, invisible weight. "Haven't your spies told you the truth yet? The people of Safara are dying. From starvation, but from this war, too. Balias will bury us all."

Aris pulled against her restraints. "Is this some strange test of loyalty? Because my loyalty to Atalanta is not nor will it ever be in question."

The man bent forward and released her arms. "We're staking our lives on that."

"Alistar." The warning in the woman's voice was clear.

Alistar. Aris filed the name away. She ran a hand over the splint on her broken wrist, wishing she could take it off, if only for a moment. The skin beneath itched.

Alistar focused on her with a frightening intensity. "Are you trying to get back to Atalanta? Is that why you're here?"

Aris eyed him warily. She didn't even know where *here* was. "I have no reason to tell you anything."

"We'll help you reach the border alive," he said, holding up a hand. "*If* you take us with you into Atalanta."

"Why?" Aris shot back.

Alistar and the woman shared a weighted look. "My sister Samira and I . . . we seek asylum," he said.

"You want to defect?" Aris's mind whirled. There was no way she could trust a thing they said, but perhaps she could leverage this somehow. If they'd let her contact Milek . . .

Samira straightened, her braids swishing. "We think of it as escaping the regime that is holding this dominion hostage."

"How do I know you don't plan to infiltrate Atalanta as spies? Or worse?" Aris watched the woman closely, looking for any hint of deceit.

"We mean no harm to Atalanta. Surely that's obvious by now? We haven't killed you. We've healed your wounds." Samira gestured to Aris's hands. "We've released you from your bonds. We'll even feed you while you're in our care."

"Okay, then. Let me have access to your comm tech," Aris demanded. "I'll have my superior retrieve me. You can discuss your petition for asylum with him."

Alistar shook his head. "Our comms have been down for months."

A weight settled in Aris's stomach. The small spark of hope that had been fighting its way to the surface died a sudden, ugly death. "What about the old telelines?"

"Balias has cut off all communications within our own dominion, aside from those used by his Military. Even within the cities." The man rubbed the back of his neck. "He wishes to isolate us."

Her mind whirled. Surely it would be common knowledge in Atalanta if Safara's local communication network was down. How had she never heard about it? "So what's your plan to reach Atalanta?"

Samira glanced toward the door, as if she'd heard a noise. Something in her face changed. The cloth rippled and a small hand crept along the wall. Without a word, Samira disappeared through the doorway, but not before Aris caught a glimpse of a tiny, wide-eyed face as the woman scooped up the child and disappeared into the dusk.

"You should rest," Alistar said. "We'll speak more in the morning." Before Aris could react, he pushed a medigun into her arm.

"What was that?" She rubbed the sore spot, swallowing back a new wave of panic.

"It will help with the pain." He pressed the button on the side of the bed and it straightened, drawing her flat.

Almost immediately, a wave of world-blurring calm swept over her. Before she faded completely, she said, "I saw your brand. You were chosen for Military. Why aren't you part of the fight?"

"I was."

Without elaborating, he left the room, and Aris fell back into darkness.

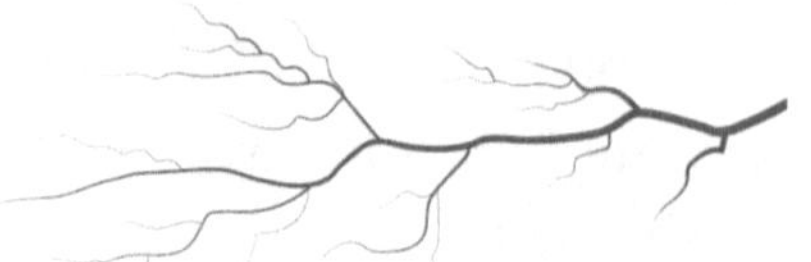

Chapter Twenty-Two

The large living room of Galena's home sat cloaked in shadows and neglect. The air smelled of the dusty remains of flowers, a scent she always associated with her grandmother, who'd died years ago.

Beside her, Pyralis hesitated on the threshold.

"Thank you for coming today," Galena said. He'd flown in that morning, for no other reason than that she'd asked him to. "I've . . . I've been meaning to do this for months, but I couldn't quite bring myself to."

"How long has it been since you've been back?" Pyralis asked as he stepped inside.

"A long time." Her voice sounded too loud in the hushed house. "When I returned from my . . . ordeal, Josef was dead and Milek living in Atalanta. I couldn't bring myself to stay."

She'd been living in a suite at the capitol ever since.

"It's okay if you need more time," Pyralis murmured.

With a sigh, Galena said, "No. I refuse to let this place haunt me."

Truthfully, it was that and more. At this moment, Milek's team was searching for Aris Haan, and so much depended on whether they found her: the integration movement, but also Milek's happiness. It was a day for distractions, for putting ghosts to rest.

Pyralis's warm brown eyes blinked into the darkness. "I understand the weight of memories."

Galena tapped the light panel and several lamps blinked on. Pale-blue walls led to a dramatically pitched ceiling. The living room's clean lines were echoed by the simple golden wood furniture. The white tiled floor was streaked with the dust.

"It's like a museum," Galena murmured, running a finger through the thick dust on the back of a chair.

"One that holds your happiest memories," Pyralis replied.

She glanced back at him. "Not all of them."

They sifted through her belongings, dividing everything into piles. Those items she wanted to keep, and those she would give away. They did the easy rooms first: the living room, where they stacked most of the furniture on the "donate" side of the room, and the kitchen, where everything but her grandmother's tea set would go.

"Milek thinks we were getting close to Elom," she said, as she stacked plates. "That's why Lieutenant Haan was shot down."

Pyralis continued collecting silverware into a large basket. "I met with Lieutenant Latza yesterday. Among other things, he mentioned that his contacts think the intel on Elom was a setup."

"A setup for what?" Galena leaned against the counter, her hands resting on either side of the stack of plates, all to be given away. She couldn't live with their reminders of the life she'd had with Josef and Milek. The quiet, distant meals, where no one knew what to say to one another.

Pyralis sighed as he ran a hand through his hair. When he met her eyes, she saw an emotion with which she was intimately familiar.

Regret.

"I think you were right about Lieutenant Haan becoming a target," he said. "We have reason to believe Elom set a trap for *her* specifically."

Galena's stomach sank. "But how did they know about the invisible wingjet?"

"I don't think they did," Pyralis said. "According to your son's report, Lieutenant Haan said the veil tech had failed. She wasn't shot until she was visible again. Someone must have warned them she was coming."

Galena stared at the swirling blue-and-gray pattern of the top plate. "So you're saying we have a spy within Spiro."

"Or a breach in our comm security. That's what Milek suspects."

She sighed. How did Elom manage to create so much destruction? "And now Safara *will* know about the invisible jet. They'll figure it out. If they develop one, we'll lose every hope of an advantage."

"Milek said his initial team retrieved the tech and burned the jet." Pyralis shrugged. "But even if they find a way to retrieve and reverse engineer the tech, we'll have a slight edge in terms of time. Our fleet of invisible wingjets is already in production. They'll be up and running within a few months."

Somehow the distraction of packing up her house was just giving her more time to ruminate. "So if it wasn't about the wingjet, then what? An attack on Lieutenant Haan herself? To strike a blow at the integration process?"

"I think it's likely. And it's worked. The protests started again immediately after we announced her death, and soldiers are risking insubordination charges by refusing to work with women."

Galena tapped her fingernails against the counter. "If that's the case, we'll strike a serious blow to their machinations if Milek's team retrieves Lieutenant Haan alive."

"Indeed." Pyralis dumped two more handfuls of silverware into the basket.

Galena cleared her throat. "Would it be of any use to speak with Bett, do you think? Perhaps she has some knowledge of Ward Balias's plans that she hasn't shared?"

Pyralis turned away as if he hadn't heard her, reaching up to grab another stack of plates from an upper cabinet. "How is Milek doing?"

Galena let it go. She rarely brought up Bett. Pyralis's wife had been the one to sell the tech that Elom had used to create a double of Galena. Bett was also the woman Pyralis had chosen over Galena, twenty-five years ago. She was not someone Galena enjoyed thinking about, and the subject was difficult for Pyralis. She just hoped they weren't missing something.

"Milek's struggling a bit, I think," she said. "It eats at

him that he couldn't go after Aris himself, but he has his unit to lead."

"Perhaps you should visit him," Pyralis suggested, as they moved upstairs.

Here they tackled the more personal items. Josef's old tunics and pants were folded neatly and stacked, labeled DONATE. Pyralis didn't say anything as Galena brushed her hands across the soft fabric, tears falling.

It was dusty, emotionally painful work, but Pyralis's presence soothed her. He was part of her past, after all. They smiled over the yellow jacket she'd worn when they first met, and the gown from her first gala as Ruslana's Ward.

"I don't know what Milek will do if he can't find Aris or . . . or if the worst has already come to pass," Galena said, sifting through a stack of letters from Pyralis during his time in Ruslana. She'd sworn to Josef that she'd thrown them away, but instead had hidden them in a small wooden box in the back of her closet. Even now, it felt like a betrayal. "He's already suffered so much."

Pyralis stacked two spindly wooden chairs along the wall. "If he's anything like you, he'll survive. He'll be even stronger for it, in the end."

She ached for Milek. He'd had to endure so much over the past year: his father's death, her disappearance and imprisonment, and now the woman he loved being in danger, possibly dead. But she ached for Pyralis, too, and the history that still drew them together.

Galena met his eyes, heart pounding in her throat as her fingers crushed the slick silco letters to her chest. "If he's anything like me, he'll hold on to hope, long after the reality shows it to be impossible."

Pyralis closed the space between them.

"Galena, you can't live in your quarters at the capitol forever. You need a home." Pyralis stopped a handbreadth away but didn't reach for her. Gently, he asked, "When this house is sold, where will you go?"

She shrugged. "I'll find a place in Sibetza, I suppose. I've only three more years in my term as Ward, and I don't think I have the stomach to run again. After that, I quite like the idea of settling outside the city."

He reached for her hands, a strange nervousness flitting across his features. "Or you could settle outside another city. Like Panthea." He tightened his grip on her fingers, like he was trying to draw strength from them. "With me."

Galena's breath froze in her throat. The sudden swirl of emotions made chaos of her thoughts. Even with their history, even knowing how he felt about her, it was the last thing she'd expected him to say. The silence between them lengthened. Her mind still couldn't provide any clarity. At last, she forced herself to say, "I . . . I don't know."

The grooves at either side of his mouth softened, and his eyes filled with a longing that nearly undid her. Galena offered him a soft, sad smile, forgetting her scars until she felt them pull along her cheeks.

How was it that her life had become a series of questions to which she had no answers?

Chapter Twenty-Three

Consciousness broke upon Aris slowly. A slash of sunlight flicked across her face each time the sheet covering the doorway rippled in the breeze, giving her no sense of time beyond that it was daylight. From outside came the faint sound of children's voices. Aris shifted and realized that at some point she'd turned onto her side. Which meant she was still unrestrained.

Before moving, she snuck a glance around the room. Empty. At least from this vantage point. She sat up in stages —rolling onto her back, pushing up on one arm. Her wrist ached, but it was a manageable pain. The splint that encased it was roughly made—wooden sticks sewn into a thick piece of canvas—but it was doing its job. She peeked under the bandage that covered the gash on her forearm; the skin was no longer puffy and red. A line of neat stitches closed the wound.

As quietly as she could, she slid the sheets off her legs and touched one toe to the rust-streaked floor. No one came running in. She made a quick, silent circuit of the room. Someone had dressed her in loose white linen pants and a thin-strapped top. There was no sign of her armor or weapon. Her uniform and shoes were missing, too.

Two long counters lined the walls, with cupboards above and below. She slid open each drawer, freezing when one squeaked. Still no one came. Many of the drawers were empty. Some contained bandages and strips of cloth. A dented can of loose cotton. No mediguns or meds, nothing she could use to defend herself. She did find a stack of soft house shoes, so she slipped on a pair. They didn't provide much protection, and they were too big, but it was better than going barefoot.

At the far end of the small room, a sheet covered another doorway. Standing off to the side so she wouldn't cast a shadow, Aris peeked around the fabric. Another room, this one much bigger, stretched out before her. It was filled with med-beds, some occupied. A woman and man in mender white flitted around their patients, speaking in soft, soothing voices. Aris didn't recognize anyone. Where had Alistar and Samira gone? Had they meant to leave her here, unshackled and alone?

Was it a trap?

Looking around her private room, she thought it must be the surgery room. There was extra equipment for more prolonged procedures, but most of it was worn and years out of date. They'd left no scalpels or knives for her to find.

Aris snuck to the doorway leading outside. She could still hear the faint sound of children laughing and calling to one another. But the view was eerily desolate. Before her a small, dusty plain edged a gray shoulder of mountain.

She'd made it to the mountains.

There were no gentle foothills here. These cliffs rose abruptly and were formidably steep. A handful of buildings clung to them, strung with narrow rope bridges that swayed precariously in the dry desert breeze. Aris studied the few other buildings gathered here on the solid ground around the plain, watching for movement, but no one appeared.

The sun hung just above the mountain, pouring heat into the bowl of the plain. It was morning, then. She hadn't lost too much time.

With quick, silent steps she snuck out of the clinic. She crept around the side of the building, keeping to the shadows. Hunger tightened her stomach, but she ignored it. As she rounded the far corner of the clinic, a screech sent her to a crouch.

In front of her, spread in haphazard lines, a group of at least twenty children played. All were dressed in dirt-streaked tunics and too-short pants. Toddlers followed bigger children through the lines, tugging on shirts so they wouldn't be left behind. The older children, some nearly her age, led the way, but Aris could tell many were lagging, showing little interest in the game. She swallowed back a gasp. Some of them were scarred, limping. One boy hopped between two metal crutches, his pants pinned up over the stub of his missing leg. All of them held wariness in their eyes like an old friend.

"Attempting an escape, are you?"

Aris stood up so fast she banged her shoulder into the wall. Alistar leaned against the building beside her. "Have you considered how you'll feed yourself? What supplies you'll be able to steal before we catch you? I assure you,

you'll need supplies. The mountains here are like Balias himself: brutal, dangerous, and entirely without mercy."

Aris didn't have an answer, so she asked a question of her own. "What happened to these children? And how are there so many, in such a small village?"

Alistar sighed. "Most of the little ones are orphans, their parents killed in battle, by Balias's men, or by starvation. Their relatives bring them here. We're known as a place of safety."

Dismay filled her. "And the older ones?"

Alistar pushed away from the wall. "When Ruslana joined the war, Balias conscripted our children." His voice shook. "Boys as young as ten. These boys . . . these are the ones who've survived. Or whose parents hid them in time."

Looking at the boy with the missing leg, Aris *couldn't* see her enemy.

In a patch of sparse grass, away from the game, a woman sat with several babies and a toddler, who climbed in and out of her lap, laughing. The long, dark braids gave her away; it was Samira. But the look on her face was a far cry from the hard, bitter glares she'd leveled at Aris the day before.

"Surprised?" Alistar asked.

"How can you and Samira leave? Are there others to care for these children? How will they—" She cut herself off. *Of course.* "It's not just you and Samira seeking asylum, is it? You want . . . you're going to . . ."

Alistar nodded. "It isn't for us. We seek true safety for our charges."

"True safety?" The rough concrete behind Aris radiated heat, making her back uncomfortably moist.

"None of these children left the Military with the proper

permission. As far as Balias is concerned, they're deserters. Deserving of death for their lack of commitment to the cause." Alistar shifted his weight, as if this knowledge physically pained him. "We can only keep them hidden for so long. We've been planning an exodus to Atalanta, hoping your people would take us in. We thought, maybe, if Atalanta knew what Balias is doing to his own people—it might help somehow."

Aris's brain spun like an out-of-control wingjet. How cowardly did Balias have to be to send ten-year-olds to war? Suddenly, she remembered the young soldier who'd died beneath the wreckage of the downed Safaran jet. Disgust turned her stomach. No wonder he'd looked like just a kid. That's exactly what he'd been. "How does Ward Balias get away with it? What about selection? Students aren't supposed to be assigned to a sector until their eighteenth year."

"Our sectors have broken down completely. There *is* no selection. Men are forced into Military while women and the elderly are left to handle everything else, with few resources and the constant fear their children will be taken from them." Alistar stepped closer, so she was forced to look him in the eye. "If you truly are an Atalantan soldier, you could be our salvation. Your word would have weight with the Atalantan authorities."

Her suspicions and distrust might have remained, were it not for the children before her. Maybe she would have felt differently if she hadn't seen that poor boy die before her eyes. "I'll do what I can to help you once we reach Atalanta," she said. "You have my word."

Alistar slumped back against the building, smiling a little at her. "Perhaps you'll deign to tell us your name now?"

Aris reached out her uninjured hand. "Lieutenant Aris Haan."

As he shook it, his eyes widened. "Lieutenant Haan? We have limited access to the news here, but everyone has heard of the woman who rescued Ward Vadim and changed Atalanta's Military laws. It's an honor to meet you."

Aris quirked a grin. "Words I never expected to hear in Safara."

Alistar watched the children playing, a new hope filling his dark eyes with warmth. "If we help you return to Atalanta, surely your people will protect us."

Aris followed his gaze. "How will they make the trip over the mountains?" she asked, her eyes caught on a skinny boy with blood-red scars running up his frail arms. He leaned heavily on a stick, limping as he attempted to follow the others down the line.

Alistar shrugged. "The stronger children will help the weaker ones. And we have several other adults who will travel with us. The rest will stay behind to care for those who find their way here after we leave."

At that moment, Samira noticed them talking. She yanked up the toddler and babe at her feet, and hurried over. "Why is she here? I told you, Alistar! She can't know—"

"And I told *you* we should tell her the truth." When Samira opened her mouth to argue, he held up a placating hand. "Sister, she's agreed to help us. *She* is Lieutenant Aris Haan."

Samira didn't look impressed as she turned her glare on Aris and tightened her grip on the children in her arms. The baby looked to be a few months old, with a silky wisp of brown hair and enormous chocolate eyes. The toddler buried his head in Samira's neck, but Aris could make out a mass of tight brown curls and round cheeks.

"Are these your children?" Aris asked. As soon as the words were out, she wished she could call them back. Samira wasn't likely to appreciate her curiosity or concern.

The woman narrowed her eyes. After studying Aris long enough to give her chills, Samira tipped her chin down to kiss the baby's head. "Hazel and Jaff are mine. Their papa was killed less than a month ago in a firefight."

Samira owned her pain with a proud ferocity. Within her confining embrace, the littlest—Hazel—squirmed.

"I'm so—" Aris started.

"Don't say you're sorry," Samira stated, her voice flat. "Your *sorry* doesn't make a damned bit of difference."

Aris leaned against the wall and drew deep ragged breaths into her lungs. It was one thing to battle a faceless enemy for your dominion, for your way of life. But now, if what Alistar said was true, Aris had to face the reality that the men—the *children*—she was fighting were as much victims of this war as the Atalantan soldiers she rescued.

What could she possibly do with this information? And what did it matter?

More importantly, how were they going to get thirty kids over the mountains into Atalanta?

Suddenly a piercing whistle silenced the scuffs and quiet laughter of the children. An older man stood panting at the edge of the clearing, signaling something with his arms. He whistled again, high and urgent, before sprinting on. Samira spun and ran across the plain, Hazel and Jaff bouncing in her arms. In a matter of seconds, all of the children disappeared, fading into the pockmarked cliffs.

Aris had no idea what was going on, but that didn't stop the panic from rising. "What's happening? Where did everyone go?"

Alistar grabbed her arm and dragged her back the way she'd come. "Hurry."

They raced along the building and burst through the doorway into the clinic. Alistar didn't stop, instead continuing on to the long room with rows of med-beds. He pushed her toward one of them.

"Alistar, please tell me what's going on," Aris pleaded as she lay down.

"I don't have time to get you to the caves, and you have to hide. *Here*." He yanked the sheets up to cover her, even part of her face. "Don't move, don't breathe. Balias's men are coming."

Chapter Twenty-Four

Dysis woke to the roar of wingjets. Before she'd reached full consciousness, she was on her feet, solagun at the ready. Daakon was on watch, and Calix was standing next to him.

The glow of dawn along the horizon outlined her companions.

"What's happening?" Dysis whispered. Through the trees, she could see pinpoints of light as the wingjets sped away.

Daakon didn't move from his position. "They finished loading the wreckage. They're leaving."

"What about Aris?" She stared down into the ravine. There was no sign of activity. Already the rush of the wingjets was fading.

Daakon stretched his neck back and forth. "I didn't see any sign of her. They didn't search the area. Hopefully that means the ruse worked and they assume she was killed in the crash."

"So what do we do now?" Calix asked. "We don't have another blood trail to follow."

Dysis couldn't be sorry about that. Less blood *hopefully* meant a less serious wound.

Daakon withdrew several nutrigel pouches and a bag of freeze-dried meat from his pack, handing the supplies around. "If you were hoping for rescue and arrived here too late, where would you go next?"

"I'd wait for reinforcements," Calix said, chewing on a piece of meat. "Maybe she's around here somewhere and now that the Safarans are gone, she'll reveal herself."

Dysis paced along the ridge. "I don't know. I don't think I'd stay. I'd be too scared the Safarans would search the area. She doesn't know we faked her death . . . she'll assume they're looking for her."

"What about her transponder? Why hasn't she triggered it?" Daakon polished off a nutrigel in a couple seconds, washing it down with a few sips of water from his flask.

"Maybe she has by now. You never know." Dysis sipped on her own pouch, the too-sweet gel making her grimace.

"Oh we'd know," Daakon replied. "There'd be Atalantan wingjets swarming all over the place."

As they talked, morning light filtered more and more brightly through the trees.

"Okay, then let's assume she *can't* activate it for some reason. Where do we search next?" Calix rolled up his thin bedroll and stuffed it into his pack, his movements jerky with nervous energy.

Dysis continued to pace, her mind racing. If it were *her* . . . if she were injured and hadn't made it to the crash site in time, if she couldn't use her beacon for help . . .

"I'd head for the border."

Daakon turned to watch her. "What?"

Dysis stopped. "If it were me, I'd try to cross into Atalanta. I'd try to get home, however I could."

"But there are *mountains* in the way," Calix said.

"Okay, *yes*. There are mountains. It'd be a long, painful hike. But what other choice would she have?" The more Dysis thought about it, the more convinced she was that she was right.

"This is all assuming she hasn't been captured," Daakon added.

Dysis grabbed her bedroll, stuffed it into her pack, and heaved the bag onto her shoulders. "We're supposed to be searching for her. I say we head east toward Atalanta. If you two actually have any *useful* suggestions, by all means offer them. Otherwise, let's get moving."

She ignored the look the two men shared. She'd hiked a few feet along the ridge, away from the crash site, before they caught up.

Dysis, Calix, and Daakon spread out and walked slowly, systematically, looking for more blood spatter or footprints in the underbrush. Every time a bird cried or a leaf rustled, Dysis's head jerked up and her heart pounded. She kept expecting to hear footsteps or Aris's voice humming an old lullaby.

It was still cool in the shade beneath the gnarled trees, but pockets of heat collected everywhere the sun touched.

"What do you think you'll do, once the war is over?" Calix's voice made her jump.

She glanced at him, eyebrow raised.

"Just . . . making conversation. These woods are getting to me."

Dysis rolled her eyes, but she understood. The trees were spindly and sickly, the underbrush interspersed with falls of rock and crumbling dirt. Everything smelled *old* somehow, like dried flowers. There was no color, no escape from the heat of the rising sun. It was like walking through a forest of skeletons.

"I have no idea," she answered. "Back home I taught mechanics, but . . . well, I hate it, to be honest. I guess I'm hoping there will still be a place for me in Military. Maybe I can work for a police detail in my village. Something where I can be close to my brother." She studied the ground as she spoke, searching for signs of passage.

"What about you?" she asked. She wasn't about to involve Daakon in the conversation. She didn't want to know about his future. Not unless he'd magically decided she should be a part of it.

Calix's features tightened. "I . . . I'm not sure either. My plans are kind of in flux right now."

Right. He was a deserter. His *plans* could very well be time in jail.

"Maybe I'll—" He stopped suddenly and dropped to his haunches. "Does this look like a footprint to anyone else?"

Dysis and Daakon hurried over. Calix pointed to a shallow impression in the dirt.

"Could be," Daakon said, straightening. "Fan out. We'll give this area a closer look."

Dysis crept forward, examining every bent leaf and broken twig. Then something else caught her eye, a suspicious smudge in the small clearing ahead.

"Hey, I think I've got something." She rushed forward.

Daakon knelt at the spot. "Someone made a fire." He touched the small circle of ash and blackened wood. "It's cold."

"Aris was here," Calix said, hope igniting in his eyes.

Daakon glanced up, his expression still serious. "Or her captors were."

Dysis made her way around the makeshift campsite, looking for other evidence. There, by the rock, a sweep of dirt. A tiny rust splotch, maybe a drop of blood?

The rising sun shone mercilessly from a cloudless sky, filling the otherwise empty clearing with heat. The trees waited, motionless, for a breeze that never came.

A faint rumble filled the air. It almost sounded like . . .

"Take cover!" she yelled and dove for a small patch of shadow beneath the trees, just as a flurry of black Safaran wingjets flew overhead. Everyone remained frozen until the sound of the jets disappeared completely. No shots were fired, and the wingjets never varied from their course.

"Was that a patrol?" Calix asked. "We need to figure out which way Aris went and get moving."

Dysis stepped in his direction, but a strange sound stopped her. She turned.

Daakon was jerking his leg up and down, clutching at his knee. He groaned again, a pained noise that slid into a high-pitched hiss. A long, golden rope hung from his ankle, rattling each time his leg moved.

Time slowed.

"Lieutenant!" Calix shouted, running toward Daakon. He slipped his utility knife from the sheath at his ankle and sliced through the rope . . .

No. Not the rope.
The snake.

Chapter Twenty-Five

The Safaran wingjets were louder than Aris expected as they landed. She kept the worn sheet up over her cheek, but she could still see most of the room. Alistar and another mender whispered in low, urgent voices. Both of the other patients had their backs to her, but she could tell by the small lumps they made under the sheets that they were probably children.

Were Balias's men here to collect them?

What if they were here for *her*?

Aris tried to keep her breathing under control but it was difficult, particularly when shouting erupted outside.

Alistar slipped from the room.

Aris strained to hear the commotion. Was that the hiss of solagun fire? She was about to sit up and sneak to the door, hoping to catch a glimpse of what was going on, when a beam of light struck her.

Someone had pulled back the scrap of fabric that covered the doorway.

Aris scrunched lower beneath the sheets and closed her eyes, feigning sleep, but her heart slammed in her chest with the power of a stampeding horse.

"Have you seen any strangers in the area?" a gruff voiced asked.

Aris held her breath. *Gods, this is it. Alistar will expose me right now.*

She braced herself. What chance did she really have?

"No strangers." Alistar's voice was calm. "We saw an explosion a few days ago, but nothing else has been out of the ordinary."

Aris released her breath quietly.

The footsteps got closer. "You always have so many patients for such a small village. Last week it was five. This week, three."

"Our water is bad. There's a lot of sickness," Alistar said smoothly.

"Three menders in such a small place. Seems like a waste of resources," the soldier growled in an offhand way, but a whisper of suspicion undercut his words.

"I'm not a true mender, Major, as you're aware." Tension crept into Alistar's voice. Aris snuck a peek through lowered lashes. The two men, hazy shadows, had almost reached her cot.

The larger man—the Major—stopped. "That's right. What *are* you exactly, Alistar?"

Silence. Aris counted it in heartbeats. *One. Two. Three. Four.*

"You know me, Major. I'm just trying to keep my people safe," Alistar said. "I'm useless for anything else."

One. Two. Three.

"They're not your people. They're Ward Balias's."

"Of course."

A slide of boot against floor. Aris opened her eyes a fraction wider. The Major had turned away. He was leaving.

For a long time, Aris remained exactly as she was, counting her heartbeats as they pounded in her temples. It wasn't until the roar of the Safaran wingjets faded into silence that she dared pulled the sheet away from her face and sit up.

When Alistar didn't return to collect her, she crept from the bed to the doorway, as cautiously as she could. Outside, the clearing was empty. Aris glanced to the blue-washed sky. Empty of clouds and wingjets.

She swayed on unsteady legs.

"Aris." Alistar appeared at her side and took her arm. "Come with me." He drew her across the clearing toward the mountain.

Alistar helped her onto a narrow path, along one of those terrifying wooden bridges strung against the rock. They passed several tiny houses, all empty, only to duck into the dark of a cave.

"Where are we going?" she asked. Her voice echoed oddly, and she couldn't help but think of the last time she'd been in a cave. She and Milek had slept side by side, just after he'd found out she was a woman.

"Most of the structures in our village are actually decoys," Alistar replied, pulling her from her memories. "We use the old clinic because our patients usually can't manage the cliffs, but for the most part we live here, in the caves."

He led her down a tunnel that burrowed deep into the cliff. Far ahead, a tiny light flickered.

"That's how you do it," Aris murmured in wonder. "You hide the children here."

The soft orange glow lined Alistar's face as he glanced back at her and grinned. "We hide everything in these caves."

A few more steps and the narrow passageway opened to a large cavern lit by old-fashioned torchlight and a small cooking fire. The air was cool and clammy against Aris's arms, a contrast to the dry heat outside. The fire sent flames toward a jagged opening in the rock, but a haze still filled the space. Long wooden tables sat in the center of the room, filled with villagers.

"When you were unconscious, I gave you fluids and liquid nutrition, but you need to eat." The ache in Aris's stomach agreed.

Alistar led her to the nearest table, occupied by several of the children she'd seen playing earlier. The boy with the limp and the blood-red scars perched on the bench across from her. He dropped his gaze as soon as he saw her looking at him. At the other end of the table, Samira breastfed Hazel. Beside her, Jaff shoveled porridge into his mouth with his hands.

Alistar walked away, reappearing with a bowl of porridge and a mug of water. "Go slowly. If this goes down alright, I'll get you some egg."

"Thank you," Aris said, meeting his eyes. His resemblance to Elom still unnerved her, but he'd had her life in his hands twice now . . . and she was still breathing.

Alistar nodded. "After you eat, we'll talk."

Aris turned her attention to her bowl. The porridge was thick, with a hint of sweetness but little taste. Not the most appetizing meal, but the first she'd eaten since the piggin the day before. She scooped it up eagerly. Beside her, a young boy grinned.

She smiled back, puffing her cheeks out as if they were stuffed with food.

He giggled and bunched up his smooth cheeks in imitation. The children next to him turned to look.

"What's your name?" she asked him. He was probably four or five years old, too young yet for Balias's conscription. So he'd probably lost his parents. The thought stole the smile from her face.

"Zeb," he said. "What's yours?"

"Aris." She forced another bite of porridge down. She'd only eaten a little but she already felt uncomfortably full.

"Why are you here?" asked the boy with the scars. His chin was raised a little too high, like he was psyching himself up to talk to her, trying to make himself look older.

She chose to answer him honestly. "My wingjet went down and Alistar saved my life."

He cocked his head. The murmurs of the other children faded. "You're a girl. And . . . and from Atalanta." He stumbled over it, like he was saying a dirty word. "You're not supposed to be here."

"That's true," Aris said. "All I want is to get back home."

The boy's arms were so thin, his brown eyes wary. Knowing he'd been in fights with Atalantan soldiers, that *his* was the face behind the blank Safaran helmets, made the porridge churn in her stomach. She took a small sip of water, trying to clear her throat.

"What's your name?" she asked.

The boy rubbed a hand across his scars. Eventually he said grudgingly, "Kori."

"When were you chosen to be a soldier?" she asked quietly.

He looked down, defiance still stiffening his narrow shoulders. "About six months ago. They came for us at night: me and a couple of my friends. My little sister was asleep in bed. I didn't get to say goodbye."

"Where is she now?" Aris tried to keep her voice steady.

Kori shrugged. "At home with my mother. Dead. I don't know. I lived in a city far from here. I don't know how to get back there." He rubbed his arm harder. "Alistar says they'll kill me if they catch me trying."

Aris gripped the edge of the heavy wooden table and fought the urge to look away.

"What happened to your face?" he asked.

"Someone tried to hurt me," she said, her fingers unconsciously tracing the scar across the bridge of her nose. "I got away."

Zeb tugged on her arm. Beside him, several other small boys were staring at her with rapt attention. "What's it like in a wingjet? I've never been."

Aris worked hard to find a smile. "I'm a flyer, so I spend a lot of time in wingjets. My favorite part is watching the ground rushing up toward me when I dive . . . it makes me feel free."

Zeb shuddered. "It sounds scary."

Farther down the bench, a little girl giggled at his reaction.

Aris smiled. "It can be. But sometimes the scary things turn out to be the most fun."

"Like climbing a tall tree?" one of the other boys asked.

"Exactly," Aris said.

Across from them, Kori stood up and shuffled away from the table. He leaned heavily on his stick; his leg hardly held his weight. Aris watched him slowly make his way to the cooking fire, his pain evident in every movement.

Her own memories of her childhood, barely surviving a fever and having to learn to walk again, sent a phantom echo of his agony through her own legs. How would he make the journey across the mountains? He could barely make it across the room.

A few minutes later, two older women gathered the children and disappeared down the dark tunnels that led from the cavern. One by one, the other adults left as well, until only Samira, her children, and Alistar remained.

Aris scooted down the bench to where they sat, abandoning her porridge. "Tell me your plan."

Samira rubbed a hand down Jaff's back. "Go with the others, love," she said. When he started to whine, she turned her steely eyes on him and he did as she'd asked, scampering into the nearest tunnel.

Alistar leaned forward, elbows on the rough wooden table. "We need to leave as soon as possible. This morning's raid gives us two or three days at most before they return."

"They come so often?" Aris asked. "What do they want?"

"They search the village for deserters, check to be sure we aren't harboring grown men or boys who could fight," he replied.

"What about you?"

Beside Aris, Samira stiffened. But Alistar didn't seem fazed. Without comment, he stood and put his left foot on the bench. He drew up the leg of his pants, exposing a metal rod enclosed in clear synthetics, molded to the shape of a man's leg.

Aris's eyes widened.

"It happened a couple years ago, just after the start of the war. It wasn't as bad back then . . . I was honorably discharged, given a new-tech prosthetic." He dropped his pant leg and sat back down. "But it won't be long until old soldiers like me are reenlisted. Ruslana's putting too much pressure on Balias. No one is safe from his conscription orders."

Aris leaned forward, rubbing her hands along the table. "But if the whole Military has been forced into service, why don't you just turn on Ward Balias?"

"Not everyone has been forced," Samira said. She held Hazel to her shoulder and rubbed her back. "There are many still loyal to Balias. Vocal dissenters often disappear. Some are even killed openly as an example to others."

Aris suppressed a shiver. "So we leave before the next raid. What happens to those left behind?"

"They'll hide in these caves," Alistar said. "We'll set part of the village on fire, make it look like we fled or were killed in the blaze. Hopefully that will buy us some time."

Aris frowned. "And how much time do you think we'll need?"

"A week." Alistar sighed. "Maybe more."

A week? Aris bit back a groan of frustration. "If only we could get our hands on a wingjet—a big one, like a transjet. We could be out in a matter of hours."

Samira looked up. "What do you mean?"

"I'm a flyer. Surely it was mentioned in the news vids?"

Alistar shrugged. "We get our news second or third-hand." Still, his expression brightened. "But this could help us."

"Do you have a wingjet we can use, then?" There hadn't been any on the village's landing pad. Aris tried not to get her hopes up.

Alistar shared a look with Samira before turning back to Aris "No. But we can get one."

Aris raised a brow.

"About twenty miles north of here, there's a stationpoint. It's where all the raids come from." Samira jiggled Hazel as she spoke; the baby was close to falling asleep against her mother's shoulder. "We have contacts there, soldiers who are loyal to the *people* of Safara, not Balias. They may be able to help."

Aris immediately balked. "No. We can't involve active Safaran soldiers."

"Lieutenant Nore's son is here," Samira explained. "He helps us with supplies and sends warnings before raids when he can. His top priority is saving his son from conscription. We can trust him. He would die before risking our exposure."

That gave Aris no reassurance that he would die before risking *her* exposure. Still, a transjet was the fastest way to Atalanta. And by far the easiest for the injured children.

"You said it'll be a couple days before the next raid. How will you contact Lieutenant Nore?" she asked.

"We have a Military radio," Alistar said. "It's so old the frequency is no longer monitored. We'll send the Lieutenant a message. He'll say he's received suspicious intel and will come 'investigate.' We'll explain what we need, and he'll give us a timeline or tell us if it's not possible."

"I thought you said there were no comms. Can we use that radio to contact my stationpoint?" Aris asked, suddenly uneasy.

Alistar shook his head. "It only works on an unused Safaran frequency. It's antiquated tech—we've tried upgrading it with no luck."

Aris shrugged, though inside her heart had plunged to her feet. She wanted to speak to Milek so badly, she could hardly bear the disappointment.

Alistar disappeared to find Gaven, the older, graying man who'd warned the village before the raid. He was, apparently, the man in charge of the radio.

Samira stood quietly, careful not to jostle Hazel, and murmured, "Follow me."

Aris left the relative familiarity of the cave for a narrow, dimly lit passageway. Samira's steps were graceful and certain, while Aris stumbled along behind, her thin cloth shoes catching on the rock beneath her feet. They wove deeper into the mountain, passing other curved tunnels lit by oily tin lanterns. At last, Samira paused before a doorway strung with a ragged scrap of fabric.

"You can rest here while we wait," she said. "Your belongings are inside, except for your weapons, of course. If we're lucky, Lieutenant Nore will be back by late afternoon. I'll come get you when he arrives."

Before Aris could protest, the woman continued down the hall.

Aris drew aside the cloth with trepidation. Inside, a small mat was draped with a single patchwork blanket made from old shirts. Her uniform and body armor rested on top.

In the corner stood a spindly table with a single jar of water and a glass.

Aris drank a glass of the oddly metallic-tasting water and shoved her belongings onto the floor before collapsing onto the thin pad. A small lantern flickered beside her on the floor. She couldn't bring herself to blow it out.

For a long time she stared up at the shadows that streaked the low ceiling. She pretended Milek was lying beside her, that his hand was inches from hers. That any second he would turn to her, wrap her in his arms, and whisper in her ear in low, fervent tones that everything would be okay.

"Don't give up hope," she whispered, not knowing whether the words were for him or for herself.

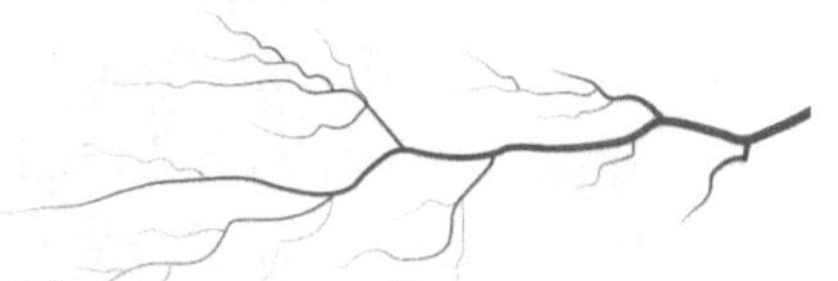

CHAPTER TWENTY-SIX

DYSIS HOVERED OVER DAAKON, MUMBLING, "IT'S okay, it's okay," even though it clearly wasn't. As much as she wanted to brush her hand across his short hair, she didn't dare touch him.

Calix knelt over Daakon's ankle, the supplies from his aid kit spread around him. He'd already removed Daakon's boot and the snake's head, but the bite was swelling rapidly, the skin turning a scary purple blue.

"What's wrong with him? Why's his leg swelling like that?" she asked, fighting down the panic. "What can I do?"

"Gods, make it stop," Daakon howled. Dysis had never seen him lose it before. His reaction was more frightening than the bite itself.

Calix stabbed him in the neck with a tiny medigun. "That should help with the pain. I hope." He glanced up at Dysis. "Help me hold him still. The snake was venomous. I need to remove the poison."

Dysis knelt next to Daakon's writhing body. "Ready?"

"Almost," Calix mumbled, concentrating on his task. He was fashioning a contraption out of a protective glove, a strip of bandaging, and a tube that had once held swabs.

"Come on, come on," Daakon grunted. He kept staring at his still-swelling leg, his eyes wide with panic and pain. Dysis took a peek and fought back a gag. Puss was starting to ooze out with the blood.

"Okay," she said, pulling herself together. She could handle this. She grabbed Daakon's face and made him look at her. "Listen to me. Focus on me, Daakon."

He tried to pull away but she wouldn't let him.

"No. I get to talk now. It's just you and me. And we have unfinished business, don't we?" She stared into his blood-shot brown eyes and kept her face calm. She couldn't let him see how scared she was.

After a moment, he nodded. At some point he'd bitten his lip; a drop of blood clung to his chin. She wiped it away with her thumb.

"You were right, the other day," she started, her underlying panic pushing out the words. "I did take advantage of you."

Behind her, Calix whispered, "Now," and Daakon jerked, groaning. She held him steady.

"I've thought about you every day since we met." She spoke faster, trying to block out the sucking sound of whatever Calix was doing. "That day, when you held me, I couldn't help trying. Even though I knew it wasn't the right thing to do." She didn't let herself think about the words as she voiced them. "And you gave me exactly what I wanted, what I'd hoped for. Then you told me you could never be with me. That everything we'd shared was all we'd *ever* share."

Daakon screamed, a primal sound that chilled Dysis to her core. She couldn't keep the fear from her face anymore; tears streamed down her cheeks. But Daakon's attention had turned inward, the whites of his eyes glaring in the darkness of his face.

"I know you were trying to help, but I'm not sure I can ever forgive you for that," Dysis sobbed. *Liar*. She couldn't say out loud that she'd forgiven him. Forgiveness was something you gave to people as they died.

He couldn't die.

Daakon's hands reached up and gripped her shoulders, digging into the muscles with all his strength. She cried out but didn't try to pull away. Instead she held him closer, both of them locked together in agony.

Without warning, Daakon went limp in her arms. She whirled toward Calix. "What happened? What did you do?"

Calix sat back on his haunches, breathing hard. He held up a sythin. The thin, rod-shaped weapon was used to render someone unconscious.

"Why the *hell* didn't you use that before? You could have saved him so much pain!" She gently let Daakon's body rest against the rocky ground, letting go in stages, her arms aching. The sun beat down on her head; they were all covered in sweat.

"I've never used a sythin in a mender procedure before. I wasn't sure how it would affect his heart rate and blood pressure." Calix slumped with exhaustion, but his hands went to work. "I needed to suck out the poisoned blood first, just in case." He removed his suctioning contraption and cleaned the wound.

Much of the swelling had gone down, but the skin around the bite was still a horrible purple blue streaked with yellow.

Dysis brushed some dirt from Daakon's uniform. His chest rose and fell shallowly, but he was breathing. She needed to get him into the shade, where it was cooler. She pointed to a spot under the trees. "Let's get him out of the sun."

Together, they dragged him into the shadows, careful not to jostle his foot.

"Is he going to be okay?" she asked.

Calix sighed. "Honestly, I don't know. I've never dealt with a venomous snakebite before. I . . . I hope I got all the poison out."

"But?" Her stomach tightened. She glanced around the clearing, as if somehow she'd find a solution there.

"But I don't have the tools to tell for sure. He needs full mender care. Possibly surgery to save his foot." Calix's fingers hovered over his chest. His emergency beacon. "We should . . ."

Dysis's heart cracked, but she shook her head. "We can't call for help yet. Not without Aris."

He dropped his hand, his face still full of doubt. "He could die, Dysis."

She gestured to Daakon's leg. "But you've done such a good job. Look, most of the swelling is gone. Chances are—"

"Chances are he'll lose the use of his foot, even if he survives," Calix said. "There were paralyzing properties in the venom. When the Lieutenant was writhing around, his foot didn't move."

Dysis paced the clearing. Major Vadim had said not to push the beacons under any circumstances unless Aris was with them. But Lieutenant Daakon was his second-in-command. And how could they continue their search, with Daakon completely incapacitated? It was only a matter of time before the Safarans found them.

And when that happened, they'd *all* be wishing for death.

The morbid thought sparked an idea. "You said he needs full mender care. What do you need to make him better?"

Calix glanced at her, then at the mender supplies still scattered on the ground. He shrugged. "I don't know . . . some kind of antivenom, probably, and antibiotics. More pain meds, clean bandages. Why?"

New hope coursed through her. It was all stuff she could carry. In a rush, she started unpacking her bag, leaving only a bottle of water and a couple nutrigel pouches inside.

"What are you doing?" Calix asked.

"You stay here with Daakon. Make sure he's comfortable. Do as much as you can for him." She heaved the nearly empty bag onto her shoulder. "I'm going to the village, the one we saw on the map. I'll sneak in after dark, grab the stuff you need, and come back. We can run searches for Aris from this campsite, while Daakon recovers."

"No way." Calix shook his head vehemently. "It's too dangerous. What if you're caught?"

Dysis crossed her arms over her chest. "Got a better idea?"

Calix opened his mouth, but nothing came out.

"Didn't think so." On impulse, she bent over Daakon and pressed a quick kiss to his sweaty forehead. His breath fluttered against her skin, a reassurance. When she stood, she gave Calix a hard look. "If I'm not back by dawn tomorrow, or . . . or if Daakon dies, you keep searching for Aris. Okay?"

Calix nodded, though he still looked like he wanted to protest.

"But don't let him die." Dysis grabbed Daakon's map and stomped out of the clearing and into the trees. She saved her tears until she was far from Calix and certain only the birds would hear.

<hr>

It took a couple hours to reach the outskirts of the village. By that point, Dysis was cloaked in sweat, her short hair dripping, her water bottle almost empty. In silence, she shifted her position to get a better view of the village.

The line of trees butted up to its north side; from her angle, she could see a small collection of ramshackle structures surrounding a dirt clearing. Through a gap in the buildings, a black Safaran wingjet gleamed in the sunlight. The mountains towered above, dotted with tiny stone houses and precarious wooden bridges.

Dysis prayed the mender clinic was on solid ground; she had no desire to dangle from one of those bridges.

After moving through the shadows to get a better vantage of the wingjet, she sat back against a scruffy tree, pulled out a nutrigel, and settled in to wait out the last of the daylight.

She focused on the different buildings and the few

villagers she saw wandering around, forcing her brain to stop reliving the moment when Daakon silently begged her to make his suffering end.

He'll be okay. You'll save him. You'll save them both.

But she couldn't shake the fear that she'd made the wrong choice, that she should have hit her transmitter. That Aris was already beyond help, and she wouldn't get back to Daakon in time.

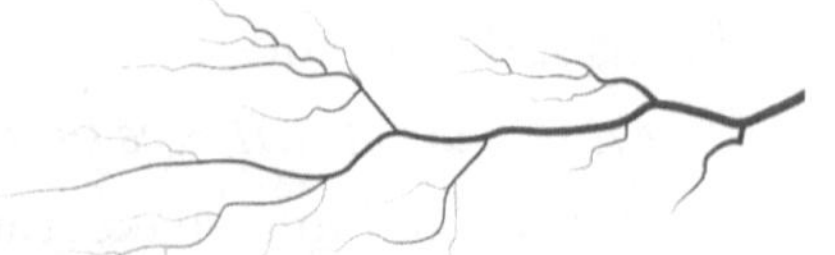

Chapter Twenty-Seven

Galena chose not to warn Milek of her impending arrival. She arranged the flight through Pyralis and Commander Nyx, and when she stepped from the executive wingjet onto Spiro's tarmac, only Nyx was there to greet her, just as she wished.

"How is he?" Galena asked as Commander Nyx fell into step beside her.

"Major Vadim has continued to conduct himself professionally, but it's obvious the mission to retrieve Lieutenant Haan is weighing heavily on him."

She was tactful, but Galena was certain Nyx knew of Milek's relationship with Aris. It was Nyx's stationpoint and her job to know everything, especially the secrets. Galena knew because she'd pried it out of him in a weak moment after Aris's wingjet went down.

The blank white corridors of Spiro reminded Galena uncomfortably of the prison camp where Elom had held her captive. At least here, the hallways weren't empty and ominously silent. As Commander Nyx led her to Milek's office, soldiers passed in haphazard clumps. Galena kept her gaze straight ahead, ignoring the looks, first of surprise, then recognition. Occasionally horror. She knew how jarring her scars could be; they still shocked her every morning when she looked in the mirror.

"Ward Vadim." A female soldier stopped suddenly in the middle of the corridor, her pale gray-blue eyes widening in surprise. A fading greenish-purple bruise marred her cheek.

"Enough gawking, Specialist." Commander Nyx gestured for the girl to move out of the way, but Galena shook her head.

"No, it's okay." This was her chance to speak to a female soldier in person. "What's your name, Specialist?"

"Tia Pallas, ma'am." The woman stood with her shoulders back and chin up. The bruise gave her a dangerous air. She was slight, but Galena guessed she was a lot stronger than she looked.

"Your role here?" Galena asked.

"A flyer," Specialist Pallas said, nervousness sneaking into her eyes. "Ward, if I may . . ."

Galena nodded. "Of course."

A furrow appeared between her brows. "You could have kept the truth buried. Forgotten us, just like everyone else." She ran a hand through her pale hair. "But you didn't. And I want to thank you for that."

Before Galena could respond, the girl continued down the hallway, her shoulders tense.

Commander Nyx resumed walking.

"It's harder for them now, even without the threat of exposure," Galena said, glancing back once, watching as

Specialist Pallas turned the corner and disappeared from view. "But are women still happy to serve openly?"

Nyx grunted. "It wasn't just about what they looked like in the mirror. They had to lie to everyone, even their families. Now . . . it's not easy." She stopped before a frosted glass door. "But most—not all, but most—women feel this sacrifice is the lighter one to bear."

Galena stared at the red scars that crisscrossed the black Military brand on the back of Commander Nyx's neck. "And you?"

Nyx tapped a panel by the door. "I think integration will fail. Sooner or later, men will find a way to remove us from Military. It's in their nature."

It was not what Galena expected. "Are you saying it's in *our* nature to let them?"

The door slid open, revealing Milek hunched over the digitablet on his desk, his head cradled in one hand.

"I think we all have a long way to go." Commander Nyx left, giving Galena no time to reply.

Without looking up, Milek said, "I asked not to be disturbed. The emergency signals could be coming any—"

"Milek, dear." After a last considering glance toward Commander Nyx's retreating back, Galena stepped into the room.

"Mother." Milek's head snapped up. He rose from his chair, his clear blue eyes—mirrors of her own—wide with worry. "You shouldn't be here. It's not safe this close to the fighting."

She wrapped her arms around him. "A minor risk, compared to what you do all day."

"That's not the point." He drew away, but his expression was far less angry than his words. "Why did you come?"

"You haven't been replying to my comms, and you missed our vid meeting yesterday." She smoothed a hand over the short golden hair above his ear, a gesture that had been a comfort to them both when he was small. She was glad Pyralis had suggested the visit. "I was worried about you. The last few days have been a far more difficult trial than you deserve."

"It's fine. I'm fine." He sank back into his chair, his eyes drawn yet again to his digitablet. "Daakon will find her."

Galena stood next to his desk and stared down at the top of his head. Weariness bent his shoulders forward, stress dug grooves in his forehead. "He will, I'm certain of it," she said. "But you'll be ill-equipped to aid him in the rescue if you don't take better care of yourself. Come eat dinner with me. Commander Nyx has reserved us a briefing room so we can have some privacy."

Milek shook his head. "Mother, I'm sorry but I can't. I need to—"

"Take the tablet with you, of course." She rested a hand on his shoulder. "I've come a long way to have dinner with my son. Would you deny me that small pleasure?" Galena smiled to soften the manipulation. She might have felt bad, if she didn't believe wholeheartedly that he needed a break and probably hadn't eaten all day.

He looked up, his tired smile crinkling the corners of his eyes. "I know what you're doing."

"Then let me do it." She squeezed his shoulder, pleased when he stood.

"Fine. One *quick* dinner. I'll reward your guilt trip this

once." His face lightened a little, even as he collected the digitablet in careful hands, as if it were something precious.

As Galena turned, a buzzer sounded, startling her. Milek pressed a button and the door slid open.

A stocky, bald soldier rushed in. "Sir, we've had a hit," he said, panting as if he'd run miles. His freckled cheeks glowed an unpleasant red.

Milek's eyes dropped to the map that glowed on the screen of his digitablet. "A hit on what, Specialist? I've had no sign that the emergency transponders have been activated."

"The name 'Elom.'"

Galena's gaze snapped back to the soldier as her stomach seized, an automatic, annoying fear response she wished would go away already.

The man continued. "A couple of Safaran units discussing his arrival."

Milek went even paler, his face as set as chiseled stone. "His arrival where?"

The young man's lips turned down. "Lieutenant Haan's crash site."

"Thank you, Specialist. You're dismissed." Milek waited approximately two seconds after the man left. Then he took off down the hall.

Galena rushed to keep up. "Milek, where are you going? What does this mean?"

He didn't answer. A few doors down, he skidded to a stop and slapped his hand against the pad on the wall.

Commander Nyx held up a hand as the door slid open. A sharp-chinned man with a pronounced Adam's apple was speaking on the vid screen. "It's getting out of hand, Commander. I've had three female flyers leave their posts this month because of harassment. I am disciplining the soldiers we know contributed, but so much of the abuse is going unreported. It's difficult to catch all the offenders."

Commander Nyx nodded. "I understand, Major. I'll be there by tomorrow's morning formation. We'll get to the bottom of this."

The man nodded. "Who'd have thought my best flyers were women all this time? And now they're leaving. I don't know what to do."

Galena half expected him to wring his hands.

Commander Nyx mumbled something under her breath, looking disgusted. Louder she said, "Send me the names of the flyers who've left, the harassers you've disciplined, and their punishments. I'll see you tomorrow."

Without waiting for a response, she ended the call. With a sigh, she turned to Milek, who was nearly hopping with impatience. Galena wanted to put a hand on his arm to calm him, but she knew it wouldn't do any good.

"What is it, Major?" Commander Nyx was rigid even while seated, her shoulders back and her posture wholly uncompromising.

"We've received intel that Elom is heading toward Aris's crash site." The words spilled from him in a hurried rush.

"And?"

Galena found Commander Nyx's unruffled response infuriating. Given Milek's reaction and her own common sense, she could guess this meant Aris and the rest of Milek's team were in greater danger.

Milek glared at the woman, his body stiff with tension.

"If Elom himself is going, that means he's found cause to question our deception. We have to move *now*."

Nyx asked, "Have your team's transmitters been activated?"

He shook his head, looking as if he wished he could yell in her face. "We need to get in there. We have a general location. If we take enough firepower—"

"No." Nyx stared him down. She ignored Galena. "You will not endanger your team by moving in on questionable information. It could well be another trap and even if it's not, your search area is too large to ensure you'll find them before Elom's men do."

"I cannot just sit by and *wait* anymore!" He pounded a fist on her desk.

Commander Nyx didn't react except to narrow her eyes. "Major Vadim, any missions that originate at my station-point originate with me. You have concerns. We all do. But you will not go against a direct order. And I order you to wait. If further intel is collected or your team hits their transmitters, we'll reevaluate."

Galena wanted to say something. She wanted to over-turn Commander Nyx's order. She wanted to give Milek what he wanted. But she couldn't. She couldn't do anything but watch him rage in silence, praying that *soon* his team would find Aris, *soon* he could come to her rescue.

"Elom is going after Aris," he growled, but Galena could see it was no use.

Commander Nyx stood her ground. "Trust your team, Milek. You picked them for a reason."

"I do trust them. But—"

Her eyes softened a hair. "But it's hard to have faith

when you can't be on the ground with them. Believe me. I know." At last, she glanced at Galena. "Go have dinner with your mother. And for Gods' sakes get some sleep. You'll be no use to Lieutenant Haan like that."

Galena understood the unspoken message in Nyx's gaze. It was her turn to take over. Milek was her responsibility now.

"Come on," she said, pulling gently on his arm. "Let's go."

They returned to his office. Galena wanted to reassure him somehow, tell him everything would be okay, but she knew the words would mean nothing. She couldn't promise anything beyond blind hope.

CHAPTER TWENTY-EIGHT

Samira came to retrieve Aris a few hours later. She scrambled to her feet, relieved to have reason to leave the tiny, dim cave. She'd napped fitfully, plagued by dreams of Elom looming over her with a knife.

Samira led her to the main cave, where one of the older female villagers gave her a small scorched flatbread, while they waited for Alistar to return with Lieutenant Nore. Aris nibbled at the bread, stomach churning, aware that she was yet again trusting Alistar with her life.

"Is it true we're leaving soon?" Zeb asked. He and a couple of the other children were scrubbing the tables, making it more a game of splashing than cleaning.

Aris wasn't sure what to say. How much did the children know?

Before she could answer, a clatter of footsteps echoed in the main tunnel. Aris turned just as Alistar and Gaven led two men clad in Safaran black into the room. She tensed as she stood to face them, her Atalantan uniform suddenly feeling like a target.

Everyone stared in wary silence for a moment before Alistar made introductions. Lieutenant Nore was the taller and thinner of the two, with a reserve that gave each of his movements extra weight. A little boy ran over yelling "Daddy!" and Nore's entire body radiated joy as he bent to give his son a hug.

The other man, Specialist Baryn, kept his eyes on Aris. His face bore several scars and a jagged, abstract tattoo that covered one cheek and part of his neck. She forced herself not to look away.

"So you need a wingjet?" Baryn asked.

Aris nodded.

Samira gestured to one of the tables—the one the children hadn't attempted to wash yet. The elderly woman led the little ones—aside from Lieutenant Nore's son—outside to play as Aris, Samira, Alistar, and the two soldiers sat down. Aris wished she could join the children for a fresh breath of air; the smoking fire dragged at her lungs.

"It has to be a transjet or maybe a large transport to fit all the children," Samira said.

Lieutenant Nore let his son sit beside him on the bench. The little boy played with the pockets of his uniform. "We'll need a reason to come with such a large wingjet," Nore said. "It can't be a regular raid."

"Tell your superior the villagers found part of the Atalantan wingjet that crashed," Aris said. She'd been thinking about it all day. The Safaran troops had certainly seemed interested in the crash site, and the retrieval team had burned the jet, so it would have been difficult to tell how much of it remained. It was a reasonable cover.

Nore thought about it for a moment, running his hand over his son's dark hair. "It'll be difficult not to throw suspicion since we were here this morning and no jet wreckage had been found."

"We went hunting this afternoon and found it a couple miles away," Alistar offered. "We dragged it back here, but it was very heavy, needed several men. Wouldn't fit in a recon."

Aris caught Specialist Baryn's eyes on her again. He didn't offer his opinion.

At last, Nore said, "Alright, I can make that work. Our commander will likely want to investigate immediately. I would guess early tomorrow morning. Can you mobilize that fast?"

Samira nodded, her expression full of determination. "We'll be ready."

"There will be six of us at least. Three who are loyal to the village," Lieutenant Nore said, as he and Baryn stood to go. "Let's try to avoid violence. Be prepared with restraints for the other soliders. Keep the children out of sight until the scene is secure."

Aris rose as well. She needed to get out of the caves for a while. The heavy, curved walls were starting to press in on her.

"Lieutenant Haan." Specialist Baryn paused at her side. "I would recommend that you stay out of sight until the village has taken control." Before she could ask why, he continued. "The world may believe you're dead, but your picture's been given out to all the soldiers of this dominion as a top target. If you're recognized, your 'resurrection' might not last long."

Aris froze. The *world* thought she was dead? Safaran soldiers had been given her picture?

Black dots danced before her eyes. She needed fresh air. *Now.*

She followed the others down the narrow tunnel and tried not to hyperventilate. When she emerged into the open, the late-day sun blasted her with heat. Gradually, her clammy skin dried and her breathing calmed. The teetering rope bridge didn't even terrify her this time; she was that relieved to be outside.

"Caves not to your liking?" Samira asked, as they wove between the clinic and another ramshackle building on their way to the landing pad.

Aris glanced at her. "Is it that obvious?"

The woman shrugged. "You're not the only one who feels claustrophobic. We try to let the children play outside every day, even if it's raining."

Aris paused and touched Samira's arm lightly. Samira drew away from the contact, but she stopped walking. "You're doing a good thing here," Aris said earnestly. "I know you don't need to hear it from me, but I need to say it. I *am* sorry about your husband, and I am sorry that these children need protection. But I'm happy they have it. *Really* happy. I . . . well, that's all."

Samira looked a little shell-shocked, so Aris jogged away, toward the wingjet. Lieutenant Nore shook her hand before climbing into the jet. Specialist Baryn climbed into the flyer's seat. Aris wondered why they hadn't asked *him* to fly them to Atalanta, and then she saw him take off.

Not his strong suit, then.

"Had you heard that I was dead?" Aris asked Alistar, as they watched the wingjet roar away.

"No, but I suppose it's no surprise. You did crash." He patted her shoulder. "Come. We have a lot to prepare for tomorrow."

Tomorrow. In mere hours, she'd see Milek again. Her chest filled with such a desperate ache she almost cried, right there in front of Alistar and Samira.

"What do we need—"

"Stay right where you are." The shout came from behind them.

Aris whirled.

Dysis stood a few feet away, the clinic at her back, her solagun trained on Alistar. Her dark hair was matted to her head, and dark circles nestled beneath her eyes.

"Oh holy, *Dysis*." Aris suddenly wasn't sure her legs would hold. Shock rocketed through her, killing every thought except for *Dysis. Dysis is here.*

She took a jerky step toward her best friend.

Alistar raised his hands to show he was unarmed. "You know this woman?"

"Don't talk," Dysis ordered, her face hard. "Aris, walk slowly toward me. Stay—"

"Put your weapon down." Gaven snuck up the alley behind Dysis, his weapon trained on her head.

CHAPTER TWENTY-NINE

DYSIS DIDN'T FLINCH, AND SHE DIDN'T LOWER HER solagun.

Aris's brain slowly moved past shock, to relief, to excitement, stuttering to a halt on *blighting hell, my new Safaran allies are about to shoot my best friend.*

"Don't hurt her, Gaven," Aris called. Dust kicked up under her feet as she ran to Dysis's side. She wanted to give her a proper hug, wanted to scream with joy at being found, at having Dysis *here.* Instead, she grabbed Dysis's shoulders, ignoring the solagun still half-raised between them.

Aris noted a lurking, frantic worry in her friend's eyes. "It's okay. I'm not in danger."

"But—" Dysis started.

"No one is a threat here, I promise," Aris said. "I'll explain everything."

It took Dysis a long time to holster her weapon, but when she did, Aris could feel the rigid tension leave her frame as she sagged with relief. "I can't believe I found you."

With the solagun out of play, Aris pulled Dysis into a hug. Tears coursed unchecked down her cheeks. Dysis tightened her arms until Aris could hardly breathe.

"Are you okay?" Dysis asked, her voice hoarse with emotion. "Major Vadim faked your death so the Safarans wouldn't look for you before we had the chance, but I thought you might be dead anyway. I'm *so* glad you're not." A laugh, edged with hysteria, spilled from her mouth.

They faked my death?

Aris's heart pounded. "Is Milek with you?"

Dysis put some space between them but kept a hold on Aris's arm. "He's waiting for you at Spiro. I think it nearly killed him not to come on the search mission." She glanced warily at the others. A small crowd had gathered. She added, "I'll tell you all about it, but first you need to explain *this*."

Aris could tell Alistar was waiting for an explanation as well. "Dysis, this is Alistar," she said, gesturing to him. "And his sister Samira. They're in charge of the village, and they're . . . well, dissenters, I guess you could say. Alistar, this is Specialist Dysis Latza, my friend and fellow soldier."

Alistar bowed. Without a word, Samira headed for the alleyway by the clinic, which led to the field where the children still played. She gave Aris a searching look as she passed.

Dysis drew Aris a few feet away. In a low voice, she said, "You're awfully buddy-buddy with these people."

Aris glanced back at Alistar and shrugged. "They saved my life."

She held up her splinted wrist. "I wandered into the village, injured and delirious, and instead of turning me in, they healed me."

Dysis took a deep breath but didn't reply. Her worry

didn't seem to be fading. She kept glancing around, not at the small cluster of villagers talking to Alistar, but toward the ramshackle buildings, as if she feared a hidden enemy.

"What's going on?" Aris shifted from one foot to another, finding Dysis's unease contagious. "Why are you alone?"

"I came here to steal med supplies." Her eyes flicked toward the villagers again. "Then I saw you, walking between those two Safaran soldiers like a prisoner. I was out of my head. I started for you, ready to take them all down, when they climbed into the jet without you." She shook her head, her disbelief still evident. "Are you sure this isn't all a trap? How come they just let you go?"

Ignoring her questions, Aris inspected Dysis more closely. "Why did you need to steal med supplies? What happened?"

"Daakon's hurt." Dysis's voice hitched, almost broke. "Dying, maybe."

A weight settled in Aris's stomach. "Where is he? What do you need?"

"He was bitten by a snake, so antivenom. Pain meds. I . . . I memorized a list." Dysis squinted up at the twilight sky. If Aris didn't know her better, she'd guess Dysis was blinking back tears.

Aris hurried to Alistar's side. "My friend's partner is injured. He needs antivenom and a mender. Can you help?"

"Of course. I'll get my things." Alistar headed for the clinic without a moment's hesitation. He called back, "Gaven, get the litter."

Dysis's eyes widened. At the sight of a flurry of Safarans rushing to save an Atalantan soldier, Aris understood her shock. She ran her good hand over her splint. She had awakened that morning thinking she was at Elom's mercy. Now . . . "It's nothing like I expected."

Dysis shook her head. "You can say that again."

In minutes, a rescue team had assembled and Dysis was leading them into the woods.

As she and Aris heaved themselves over a tumble of boulders, Dysis said, "There's something you should know."

"What?" Aris scrambled to keep up.

"Daakon and I aren't the only ones on this mission." Dysis shot her an unreadable look. "Calix is here, too."

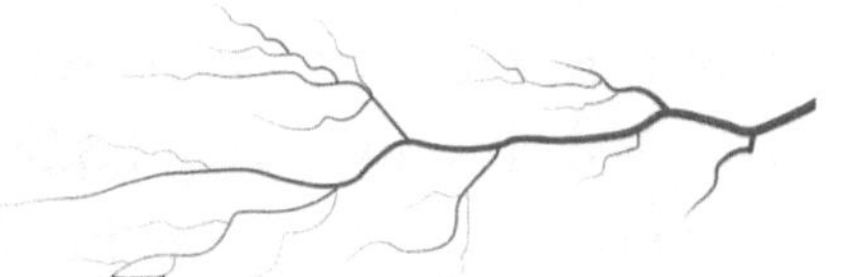

CHAPTER THIRTY

OF ALL THE PEOPLE ARIS MIGHT HAVE IMAGINED on a rescue mission for her, Calix wasn't even on the list. It was nearly dark by the time they reached the campsite, but Calix's eyes locked onto hers immediately, widening in shock. There was still enough light to reveal his brown hair, tawny skin, and the leaf-green eyes she'd once lost herself in.

"Aris." Calix stood up and took a step toward her. He opened his mouth to say something, and then seemed to change his mind.

Memories flooded her without warning, and inappropriate tears pricked her eyes. They hadn't spoken in months, he'd broken her heart, but they were still connected. She still cared.

Dysis ran to the still form on the ground. "How is he? Is he . . . ?"

Calix stared at Aris for a half second longer before dropping down next to Dysis. "He's still alive, but he hasn't regained consciousness, and he should have by now. The leg is starting to swell again."

Alistar moved to kneel on Lieutenant Daakon's other side. Daakon's unmoving body looked oddly small with so many people huddling over it.

"How long ago was he bitten?" Alistar asked, studying the wound. Gaven stood behind him with a folded length of fabric and two long poles.

Calix seemed to have just noticed that Dysis and Aris did not arrive alone. He looked like he might pull his weapon. "Who are you?"

"It's okay, Calix," Aris said. "Alistar and Gaven are here to help."

He glanced at her over his shoulder and couldn't seem to look away. "He doesn't need help. He needs to get out of here. Now that we've found you, we can let Major Vadim know where to retrieve us."

"Milek isn't on his way already?" Aris's pulse quickened. If Milek hadn't left Spiro, they could tell him to bring several transports. They could evacuate the village *now* instead of waiting for morning.

"No, not yet." Dysis rubbed a gentle hand along Daakon's forehead, as Alistar worked on his ankle. "We don't have a way to reach him except by pressing our emergency transmitters."

Dismay filled Aris. "You don't have comms?"

Calix shook his head. "No. Major Vadim thinks Safara has hacked into our comm system. It wasn't safe to communicate that way."

Aris struggled not to let her disappointment show. "Do

you know what kind of team he's bringing for the extraction?"

Confusion overtook Calix's features. "Just a single recon and transport. He wants to get in and out before Safaran forces see us."

One transport wouldn't be enough for all of them. The Safaran cargo jet they planned to commandeer could hold twenty-five or more safely, but Atalantan transports only held eight or nine people. Maybe once Milek got here, she could ask him to radio for reinforcements. . . .

No. There wouldn't be time. Safaran troops would lock onto their position, like they'd done when she crashed. There'd only be minutes to get in and out.

Calix reached for his transmitter.

"Don't touch that!" Aris said, snapping out of her thoughts and lurching toward him. "You can't contact Milek yet."

"But we have to let Major Vadim know we found you," Calix said. "He's awaiting our signal to retrieve you."

"You can't yet, Calix," she said, tension feeding every muscle. If Calix hit that beacon, Milek would arrive, guns blazing, and there'd be no way to save the village's children. Not with only one transport and no warning. As much as she wanted Milek to be here, *now*, she'd given her word. She wouldn't abandon her mission. "Please. Just wait until I can tell you everything."

For a charged second, Calix stared at her, his hand still resting on his beacon. Aris stared back, a little dazed.

"I'm afraid you don't have time to wait for your reinforcements," Alistar interjected. He glanced at Calix. "This kind of bite usually kills within minutes. You saved this man's life, but he's still in danger. He needs fluids and a blood transfusion. Possibly surgery on his ankle. I won't know until I get him back to the clinic." He rocked back on his heels, considering. "We need to move him quickly."

Gaven was already assembling the litter.

Dysis stood, using Calix's shoulder to push herself up. "Don't worry. As soon as Daakon's stable, we'll hit our transmitters. Let's just make sure he's going to be okay first, alright?"

"Actually," Aris said, already anticipating a fight, "I have another plan to get us out of here."

ARIS TOLD Calix and Dysis about the village's hidden children, but she waited to tell them the evacuation plan until after Lieutenant Daakon stabilized. They were all sitting at one of the long wooden tables in the main cavern. Dinnertime had come and gone before they made it to the clammy, fire-lit cave, so the room was nearly empty. It had been a trial convincing Dysis to leave Daakon in the capable hands of the village's menders, but his improving color and the fact that he'd both regained consciousness and could move his toes gave her some reassurance.

Aris hadn't gotten a chance to talk to Calix about what he was doing here. Truth be told, she was reluctant to ask. She suspected why he'd come—she'd gone on a similar journey herself once—and wasn't sure what she would say when he told her.

A few of the older children lingered over half-empty bowls of roasted potato and wild turkey, talking quietly and sneaking frequent glances at the newcomers. Aris caught a glimpse of Kori; he sat with his head down, his thin, scarred arms framing his bowl as he concentrated on his food.

"Alright, here's the plan," she said, dragging her eyes from the children. "We're taking these kids with us to Atalanta."

"What?" The word exploded from Calix's mouth.

Aris held up a hand. "Alistar has friends in the Military. Tomorrow a group of soldiers, some loyal to us, some not, will arrive with a cargo jet, ostensibly to retrieve a broken piece of my wingjet. We'll then commandeer the jet and transport the children to Spiro."

"What about Major Vadim?" Dysis asked. Her voice was hoarse, as if she'd recently been crying. "Why not contact him now? He could help with the retrieval."

Aris shook her head regretfully. "I want to, believe me. But all he'll bring is a recon and transport, like you said. There won't be room for everyone, and no time to comm for a bigger jet. As soon as Milek enters Safaran airspace, Balias's men will engage." *Only a few hours.* She could wait a few more hours to see him. "We don't want any violence. We can't risk putting these children in danger."

Calix stood up from the table. "But you may be putting *yourself* in danger. We saw them removing the wreckage of your jet. What if they figure out it's a trap? What if they suspect you're still alive? A lot of people went to great lengths to protect you from Ward Balias and his men. I went to your *burning*, Aris."

Aris swallowed, remembering what Specialist Baryn said about soldiers being given her picture. "I'll stay out of sight until we have control of the situation." She leaned forward. "It's a solid plan, Calix. With you and Dysis here, we've an even greater chance of everything going smoothly. There will be six men on the jet; only three of them are loyal to Ward Balias. We've only got to overpower *three* men and we'll be able to get out of here."

Calix backed away from the table. "And what would *Milek* say?"

Her breath caught in her throat. "What do you mean?"

His tanned face twisted for an instant before smoothing into calmer lines. Aris stared at him, guilt and regret wriggling within her like a mess of snakes. He knew about Milek. "He doesn't know you're safe, Aris," Calix continued. "Doesn't that bother you?"

She could see how hard it was for Calix to say those words, and she tried to be gentle. "Milek would understand. He *will* understand. I'm a soldier. My job is to rescue those in harm's way, Calix. My safety is *not* more important than Kori's"—she pointed toward the group of boys at the end of the table—"or Samira and her children's. I will not let you make this about me. This is a *mission*."

Calix backed farther away. No one else spoke. It was as if the whole cavern held its breath. His hand moved to the beacon on his chest. "You're right. It *is* a mission. And I have my orders."

Aris stood so fast she knocked her hips against the table. Beside her, Samira and Alistar stood, too.

"Calix," Aris said, her voice shaking. "I am asking you to accept me and my choices. You don't have to understand or agree with them, and you can worry. We all worry. But I'd like you on my team for once. This is your choice, right now." Her face hardened with the strength of her conviction. "If you press that transmitter, you are dead to me. As dead as if I'd been to *your* burning. So choose."

For a long time he stared at her, weighing his truth against hers. Aris's heart pounded in her chest. He'd never trusted her to make her own choices. He'd turned his back on her in Mekia, when he'd found out she was a member of Military. He always followed the rules.

"I don't see you the way you wish I could, you're right," Calix said. With an exhale, his hand dropped to his side. "But I *am* trying. If this is what you feel is right . . . I won't fight you."

Aris should have been relieved, but his response bothered her. "I'm glad you won't fight me. But don't you care at all? Is this really *just* about me? What about saving these kids? Exposing Ward Balias's crimes to the world? Doesn't that matter at all?"

Calix shrugged and smiled sadly. "It does matter to me, but not more than you do."

Aris swallowed back her surprise. It was eerie how closely his words echoed what she'd thought when she'd first joined Military. When Dianthe had told her it wasn't about Calix but something much bigger, Aris hadn't seen it that way. But now she did.

"Well, now that you've resolved that little drama in the most awkward way possible," Dysis broke in, "I'm going to go check on Lieutenant Daakon. And we need to get ready for tomorrow morning."

With a glare in Calix's direction, Samira left to show Dysis the way out of the caves.

Zeb ran up beside Aris and pulled on her wrist. His halo

of black hair stood up, electrified. "Come on! You have to see it!"

"See what?" Aris let the small boy pull her toward the tunneled entrance. She glanced back at Calix, who stood by the table. "You coming?"

When they reached open air, the chill raised goosebumps along her arms. The heat of the day had disappeared with the sun. Zeb led her along the rickety rope bridge, nimble and completely unconcerned with the darkness. She held her breath until her feet touched solid ground.

When they reached the open field where the children often played, Zeb pointed toward the horizon. A large swirling glow arced into the night sky.

"What is it?" Aris asked, not sure whether to feel awe or terror. She'd seen the strange light before, when she'd stumbled into the village two nights before. She'd just assumed it was a hallucination.

"The flaming scorpion!" Zeb said, squealing as another explosion of curling light shot into the air. The tails of yellowy red did vaguely resemble the curving points of scorpion tails.

"It looks like a firebomb," Calix said, coming up beside her.

Aris shook her head. "A bit, but there's no concussion. And it's moving almost like smoke, sort of slow and undulating."

"Maybe we're too far away to feel the blast?"

Alistar walked toward them. "It's not a firebomb. We're not sure what it is. The 'flaming scorpion' has lit the night sky on and off for months. Always in the same place. It's a mystery."

Aris patted Zeb's head as he released her wrist and scampered over to where the other children gathered to watch the show.

"During a war," she said, a chill running along her arms, "mystery is never a good thing."

Chapter Thirty-One

For a long time, Dysis sat on the edge of Daakon's med-bed and watched him sleep. His skin was ashy, with dark hollows under his eyes, but his breathing had steadied. Alistar had wrapped his ankle with a thick white bandage.

She wished he'd wake, so she could tell him she was sorry. Daakon didn't need to know he'd broken her heart; it didn't do either of them any good.

When she emerged from the ramshackle clinic, the sound of voices drew her to the back of the building. There, in the dim light of two flickering street lights, a group of children stared in awe at the sky. A few yards away, Calix stood with Alistar. She followed their line of sight to the red-gold swirl undulating across the sky.

"What is that?" she asked as she reached the two men.

Calix glanced at her, his face darkened by shadow and the beginnings of a beard. "The children call it the flaming scorpion."

"Huh. Sounds ominous." She almost laughed. What wasn't ominous, these days?

Alistar drifted away, gathering up the children and shuttling them toward the caves.

Dysis crossed her arms over her chest, a protection against the chill night air. "Where's Aris?"

"She went to help Samira get the children's belongings together," Calix replied. "They don't have much, but some have things they want to bring with them . . . mementos from their families."

Dysis dropped to the sandy ground, her eyes still on the strange light in the sky. "We should probably be doing something to help."

Calix sat beside her. "In a minute."

She got the sense that he understood that she *needed* that minute. Just to sit. Breathe. Acknowledge to the stars that both her best friend and the man she loved had cheated death. That, even here in enemy lands, she was lucky.

She snuck a look at Calix. She'd assumed he'd be a coward. The kind of man who would feel threatened by a strong woman. Why else would he turn his back on Aris?

But the way he'd reacted when Daakon was hurt—killing that snake, sucking out the venom—those were not cowardly acts. And she never imagined she'd be grateful to him.

"How did it feel?" she asked, hoping to put him on edge as he'd done to her.

"How did what feel?" Calix glanced at her, a patch of light catching his cheekbone.

"Breaking the rules. Again." She smirked. "You're a deserter *and* a rule breaker. One might even call you a rebel."

He smiled ruefully at his knees. "I wouldn't say that."

"Doesn't it feel good to use your *own* brain once in a while?" She swept a hand along the ground, making small finger-shaped tracks in the dirt.

"I have respect for the laws and traditions of our dominion. That doesn't deserve ridicule." His face tightened as he looked up at the sky, where the last swirls of the flaming scorpion faded into the darkness. "Without law, without respect, this is what you get. A dominion where its own people feel victimized and alone."

"Not all rules should be followed," Dysis protested, shifting uncomfortably.

Calix turned to her, his gaze piercing. "And you think *you* should be the one to decide which ones are worthy? The Peace Accords might not be perfect, but they—"

"Hey, you're the one breaking all the rules these days," she interrupted. "I wasn't trying to start a political discussion. I just think you're uptight and *wrong* about Aris. And me, for that matter. We deserve the right to do this job. Things *do* change, Calix. Rules change. *People* change."

She wanted to get up and leave. She shouldn't have to defend herself. But, in the end, she decided to stare him down instead.

He looked away first.

"You're right. Aris and I are living proof." He stood, slowly, as if the movement pained him. "The thing is, I'm not sure I *can* see Aris that way, as much as I want to."

"What do you mean?" Dysis stood, too. A cool finger of breeze slid across her neck.

"I know she's independent now. Strong, like you." He

scuffed a boot against the ground. "But as hard as I try, all I see is the Aris I grew up with. The one I need to protect, take care of. I don't know if that feeling will ever go away."

"You did a good job tonight, respecting her wishes."

He didn't reply.

She cleared her throat. "I should find her. There's a lot to do before tomorrow." She hurried away, focusing on the small points of light that stood vigil in the dark.

Behind her, his voice, gruff and desperate, begged, "Don't tell Aris I deserted. Please."

WITH GAVEN'S HELP, Dysis found the long, low-ceilinged cave where the children slept. Aris and Samira huddled near the entrance, surrounded by small hemp bags. Beyond them, the children slept on pallets, their meager belongings stacked neatly at the end of each bed. Dysis leaned against the rough stone, just outside the dim lantern light, and watched as Aris snuck down the line of beds, gathering each child's things one by one. She delivered them to Samira, who catalogued everything before placing it in a bag with the child's name written in heavy black ink.

Most items were commonplace—tattered clothes, a collection of smooth stones, a cracked digitablet—but they were all treated as treasures. Some, like a necklace set with polished bloodstones and an intricately carved wooden doll, were valuable for more than their memories.

"Do these children have any money?" Aris whispered, as Dysis eavesdropped. Samira lovingly wrapped the doll in its owner's softest dress. "How will you afford a place for them to live?"

Samira didn't look up. "Not much. Our hope is that we'll be taken in as refugees until it's safe to return to our families."

"And the orphans?" Aris ran her thumb across the rough edge of a crude wooden box.

Samira glared at her. "They will not be abandoned."

"Of course not." Aris sat back on her heels and sighed. "I keep saying the wrong thing."

Samira's busy hands paused. After a moment, she said, "You could have let your friend hit his beacon. You didn't need us to get back to Atalanta, but you stayed. Why?"

Dysis shifted, trying to get a better view of the woman's face.

"I gave you my word that I would help." Aris studied the box she held.

"Words are just words. But . . . thank you," Samira said grudgingly.

Dysis could use a little more reassurance that her friend wasn't being coerced into helping, but she'd heard enough. She emerged from the narrow tunnel and into the flickering lantern light.

Aris smiled. "Hey Dysis. How's Daakon?"

"Better." Dysis jerked her head back toward the tunnel. "Can we talk? Privately?"

Aris glanced at Samira. "How much more do we have?"

Samira waved a hand. "Only two more. I'll finish up." She looked a little relieved to be rid of Aris. "Take these bags to the common room, if you would. We'll be staging the exodus from there."

Aris nodded.

Dysis helped her collect several of the small satchels and filed into the dark. Lanterns were hung at wide enough intervals that whole swaths of tunnel filled with shadow.

"Where's Calix?" Aris asked. She let Dysis lead the way.

"Daakon and I had sex," Dysis blurted, the words echoing too loudly against the stone. She didn't know why she said it. She'd wanted privacy to discuss the Safarans, but somehow *that* was what came out.

"*What?*" Aris yanked Dysis to a stop in a patch of darkness before they reached the next lantern. "When?"

"Right after I found out you were dead. Or, at least, when I *thought* you were dead." Her breath hissed through her teeth. Talking here, in the complete darkness, without facial expressions or body language to read, almost felt like their conversations while cramped in a wingjet cabin.

"Um . . . so . . . are you okay?"Aris's voice stuttered through the inky black.

"Do you believe people can change? *Shouldn't* we be able to change?" Dysis clipped the words.

"Do you think Daakon has? I mean, if you two, you know . . ."

Dysis shrugged, the fabric of her jacket whispered against the rock. "He was trying to comfort me, I think, but he is who he is. I *wanted* it to change things, but it didn't. I'm trying to respect that."

"I'm sorry." Aris touched her arm, but Dysis moved away. She didn't want to be comforted like a child.

"Now I have to move on all over again." She made a noise that was part frustration and part sadness.

"Had you? Moved on, I mean? Before you came back?"

Dysis sighed. "I was trying. It was easier, thinking I'd never see him again, not knowing how he'd reacted to finding out the truth about me." Her voice hardened, even as the shattered pieces of her heart ground together. "Now I know. And it's not better."

"But it's closure, right?" Aris sounded hesitant, like she wasn't sure if Dysis wanted questions.

"It's closure for *him*. For me, it's . . . something else."

It's agony. But that was a truth she kept locked away.

Aris whistled softly under her breath.

"Have *you* gotten closure?" Dysis asked. "With Calix?"

"We haven't had a chance to talk yet. I'm . . . I'm a little nervous to, honestly."

"It's easier for you, isn't it? Because you're in love with someone else." Dysis's words fired into the dark cave.

Aris shifted and sighed, her arm brushing Dysis's in the dark. "Does everyone know?"

"I doubt it," Dysis said, amusement filtering through the words. "You and Major Vadim have kept your secret well. But Calix and I, we know you."

"So why is Calix here?"

Dysis started walking. "That's a question you'll have to ask him."

As they emerged into the light of the main cave, she shifted the hemp bags to one hand and grabbed Aris's shoulder, emotion surfacing in her eyes. "I'm glad we got to talk. I didn't think I'd get the chance."

Aris gave her a quick hug and for once, Dysis didn't stiffen or pull away. "Me too."

"I didn't want to wait," Dysis added, "you know, until after tomorrow."

The words she left unspoken echoed in her mind. *In case the rescue doesn't go to plan.*

In case we don't get another chance.

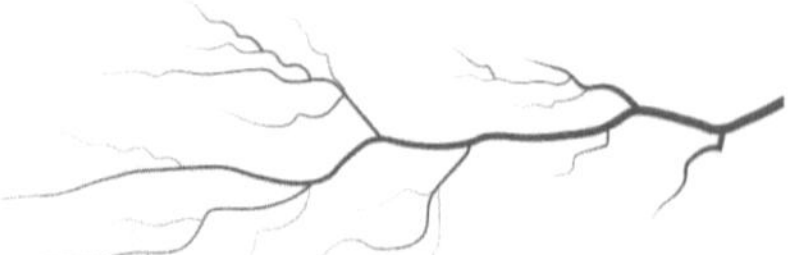

Chapter Thirty-Two

Pyralis stared at the silver windowless door and took a deep breath. He really didn't want to do this. But Galena's question haunted him. What if Bett *did* know something?

He couldn't let himself be the coward who didn't ask.

"Open the door, please," he said.

Two guards held up scanners to the pads on either side of the door, then pressed the devices to the wall simultaneously. With a shimmer, the silver door became transparent, revealing the prisoner inside.

Bett sat on the bed against the far wall of the small, unadorned room, staring straight ahead. When she saw him, she looked down at her hands, clasped demurely in her lap. Her thick black hair—once her self-declared finest feature— was pulled into a single, messy braid. In the bright light, Pyralis could see her first streaks of gray. Bett's fine clothes and extravagant jewelry had been replaced with an unflattering gray jumpsuit.

As Pyralis and the guards entered the room, a transparent partition slid into the wall behind them and locked into place with an eerie, echoing thud.

"It's been four months and three days." Bett's voice was hoarse, as if it'd been that long since she'd last spoken. She didn't look up.

Pyralis stood before her, staring down at her bowed head, and wondered how the hell they'd gotten here. When Bett had confessed to giving the diatous-veil tech to Elom, she'd told Pyralis it was his fault. He'd been so beaten down by the war, she felt she had to *do* something. She'd wanted to help. That's what she said, anyway. According to her, Elom had promised that once a replacement was in place for Galena Vadim, the war would end. Atalanta would be left alone.

Pyralis still didn't entirely believe her story. She'd never struck him as someone so gullible as to believe such ridiculous assertions. And she had to have known, whether she admitted it or not, that Galena would be put in danger.

"Hello, Bett." He kept his voice neutral with great effort; the last months hadn't cooled his anger.

At last, at the sound of his voice, she looked up.

Four months and three days ago, when he'd last visited, she had begged him for mercy. He'd explained her punishment wasn't up to him but to the official tribunal, but she'd begged anyway. Said she loved him. Told him she'd die without his forgiveness.

Now her dark eyes stared through him, full of hate.

"I need to ask you a couple of questions," he began, taken aback. Her letters—the ones he'd read—had been filled with a wild lack of control, not this quiet calm.

"I will die in here, in this empty, blank room. And what will you do?" Her voice was flat. Dead. "Will you cry?"

"Bett, tell me what you know about—"

"Of course you won't cry." Bett tried to laugh, but it sounded like a screech. She turned her head, slowly, to look at the walls of her prison. "You will rejoice to be rid of me at last."

He took a step closer. He didn't have time for her guilt trips and manipulation. "How did Elom contact you? Did you ever interact with Safaran spies? Who exactly did you speak to?"

She ignored him, lost in whatever she saw as she stared at the blank wall. "I wanted you from the moment we met. I *wanted* you." She looked at him then, a remembered joy momentarily eclipsing the hatred. "You had me, all of me, the moment you asked. And then you went to Ruslana and when you came back, nothing was the same."

Pyralis shook his head. "I can't talk to you about this now, Bett. I need information. I'm not here for us."

"I have nothing *but* us! Nothing to think about, nothing to *do* but remember the way you died a little inside, each time you looked at me." She stood up, the back of her legs banging against the bed. The guards tensed at the sudden movement. "Did you think I couldn't see?"

"Bett—" he warned.

He shouldn't have come. There was relief in that, seeing her behave as he had expected. At least he knew he wasn't missing something.

"Why did you marry me, Pyralis? Why did you have to be such an honor-bound, idiotic child? Don't you know what you did?" Her face looked sunken, skeletal in the garish light. The words poured out of her, fast and messy, as if she'd been holding onto them for years, waiting for a moment to finally speak. "Why didn't you just break our Promise? I thought I could love you into loving me again, so I chose you. I had *hope*. But you killed it! You killed *me*. Look at me, look at this life you've given me. Why didn't you just let me *go*?"

He forced himself to do as she asked. He looked at her, really *looked* at her gaunt frame and shattered eyes, and faced the truth in what she said.

"I shouldn't have married you. You're right." He'd never admitted it to her before. Maybe hadn't admitted it to himself either. He'd thought it better to make the best of things, to honor his promises. To try. "Truly, Bett, I never meant to hurt you. For that, I am sorry."

She slumped back onto the bed, all the fight and passion sucked away.

"You're never coming back. For the rest of my life I'll be in this room, and I'll never see you again."

Pyralis turned to face the door, still transparent, showing the empty hall. "Goodbye, Bett."

From behind him, her voice, as tragic as the small, empty room: "Balias has eyes everywhere. If you think you're safe, that your plans are secret . . . they're not."

Pyralis spun to ask her more, but Bett turned her face to the wall and wept.

CHAPTER THIRTY-THREE

Aris had already gathered with Calix, Samira, and Alistar in the large, central cavern when Dysis joined them. As far as Aris knew, she'd slept in the clinic, keeping watch over Daakon.

In the tiny cave Aris had been assigned to, the night-mares had kept watch over her.

Samira spread an impressive array of weapons across one of the tables, including the ones that had been taken from Aris when she first came to the village, and started passing them out to the adults. Aris reclaimed her solagun and utility knife. Dysis reached for a long-range solagun.

Kori sidled up to the table and tried to grab a solagun, but Samira stopped him. "No, sir. You're staying here."

He crossed his frail arms across his chest. "You can't keep me from fighting."

Samira put a hand on his cheek. "We're doing this so that you don't *have* to fight. Please stay with the others. It'll be your task to protect them if something goes wrong. Okay?"

"Besides," Aris offered, smiling at him, "if we do our jobs properly, there won't be any fighting at all. Just a short conversation, and then we'll all be on our way."

The boy turned away, his cheeks flushing. "What if I don't want to go to Atalanta?"

Aris remembered what he'd said about his mother and sister, and her heart broke a little. She pulled him aside.

"Kori, leaving Safara does *not* mean you're abandoning your family," she said, ducking so she was on his level. "The only way you'll be reunited with them is if you keep yourself safe. I promise I'll do whatever I can to help you find them."

He wouldn't look at her. "Why do you care, anyway?"

She shrugged. Truthfully, she wasn't sure. But there was something about him that made her desperate to help. She squeezed his shoulder. "I'm a search and rescue flyer. Finding people is what I do."

With a half shrug, Kori hobbled off to join the other children. They were collecting their bags of belongings, the bigger kids helping the smaller ones. An old woman gave each child a small loaf of bread and a wrinkled orange fruit.

Dysis bumped her arm. "Morning."

"How's Lieutenant Daakon doing?" Aris asked.

"Better. Not well enough to get out of bed yet, though."

Aris nodded. "Alistar said it would take some time for the effects of the venom to fade, even with the antivenom."

"Can I ask you something?" Dysis didn't look at Aris, her eyes following the milling children. Someone was helping the boy with the missing leg negotiate his crutches and the small hemp bag that held all he had in the world.

"Sure," Aris said.

"Why are you doing this, really? You don't owe them this, Aris. Even for saving your life."

Aris glanced at Kori, who brightened a little at something one of the smaller kids said. A few feet away, Samira was rubbing Hazel's back and shooing Jaff back to the group as she handed out the last of the weapons.

She tried to find the words to explain. "I've spent the last year fighting a faceless enemy," she began. "No, not faceless. An enemy that looked like Ward Balias and Elom. Now . . . now I feel sick, knowing our 'enemies' are victims themselves. I don't know what good it will do—we have to protect Atalanta above all—but maybe if the world knows how the Ward persecutes his own people, maybe the other dominions will help us end this. Maybe we can save some innocent Safarans, too."

"Pretty speech," Dysis said, the words sounding more serious than sarcastic. She slung an arm across Aris's shoulders.

Calix approached. "Time to take our positions. Where's your body armor, Dysis?"

She shifted the gun in her hands. "Back in the clinic. Heading there now."

Before they parted, the girls shared a quick hug. Dysis grinned. "We've got this, Hummingbird."

Aris smiled as she watched Dysis disappear into the tunnel.

"Hummingbird?" Calix asked mildly, though a current of something deeper ran through the word.

Aris double-checked her body armor and holstered her

solagun. She didn't look at him. "I told her the story a long time ago. She thinks it's funny."

"Ah. I see."

Without saying more, they headed out into open air themselves. Light broke over the mountains behind them in a bright wave. They walked together to a small storage building with dirty windows that overlooked the landing pad. Aris knew she had to stay out of sight until Balias's men were in custody, but she wanted to be close so she could examine the cargo jet as quickly as possible. She'd need plenty of time to acclimate herself if the controls were unfamiliar. Calix had asked to walk her over, though he would spend the exchange in the caves to protect the children in case things went wrong. Samira would be there, too, ready to defend them to the death.

Aris had gone searching for Calix the night before, but he'd already gone to bed. It was strange to be this close to him after so long.

They reached the building. Aris turned to him, observing the new seriousness in his eyes, the roughness the scruff along his jaw gave him. Her feelings had changed over the past year, but she could still appreciate how handsome he was.

She knew this was her chance to clear the air, but that didn't make it easy. The most obvious question turned out to be the hardest to ask. "Why are you here?"

Calix took her hands. She almost didn't let him. Yet somehow the gesture still felt natural.

He cleared his throat. "When I heard you'd died, I realized what a fool I'd been. It crushed me, knowing I'd never get the chance to tell you how sorry I am."

Aris tightened her grip on his hands. "Calix, you—"

He shook his head. "I was wrong. I should have supported you. I should have told you I'd wait. I should have given you a chance to explain *why*. But I didn't. And because of that, I lost you."

Seeing the longing in his eyes—the love—she wanted to deny it. She wanted to curl herself into his arms like she'd done so many times before. She wanted to go back to the night before he left for Military sector, when they'd kissed in the rain. She'd held him so tightly that night, *knowing* she'd never want anything else in this life but the feel of his skin and the searing pressure of his lips on hers.

She wanted to tell him nothing was lost. That it wasn't too late.

But she couldn't. Because the words would be for him, and for him only. She knew that for certain now, as she looked into his familiar green eyes. The part of her life that was marked by loving him was over. He *had* lost her. Maybe it had happened when he wouldn't wait for her. Maybe her feelings had changed before that, when she'd realized her own strength.

"I'm sorry, too, Calix." She let go of his hands.

Something in his eyes faded.

She smiled gently, thinking of the certainty of that night so long ago. "In another life, there is no war. We Promise the night of Selection, and we live happily, quietly, in Lux for the rest of our days, with children and olive groves and wine on the beach throughout long summer evenings. We're old, and happy, and at peace."

He returned her smile, though sorrow still lingered on his face. "It would have been a good life."

The moment, that life they might have had, lingered between them, before fading into the heat of the rising sun.

Aris reached up and kissed his cheek. "Thank you for coming to find me. I don't know how you did it, or what possessed Milek to let you, but I'm glad he did."

They walked into the dusty building together. Aris found a spot by the window, where she could sit on an old desk and watch the proceedings from the shadows. No one would see her.

"He knew I would give my life for you if necessary," Calix said.

Aris didn't know to respond. Instead, she watched the villagers disappearing into doorways and around corners as they took position.

"Remember," Calix said, pausing at the door. "Don't move into the open until the enemy is secure. Promise me."

Aris nodded. "Don't worry. I'll be safe."

With a last, long look, Calix said, "Good luck," and closed the metal door.

Her breath was loud and too fast in the empty room.

Faintly, she heard Gaven's piercing whistle.

The Safaran soldiers were here.

Chapter Thirty-Four

Dysis strapped on her body armor, each familiar clip and cinch a ward against the waiting dark. The Safaran jet would be here any minute. Dysis wanted to believe Aris's plan would go smoothly—she *did* think that saving those children was worth the risk—but unnamed misgivings settled like an anvil in her stomach anyway.

"I should be out there with you," Daakon said, looking up at her from his med-bed, his face drawn into lines of worry.

Dysis patted his knee, her sweaty fingers clinging to the thin sheet. "Now that you're stable, you need to rest. Alistar thinks you'll improve quickly once we get you back to Atalanta. Our meds are better." Her grin was crooked, not quite as confident as she was going for.

And, of course, he saw right through her. "Don't worry about me, Dysis. I'm *fine*. Or I will be." He reached out and grabbed her hand, surprising her. "Focus on the mission. Keep yourself safe."

Dysis pulled away and retrieved Daakon's solagun from his pack. "Here." She handed it to him. "There shouldn't be any issues, but you never know."

She shifted the long-range solagun in the harness on her back as she turned to go.

"I'm sorry." Daakon's voice was quiet behind her. Dysis didn't turn around. "I never meant to break your heart."

She glanced over her shoulder with a wry—if sad—smile. "And I didn't mean what I said, about not forgiving you."

She left without saying anything more.

Dysis waited below an overhang at the far edge of the clinic. She couldn't climb to her position on its roof until the cargo jet landed or they'd see her. Even in the shade, heat blasted her from all sides, drawing out sweat across her forehead. It would be worse soon, when she'd be lying in direct sunlight.

Think cold, wet thoughts.

A whistle split the morning air. Before it faded, the rumble of a wingjet drowned it out.

When the bulbous nose and swollen sides of the cargo jet came into view, she tightened her grip on her gun. Alistar stepped out onto the plain with Gaven. They waited as the wingjet landed, shielding their eyes from the blowing sand.

As soon as the jet touched down, Dysis scrambled up the rungs of the rusted emergency ladder fixed to the side of the building, grateful her solagun was harnessed securely to her back.

By the time the dome and cargo bay of the wingjet hissed open, she was in position.

As promised, six soldiers emerged from the wingjet,

beetle-like in their black uniforms. Dysis tried to remember that three of those men were their allies, but her finger twitched on the trigger anyway. Every muscle tensed as she watched them gather before Alistar.

"Where's the wreckage?" one of the men asked. His voice carried easily throughout the clearing. He looked around. "We were told we needed to pick up evidence of some kind."

Dysis focused every fiber of her being on the soldiers below her. The moment sharpened; this was it. From this heartbeat to the next, everything would change.

Alistar cocked his head. "You were misinformed."

Gaven stepped back at the same instant three of the Safaran soldiers separated themselves from the group. One by one, they raised their weapons.

Dysis held her breath.

"Don't move," the tallest soldier said, pointing his solagun at the man who'd spoken.

From this distance, Dysis couldn't see facial expressions that clearly, but she could read body language well enough. And the leader was standing his ground.

"What exactly are you doing?" he asked, not sounding nearly concerned enough.

The men with the raised guns said nothing. Alistar stepped forward. "Put your weapons down. We've no wish to harm you, but we will, if it comes to that."

Dysis was impressed at the steadiness of his voice. He spoke as he would to a patient, with a soothing calm. She never would guess that the lives of more than thirty people, most of them children, were riding on him. It was the single most important moment of his life, and he was owning it entirely.

One of the soldiers loyal to Ward Balias moved, his hand creeping toward his solagun, clearly not prepared to surrender.

It wasn't part of the plan—Aris didn't want to risk any retaliation—but the sooner these men relinquished their weapons, the sooner Dysis could be gone from here. She sighted down her long-range solagun, aiming for the light a few feet away from the assemblage. But before she could take the shot, more villagers appeared.

They all held up weapons, calmly stalking toward the three soldiers.

Balias's men looked at each other. For an instant, Dysis was sure there would be a firefight.

But the one who'd been reaching for his solagun took the weapon and dropped it on the ground, raising his hands. The leader was the last to surrender.

"Why the hell are you doing this? You realize this is treason," he yelled. "You've signed a death sentence for your family. And for what?" His voice rose as the villagers restrained him. When all three men were secured, the leader still yelling, Gaven and Alistar marched them to the small building at the opposite edge of the clearing that served as the village's jail. The noise didn't stop until the cell door closed.

With silence restored, Dysis let out a heavy breath. That had been easy, as Aris had promised. Two villagers searched the cargo jet while the rebel soldiers stood in the clearing, waiting to help the children onto the jet. Aris emerged from her hiding place and climbed into the cabin to inspect the controls. Hopping down, she grinned so wide Dysis could make out the expression, even from a distance.

"Flying this beast will be no problem," Aris said triumphantly.

A flurry of activity ensued. Alistar and one of the soldiers—the one with a child here—ran toward the caves.

Dysis stood and headed for the ladder.

There was no warning this time.

Dysis barely made it to the ground as a wingjet screamed overhead, sowing fire in its wake. The jail exploded. As she watched, horror-stricken, part of the clinic caught fire.

Daakon.

Without a second's hesitation, she pounded the emergency transmitter on her chest.

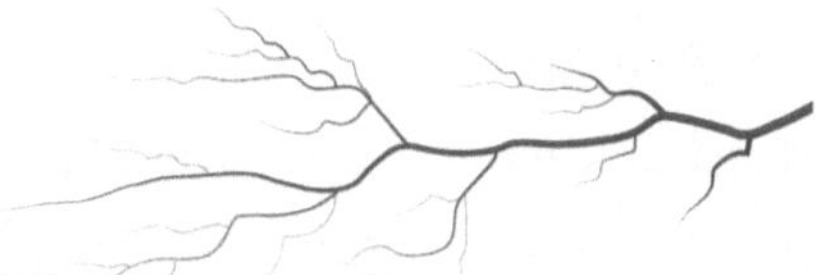

Chapter Thirty-Five

Aris ducked, covering her head to protect it from the burning rubble. The wingjet did another pass, dropping a firebomb on a small collection of houses at the edge of the landing pad, only a few feet from the field where she'd watched Kori and the others play. Flames burst into the sky as Aris crawled to Gaven.

He was lying on the ground, a chunk of concrete wedged against his stomach. His eyes were closed. She touched his face, but he didn't respond. That's when she noticed the blood pooling beneath his head. Stomach twisting, she checked his pulse.

Nothing.

The whine of the wingjet's missiles stopped. Aris looked up. The sleek black jet hovered ominously for a few seconds before dropping to the ground. Another, smaller, wingjet appeared and began circling the village. Aris shot a look at the cargo jet. It didn't appear to be damaged, but the clinic and jail were on fire. It wouldn't be long before flames engulfed the jet, too. She scoured the edge of the clinic's roof. Where was Dysis? Daakon? Calix?

A shout caught her attention. Specialist Baryn and the third soldier who'd helped them gestured to her, partially protected by a ragged half wall. With an inner sigh, Aris said goodbye to Gaven. Then she removed her solagun from its holster and scrambled over to the soldiers.

The wingjet had stopped shooting, but it would no doubt be a brief reprieve.

"What's going on?" Aris gasped. "Did you know there were other wingjets in the area? Why are they attacking the village?"

The soldier she hadn't met shook his head. "Those men aren't with us. I don't know—"

There was a flash of light.

The man crumpled slowly, surprise burned into his expression, a solagun-shot smoking at his throat.

Aris froze, watching his collapse with horror. "What—"

Baryn lowered his gun and yanked hers out of her hand before she had time to process what was happening. Then he grabbed her, his fingers digging savagely into her arm. "Let's go."

Aris couldn't speak. They'd trusted that Baryn was loyal to this village. To Samira and Alistar.

We were wrong.

"Why are you *doing* this?" Aris struggled against Baryn's grip, craning her whole body toward the caves. Had Lieutenant Nore betrayed them, too? What about his son? She combed the broken buildings with her eyes, looking for small, scared faces.

There was no sign of the children. Villagers fired toward

the wingjet in the center of the clearing. A swarm of black-clad soldiers spilled from the back of the jet, returning fire as they moved farther into the village.

Baryn wrenched her arm, pulling her toward the jet. "I told you to stay out of sight, remember? Not that it would have mattered. As soon as I saw you, I knew it would mean big things for me," he said. "You're quite the prize."

Aris tried to break Baryn's hold, twisting with a kick toward his knee. He grabbed her splinted wrist and yanked. She screamed.

In a daze, she stumbled toward the wingjet, dragging against Baryn's grip. In the center of the flurry of Safaran soldiers, a flash of white caught her eye. A tall, dark-skinned man in a flowing white tunic walked calmly down the wingjet's ramp, and even before he turned and met her eyes across the plain, Aris knew.

It was Elom.

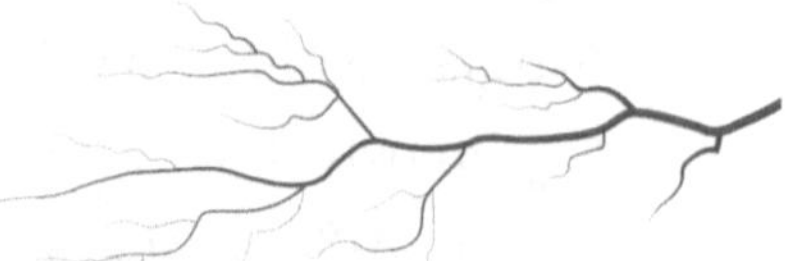

CHAPTER THIRTY-SIX

DYSIS RAN ALONG THE SIDE OF THE CLINIC, PANIC keeping pace. Acrid smoke burned her nose, and the sounds of solagun fire and people shouting assaulted her. When she reached the clearing, the scene on the landing pad sprang into unforgiving detail. There were only four or five villagers still fighting the swarm of Safaran soldiers. And there, being dragged across the plain . . .

Without thinking, Dysis dropped to her knee and sighted along her gun. Aris's captor fell a second later. Aris wrenched free from his body, her eyes wildly scanning her surroundings. Then she ran like hell into the shadows between two buildings. Dysis couldn't tell if Aris had seen her or not. But a couple of the other soldiers had. In quick, merciless succession, she brought them down.

The others soldiers, realizing there was a new threat, found cover behind the wingjets, around the corners of buildings. The hiss of solagun fire slowed.

At least she'd bought the villagers a little time.

She swung the long-range gun onto her back, pulled her smaller solagun, and ran around the front of the building. She slipped through the doorway and into the clinic. Behind the flapping fabric door, the smoky room glowed red.

"Daakon?" she yelled. Fire licked along the ceiling.

She made it to his med-bed, but he wasn't there.

"Dysis, help me."

She held an arm up to cover her nose and mouth. Daakon was hunched over another med-bed, the small form of a child under the sheets. The bed shook with the force of the boy's coughing.

"Can you carry him?" Daakon asked, turning a soot-streaked face toward her. His eyes ran with tears from the smoke. "He can't walk."

"Neither can you," Dysis said, noticing how heavily he leaned against the bed.

He shook off her concerns. "I can manage. Help him. We don't—" The fire roared as part of the roof collapsed, drowning his words. A thick wave of smoke engulfed them.

Dysis threw Daakon the smaller solagun and gathered the painfully thin boy into her arms. His bony fingers dug into her arm.

"Anyone else?" Smoke burned its way down to her lungs. She coughed, shoulders shaking.

"No," Daakon said, staring into the heat of the fire. The beds at the end of the room were burning.

They turned and made their way toward the door. Daakon limped heavily, his injured leg almost entirely useless. The boy in her arms whimpered.

They reached the doorway just as the rest of the roof collapsed. The force of the falling rubble blasted against them, pushing them into the open. Daakon went down on one knee. Dysis stumbled forward, tangled in the tattered cloth covering the doorway. Desperately, she clutched the child closer as she fought to see, afraid she'd drop him.

Finally, she tore free of the fabric. All around her was the hiss of solagun fire.

"Come on, Daakon," she said, shifting the boy in her arms to free a hand. She pulled on Daakon's arm. "We need to get out of range."

He didn't answer.

"Come *on*." Dysis yanked harder as she turned toward him.

The small, round hole in his forehead stared back at her as his body tumbled onto the ground.

For a second, the whole world froze.

Her breath. Her beating heart.

Everything.

A flash of solagun fire grazed her shoulder. In her arms, the boy cried. Something inside Dysis broke apart. She wrenched her long-range solagun from across her back. In seconds, the man who'd killed Daakon was dead himself, along with two of his friends.

Dysis clutched the boy closer to her and lurched around the corner of the building. The act of leaving Daakon behind burned more painfully than the scorched flesh of her shoulder.

As soon as they were out of range of the fighters, Dysis dropped to the ground, easing the boy to the dirt beside her. He propped himself against the wall, his breathing ragged. His face was black with soot, the whites of his eyes wide. He hugged his arms across his chest as if it would hold him together.

Dysis stared at the gap between buildings, where solagun fire still hissed. The second Safaran wingjet made another pass, and another building burst into flames.

It came out of nowhere. One second her solagun was up, and her eyes were surveying their position for danger, the next she was curled into a ball, weeping.

For a long time, she could do nothing but sob into her knees, oblivious to the boy beside her. To her own safety.

At the *woosh* of an incoming wingjet, Dysis finally lifted her head. Her eyes had dried to burning disks and her throat was raw. Above the village, two silver Atalantan wingjets cut through the white-hot sky. A new, grim resolve filled her.

"You okay?" Dysis leaned toward the boy she'd saved.

He gave her a shaky nod.

She inched along the wall to the entrance of the alleyway. She needed to return to the fight.

In the sky, the Atalantan recon drew the Safaran wingjet away from the village and shot it down. An explosion rattled the ground, throwing Dysis off-balance. More smoke billowed into the already caustic air. She didn't see the transport.

As she reached the clearing, a cough, too loud to be the boy's, echoed behind her. She whirled back into the alley, raising her solagun. Three figures stood a few yards beyond the boy, half-hidden by the smoke.

A split second before she pulled the trigger, one of the figures raised his hands. "Specialist Latza."

She recognized the voice. Dysis lowered her weapon slowly. "Major Vadim. You made it."

The major's pale skin had a grayish tinge. Specialist Mann's stocky, muscular form emerged from the smoke beside him. Otto came into focus last, his eyes wide as he took in the devastation.

"Where is Aris?" Major Vadim asked. He was surprisingly calm for having landed in a war zone. This couldn't have been what he'd expected. "What's happening here?"

"Last I saw, Aris was on the other side of the village," Dysis reported. "Balias's men showed up. . . . I think they're here for her. The villagers are fighting back. They're trying to help us." She said it agin, to be sure they understood. "Our fight is *only* with the soldiers. The villagers are on our side. Don't hurt them."

Vadim nodded. He glanced at the boy huddled against the wall. "And who is—"

"Lieutenant Daakon's dead," she said in a rush, swallowing back a sob. The words made it real and irreversible. *Daakon was dead.*

Major Vadim's breath hissed out, as if she'd punched him. "Daakon . . ."

A blast of solagun fire ripped across the concrete wall above them. Vadim crouched, searching for the source of the threat.

"I need to get to Aris!" Major Vadim yelled over the sound of renewed battle.

Dysis pointed to the entrance of the alley. "That way."

Another blast pounded above them.

The boy, still huddled against the wall, whimpered. Dysis caught Specialist Mann's eye. "Can you carry this kid toward the mountains? There are caves . . . Other children.

Ask for Alistar or Samira. They'll help you get him to safety."

Mann nodded and reached for the boy.

Major Vadim edged toward the entrance of the alley, braced for more solagun fire. Dysis joined him, her hands gripping her weapon tightly. Behind her, she heard footsteps as Otto followed suit.

"Pallas and Baksen are still up in the air. They'll provide as much support as they can. As soon as I saw the fighting, I also called for reinforcements," Major Vadim said. "We should have more help soon. In the meantime—"

"Go. Find Aris," Dysis said, raising her weapon. "I'll cover you."

CHAPTER THIRTY-SEVEN

IN A ONE-ROOM SHACK NEAR THE BURNING remnants of the jail, Aris fought to control her panic. She had no weapon. No way out. And Elom was after her. She'd run when Baryn went down, but the bright sunshine and rapidly exchanged fire had been disorienting. This was the first shelter she'd come to, and it had no door beyond a tattered sheet. It was out of the line of solagun fire, but if Elom or one of his soldiers found her, there'd be nowhere to go.

Calix and Samira hadn't brought out the children when the second wingjet screamed out of nowhere; hopefully they were safe in the caves with Alistar. Of course, she couldn't imagine either of them *staying* safe in the caves. They'd be out fighting soon, if they weren't already.

Aris pressed her back against the wall beside the doorway and snuck glances outside. Not long ago, two Atalantan wingjets had appeared and taken out the airborne Safaran jet. But Elom and his men were still on the ground. Shouts and the hiss of weaponry still sent adrenaline coursing through her.

This wasn't how it was supposed to go.

Anger and frustration increased the tension between her shoulder blades. Baryn had sold her out—all this death and destruction could have been avoided if they'd known not to trust him. Just one person, and everything was ruined.

She snuck another peek into the alley, just as two Safaran soldiers rounded the corner. She ducked back inside, but one of them spotted her. "Over here!" he yelled.

She scrambled farther from the door, as deep into the darkness of the windowless shack as she could get. *Blight it.*

If only she had a *weapon*: a sythin, a stone, *anything*.

Aris put her fists up as the men burst through the tattered fabric door. She would have settled for Dysis's lethal combat skills.

Suddenly the men jerked to a stop. She heard a clank of metal, a grunt, a thud. In the darkness, she couldn't tell what was happening, but no one grabbed or shot at her. Hopefully that was a good sign.

"Alistar?" she whispered.

Just then, a breeze blew the door covering askew, letting in a finger of sunlight. The Safaran soldiers were black-uniformed heaps on the ground. And, standing over them . . .

It wasn't Alistar.

Milek and Otto stared back at her, their faces drawn.

"Aris." Exhaustion and worry had left their mark on Milek. His clear blue eyes looked enormous in the low light, weighed down by the purple shadows beneath them.

Relief made her dizzy. "Oh holy, you're here."

Their arms were around each other in an instant, mouths pressed desperately together. Aris couldn't get over how *real* he felt, how solid and substantial his body was against hers.

From behind them, Otto whistled. "Remind me never to get in the way of true love."

Aris tried to pull away, but Milek held her fast. Against her mouth, he whispered, in wonder, "You're alive."

She tightened her grip on him for an instant before forcing space between them. "For now. Elom is here, Milek. He came for me."

Milek's expression became all business, as he turned his attention to their situation. "I was worried he might be looking for you. We received reports he was in the area." He moved to the doorway, using the wall as cover to peer into the alleyway. "Are you sure we can trust these villagers?"

Aris gave Otto a quick hug.

"Glad to see you," he whispered.

"Yes, we can trust them," Aris said, stepping over the prostrate soldiers to stand at Milek's shoulder. "I promised to help evacuate their children." More explanations would have to wait.

He kept his eyes trained on the alley. "We need to find Elom."

"Last I saw, he was in the clearing where the fighting was fiercest. But he may have followed me into this part of the village."

"Specialist Otto, you head to the left, toward the landing field," Milek said. "I'll go right and search these buildings. It's possible he's found cover."

"Yes, sir," Otto said. His habitual humor dropped from

his voice, and his eyes held a seriousness Aris was unused to seeing.

"Be safe," she said, squeezing his arm. He had a wife at home, like Galec had. Then again, they all had loved ones waiting.

Otto slipped around the corner, his solagun steady in his hands. Milek turned toward her, searching for her face in the shadows. "You stay here. As soon as I've got Elom, I'll come back for you."

She laughed. "No chance."

To his credit, he didn't bother arguing. "It was worth a try."

With another fast, hard kiss they crept together into the sunlight.

Almost immediately, gravel clattered as someone rounded the edge of a building in front of them.

Milek raised his weapon, just as Calix came into view.

He leaned heavily against the wall. One side of his face was purple and swollen with bruising.

Aris gasped and ran to his side. He put a heavy hand on her shoulder, gripping tightly as his whole body sagged. He licked his bloody bottom lip and cleared his throat. "Are you okay? I've been looking for you."

She ducked under his arm to help him stand. "Why didn't you stay with the children? You shouldn't have—"

"I came here for you, Aris. Of course I was going to try to find you." His eyes met Milek's, and something Aris didn't quite understand seemed to pass between them.

Milek threaded Calix's other arm over his shoulders. "We need to get you somewhere safe. You're no use to us like this."

"I'm okay," Calix protested. "Leave me be. You have more important—"

"We're not leaving you, Calix," Aris said, her voice hard. To this, there would be no argument.

Two turns and a narrow alleyway later, concrete exploded above them in a shower of dust and debris. They dropped to the ground.

Up ahead, through the haze, Aris saw a flash of white. Instinct and a raging fury took over. She grabbed Calix's solagun from its holster and sprinted down the alley.

"Aris!" She couldn't tell if it was Calix or Milek who called out behind her. It didn't matter. She kept running.

When she reached the corner, she raised her weapon.

There, midway down an open dirt road leading to the landing pad: a tall, dark-skinned figure dressed in a neat white tunic.

"Stop!" Aris cried.

Elom froze. Slowly, he turned. Smiled, white teeth flashing.

Fear broke in a wave over her, even though she was the one holding the solagun.

"Ah. I'd say the deception is officially over." He showed little concern for his predicament, his voice light and easy. But Aris noted the tiny shift as he put his weight on one foot. Preparing to run. "The lovely Aris Haan is most certainly alive. For now, anyway."

Something in his eyes—the arrogance, maybe—cooled her fear. Her hands were dead steady on the weapon. And it was pointed at his heart. "Don't move. Ward Vadim doesn't want you dead, but I have no such qualms."

She raised her chin, the sunlight falling on her face—and on the scar he'd left there.

His smile twisted as his gaze flicked to a spot beyond her. "Major Vadim, you look taller in the news vids."

Aris whirled. A few yards behind her, a Safaran soldier dragged Milek toward her, his weapon pressed against Milek's temple.

She didn't hesitate. The blast of solagun fire hit the soldier square in the face, where there was no helmet or armor to protect him. He fell backward, as Milek wrenched himself away.

"Aris—" His eyes widened.

She turned again, in time to see Elom leveling a solagun at her chest.

Oh holy.

But instead of taking the shot, he sank to the ground, mouth open in surprise.

Otto stood behind him, holding a chunk of concrete. "I would have shot him," he said, a shaky smile flashing across his lips, "but a blighting villager stole my gun."

CHAPTER THIRTY-EIGHT

BY THE TIME DYSIS FOUND THE OTHERS, STANDING in a wide alleyway near the burnt-out jail with an unconscious Elom at their feet, the rest of the Safaran soldiers were dead. But vengeance couldn't bring Daakon back to her.

He wasn't yours, she kept telling herself. That didn't help either.

Specialist Pallas landed her recon next to Mann's transport on the children's playing field, away from the carnage of the landing pad. She and Baksen helped Dysis wrap Daakon's body in a singed sheet from the clinic and carry it to the transport. Dysis wanted to stay there, holding vigil, but more work had to be done before they could head back to Spiro.

The cargo jet wasn't damaged, thankfully, so the children and injured villagers could be transported as planned, with Aris as their flyer. The only Safaran soldier to survive the battle was Lieutenant Nore, who'd gone to check on his son among the children. He joined the other villagers in their exodus.

Major Vadim's reinforcements arrived after the battle was over, so they helped organize the children and bury the bodies of the Safaran soldiers and villagers. A couple of recons patrolled the sky for more Safaran forces, but none appeared.

The sun had begun its descent when the team finally departed. Dysis rode beside Calix in the transport, her gun poised over Elom in case he woke up, even though they'd bound his hands and stuck him with a sythin for good measure. Daakon lay beside him, wrapped in his soot-streaked shroud.

She and Calix didn't speak. She'd never admit that the warmth of his arm against hers was not unwelcome.

When they landed at Spiro an hour later, Dysis and Calix filed off of the transport into a scene of chaos. Children milled across the landing pad, and injured Safaran villagers were helped to the tarmac. Milek had commed ahead, so a contingent of menders from Mekia were waiting.

Dysis and Calix leaned against the rounded building, out of the way, as soldiers and menders streamed past. Commander Nyx and another woman greeted Major Vadim. Even from a distance Dysis recognized Ward Vadim's scarred face. The woman hugged her son right there, in front of all his subordinates.

"You should have someone look at your shoulder," Calix said. "That solagun wound won't heal itself." One of his eyes was nearly swollen shut. She was surprised he could even talk, with the bruising around his mouth.

"Speak for yourself," she replied gruffly. Her shoulder burned, but she wasn't about to tell him that.

He made an attempt at a smile, though it came out more like a grimace. His eyes found Aris in the crowd, but he didn't leave Dysis's side. She wished he would.

"I'm sorry about Lieutenant Daakon."

She shrugged and kept her face a mask.

"He was a strong son of a bitch," Calix said. "I still can't believe he stayed conscious after that snake bit him. When I was getting the venom out . . ." He cleared his throat. "The only way he was going down was a shot to the head. Nothing else could have stopped him."

Dysis's mouth opened but nothing came out. She wanted to be infuriated, but somehow she was comforted instead. Daakon *was* a strong son of a bitch.

Several stern-faced, unfamiliar soldiers approached, weaving through the crowd.

Calix sighed. "They're for me, I imagine."

"For you?" Dysis asked. One of the men was carrying restraints. Surely he was here for Elom.

Calix shot a look at her. "Remember how I got here?" When she nodded, he smiled grimly. "Well, this is my reckoning."

"Specialist Calix Pavlos, we have authorization to detain you for desertion," one of the men said when he reached them.

"Yes, sir." Calix held out his hands.

"Wait!" Aris ran across the tarmac, dodging children and soldiers alike. "What are you doing?" she asked angrily. "He's allowed to be here. You can't—"

"It's okay," Calix said, as the soldier snapped on the restraints. "They have to."

Her eyes filled with panic. "Why? I don't understand."

He smiled as they began to lead him away. "You were right, Aris. Some things are worth breaking the rules for."

Dysis saw the moment when understanding dawned. Aris moved to go after him, but Dysis grabbed her arm. "There's nothing you can do. Not now, anyway."

"But . . . why would he do that? I just . . ." Aris stopped straining against Dysis's grip. Her shoulders slumped. "Gods, I'm tired."

Dysis released her. She was tired, too. Bone tired.

Numb.

"I'm sorry about Daakon," Aris murmured, the words barely audible over the rumble of voices on the landing pad.

"I know." Dysis bumped her arm, the only physical contact she could handle right now.

"Maybe if we'd—"

"No. Don't do that," Dysis cut her off. "We did what we did. None of us get to choose how our story ends. But it *does* end, always."

Aris's eyes filled with tears, but she smiled a little. "I'm grateful my story didn't end today. It would have if you hadn't found me." She leaned against Dysis. "Thank you."

Dysis couldn't speak around the lump in her throat. Her mother had once told her that good never appeared without a little bad thrown in, and vice versa. When she'd died, so soon after Dysis's father, it had been difficult to find that little bit of good.

But Aris was right about today. There was good in this.

Samira and Alistar arranged the children in two lines on

the landing pad as the injured adults were taken inside. "What will happen to them?" Dysis asked, when she could speak again, nodding toward the Safarans.

"They'll go to a refugee camp," Aris replied, her gaze following Dysis's. "Alistar and Samira will speak to the authorities, offer whatever intel they can, in exchange for asylum."

"Will it make a difference, do you think?"

Aris crossed her arms over her chest. "The fact that we captured Elom will."

A small child ran up to Aris and pulled on her arm until she stooped to his level. His puff of dark hair wobbled as he said, "I did it! I rode in a wingjet! And it wasn't scary at all!"

Aris smiled and gently touched his face. "I'm glad, Zeb."

When he ran back to the others, he lifted his arms out from his sides and *zoomed*, as if he were a wingjet himself.

Suddenly, the shifting bodies and quiet murmurs of the children fell silent. All heads turned in the same direction.

Major Vadim and Commander Nyx led Elom, bound and blindfolded, from the transport. His flowing tunic and pants had somehow remained a pristine white, with the exception of a single splash of red down his back. Blood from the head wound Otto had given him.

The man had been captured, injured, and was at their mercy . . . and yet he still wore a smug, self-satisfied smile.

Dysis's breath caught. Because standing right there on the tarmac before him, Ward Vadim faced her torturer for the first time.

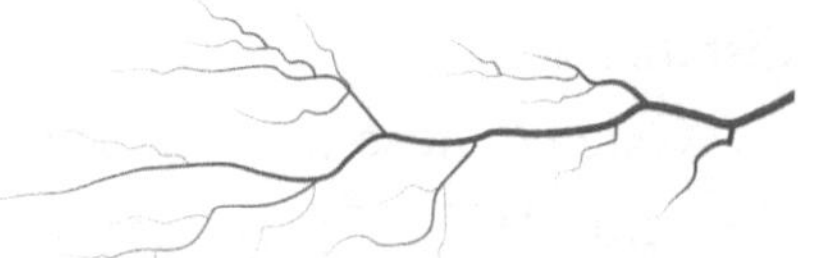

CHAPTER THIRTY-NINE

It was a moment she'd been waiting months for. Galena had about a minute's warning before Commander Nyx and Milek led Elom off the transport. He couldn't see her and she didn't speak, but somehow it felt like he *knew* she was there. Maybe it was his careless smile, the one he'd flashed when he'd first kissed her face with fire.

Galena wanted to spit on him. Pound him with her fists. Break him.

But she had an audience and a responsibility to her dominion.

Milek watched her closely, but she kept her chin high and gave nothing away.

Galena followed Elom's procession down a series of featureless hallways. All stationpoints were equipped with several small holding cells, and she wanted to see him locked away with her own eyes. It would be better once he was transferred to a high-security facility, but the blank white door sliding shut in his face was still satisfying.

"How are you?" Milek asked, as they returned to the main corridor. Commander Nyx walked a respectful distance ahead.

Galena chose to answer him honestly. "I hardly know," she said. "When I decided to visit you, I certainly didn't expect to witness Lieutenant Haan's return, let alone Elom's capture." She laughed a little. "I truly don't quite know what to do."

"It's been a long time since we've had good news." Milek smiled, but his joy was tempered with grief, and Galena knew why. Lieutenant Daakon had been his oldest friend. She could still clearly picture them as children, running to the end of the street to join in a snowball battle with their band of local boys. Throughout their lives, Milek and Daakon had stayed thick as brothers. When Milek had been selected for Military, Daakon had volunteered.

"What happens now?" Milek asked. "With Elom and Aris, there's a lot of news to share with the world."

"Indeed." Galena bit back a sigh at the thought of all the statements and questions in her future. "I'll need to head back to Panthea soon. But first I'll contact Ward Nekos, and we'll arrange for Elom's transfer to a more secure facility. Once I get back to the city, we'll announce Aris's resurrection. Maybe have the ceremony after all."

Milek nodded, his mind clearly elsewhere.

"Go find Lieutenant Haan. She deserves a warm welcome after the week she's had." His eyes brightened. Galena squeezed his hand. "And for Gods' sakes, get that girl a vid comm to her poor parents. They need to see the miracle for themselves."

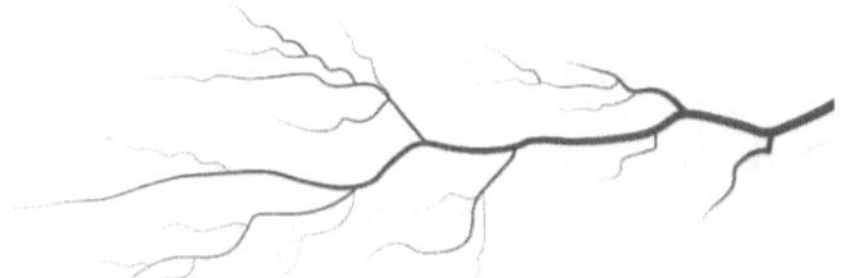

Chapter Forty

Calix's conduct hearing was held in Mekia two days later. An indoor training space had been transformed into a makeshift courtroom, with three tables arranged at one end and a row of chairs a few feet away.

Dysis slipped into the chair at the end of the row. Only two other chairs were occupied. The other character advocates. She didn't recognize either soldier. A few minutes later the commander of the base strode in, followed by Calix's direct supervisor, then Calix himself. He was unshackled but tired looking, his tan skin made haggard by the bright solar lights.

Each man sat behind one of the tables. When Calix saw her, his eyes widened.

The base commander, Commander Helos, began with a short statement. "We are here to hear testimony concerning Specialist Calix Pavlos. On the eighth day of this month, Specialist Pavlos vacated his post without authorization to attend the funeral of one—" the grizzled soldier consulted his notes "—Aris Haan."

Dysis wanted to shout, "That's *Lieutenant* Aris Haan," but she kept her lips pressed together.

Commander Helos continued. "Specialist Pavlos then proceeded to insinuate himself on a highly sensitive mission under false pretenses. We will first hear the full facts of the case, and then open the floor to advocates for and against Specialist Pavlos. As ranking officer at this stationpoint, I will recommend a course of action. Do you understand this process as it has been explained to you?" He turned to catch Calix's eye.

Calix nodded. "Yes, sir."

Commander Helos then nodded at Calix's superior officer, who proceeded to share a complete recounting of the desertion and mission to retrieve Aris.

Then the two other soldiers took turns describing Calix's honesty, integrity, and skill as a mender. There were no advocates against. One soldier, Calix's sectormate, tried to explain why Calix would have gone to such great lengths to attend the funeral. "Specialist Pavlos spoke on many occasions about the depth of his affection for Lieutenant Haan," the man said, looking a little sheepish. He spoke in a nervous, stilted manner that suggested he'd memorized his speech. "It is my belief that while Specialist Pavlos knew he was breaking the law, he was not doing it out of malicious or unlawful intent. His feelings for Lieutenant Haan overcame his good sense and he made a regrettable mistake."

When it was Dysis's turn to provide her testimony, she dropped a packet of silco onto Helos's table. She didn't bother sitting back down. "Here are some documents from

Major Vadim, on Spiro Stationpoint. It is his recommendation that Specialist Pavlos receive the most lenient punishment available for his crimes. As for me," she banged a hand on the table in front of Calix, making him jump. "I personally think you should give the guy an award of some kind. Sure, he left his stationpoint without authorization, but he did it to honor a fallen comrade and comfort that soldier's family. And, upon learning that this soldier, *Lieutenant* Aris Haan, might still be alive, he chose to join a dangerous mission to retrieve her. Specialist Pavlos's efforts were crucial to the mission's success and directly contributed to the saving of lives."

She described in her own words what it'd been like to watch Calix save Daakon, from killing the venomous snake to making a contraption to suck the poison out of the wound. As she spoke, she and Calix shared a look, bearing witness to Daakon's first brush with death.

She remembered what Calix had said about Daakon's strength, and it bolstered her as she explained why the Lieutenant couldn't offer advocacy himself.

When she was finished, Commander Helos took Major Vadim's statement and retreated briefly to review it with the other officer. They returned and asked Calix to stand.

Dysis was impressed at the serenity in his face. He knew he'd done something wrong and was prepared to accept the consequences. He neither begged nor argued, just waited patiently, hands relaxed at his sides.

At last, Commander Helos spoke. "The maximum penalty for Specialist Pavlos's crime is six months' confinement, an additional six months' probabtion, and forfeiture of pay. However, in light of Specialist Pavlos's unique circumstances and obvious commitment to the Atalantan Military, I will instead recommend to my superiors that he be allowed to remain on point and serve probation, rather than the full sentence. Specialist, you will lose all bonuses, award for service, and accrued leave." He consulted his notes. "In addition, Major Vadim has requested your presence at the ceremony to honor Lieutenant Haan tomorrow. I will grant you a two-day pass to attend. But you will not be eligible for any award or bonuses related to this mission. Do you understand these penalties as they've been relayed to you?"

Calix nodded, his expression never changing. Dysis rolled her eyes. He'd just gotten the equivalent of a slap on the wrist and he didn't even *smile*.

After the commander dismissed him, Calix shook the hands of his other advocates, thanking them for their kind words. Dysis had almost made it to the door when he stopped her.

"Thank you for coming, Dysis."

Shrugging, she said, "It was an order. Aris and Major Vadim are already in Ruslana preparing for the ceremony. They would have come if they could."

"Still." He studied her with an unreadable expression. "I appreciate it."

"Well, I, uh . . . appreciate what you did for Daakon," she said grudgingly.

She could have told him she'd been wrong about him. That he'd earned her respect. But she turned on her heel and left the room instead.

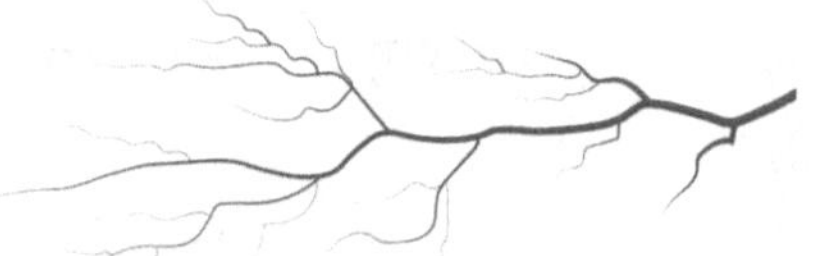

CHAPTER FORTY-ONE

ARIS HAD SEEN THE RUSLANAN CAPITOL BUILDING on news vids plenty of times—the tall arching windows, the swirls of mosaic flooring, the colorful dresses of foreign dignitaries. But somehow, standing there in the center of all the finery, it was all so much bigger—so much *more*—than she expected. She and Milek were hidden in an antechamber, but its frosted glass wall had etchings she could peek through. Her eyes scoured the crowd for her parents. She'd spoken to them several times over comms in the last few days, but this would be the first time she'd see them in person.

Aris turned to Milek, who looked dashing in his trim dress uniform. "Do I look okay?"

She'd never cared much about clothes or hair or any of that—not like her old friends from home, who could spend hours debating the latest fashions. But then, she'd never been the honored guest at a ceremony in a foreign capital either. Her hands darted nervously to her close-cropped hair.

Milek put a warm hand on her exposed shoulder. "You look beautiful." His gaze traveled from her eyes, heavy with sparkling makeup, to her sweeping off-the-shoulder emerald gown. "Perfect."

"I feel silly," she said.

Milek's mouth quirked in a little grin. "Doesn't seem real, does it? After months in the field, everything is so . . ."

"Bright?" she offered. His admission calmed her racing heart. It was a comfort knowing he wasn't feeling entirely at ease either.

"I was going to say clean."

Aris laughed.

"Aris?" The tentative voice drifted from the doorway. She turned, and her smile widened.

"Mother?" Aris stared in awe. Krissa had traded her worn apron for a glittering fuchsia gown, her soft auburn curls twisted into an elaborate updo. Beside her, Gus, Aris's father, shifted awkwardly from foot to foot in a stylish tunic and flowing pants.

"Oh *dear*." Krissa swept forward and folded Aris into a warm, solid, *real* hug. "Oh Gods." Her body began to shake with silent sobs.

"I know, Mother. I know." Aris breathed in Krissa's scent. Even here, she still smelled of basilis and browned butter, as if she'd just finished making dinner. Aris clung to her.

A hand squeezed her shoulder. She looked up to her father gazing down at her. He'd aged since she'd seen him last. His pale hair was thinner, and the weathered grooves of his face had deepened. But the quiet joy of his smile was unmistakable. Aris threw her arms around him.

"I'm so glad you're here," Aris said at last, stepping back. She drank them in, appreciated their familiar faces, and loved them all the more. The last few weeks had taught her to value every single moment with the people she loved.

"How I'll enjoy seeing *our* daughter being honored by the Ward of Ruslana!" Krissa exclaimed, squeezing Aris's shoulders. The affectionate gesture also served as a not-so-subtle reminder to stand up straight.

For once, Aris found it more endearing than annoying. Amazing how distance and almost-death softened her toward her parents. Beside her, Milek cleared his throat.

"Oh!" Aris stepped back to include Milek in their little circle. "Major Vadim, you remember my parents from the . . . ah . . . funeral?"

Milek bowed to her father, who returned the gesture. "It's a pleasure to see you under better circumstances." He turned back to her. "Lieutenant, the ceremony will be starting soon. May I escort you to your seat?"

Aris nodded. She gave her parents each another quick hug. "I'll see you afterward. Come find me."

They nodded with pride and relief and wistfulness. Something in their eyes told her they were at least *trying* to understand this new life of hers and why it was so important.

Milek took her arm and led her through the milling crowd. He walked with his back straight and his movements precise, befitting an officer escorting an honored guest, but she knew he held her tighter than was strictly necessary. Being so close to him here, after their short but agonizing separation, made her ache to touch him even more. Her fingers drifted back and forth against the smooth fabric of his jacket, tracing small circles.

Despite the opulence around them, the war raged just as violently as ever beyond these walls. But Aris couldn't connect to that horror right now. It was always there, dogging her, along with the memory of Daakon's shrouded body. But here, in this beautiful room filled with clinking glasses, swishing dresses, and tinkling music, her brain took a momentary holiday. Her eyes drank in the colors, so cheerful. The women in swirling gowns, the smiles, the voices raised in laughter, not in pain. It was okay that people were having fun, enjoying this moment. For once, there were things to celebrate. It was okay that Aris found herself happy. Milek pulled her just the slightest bit closer to him. She glanced up and caught his quick, private smile.

They stepped onto the raised dais at the end of the room, where two rows of chairs sat to one side of the podium. Several of the chairs were already filled: Dysis, her brother Jax, Otto, Pallas, Mann, Baksen, even Calix, who'd been allowed to attend the ceremony, though he wouldn't receive any formal award for his part in recent events.

Milek led Aris to a seat in the first row between Pallas and Dysis. He took the seat directly behind her. Dysis leaned into her shoulder for a split second, and the two girls shared a smile.

Aris's best friend looked positively regal in her silver-green dress. She'd applied little makeup, except to highlight the key-shaped Tech brand on her temple with silver glitter.

On Aris's other side, Pallas whispered, "Can't believe I'm here. And in a dress!"

At that moment, the lights dimmed, darkness pressing in from outside the tall windows. Voices quieted, bodies shifted to face the dais. By the time Ward Vadim and Ward Nekos took the stage, the room was silent. Ward Vadim approached the podium.

"Good evening," she said. "Thank you for joining me as we honor Lieutenant Haan and the rest of her brave team for their part in my rescue and in the apprehension of my abductor."

Ward Vadim raised a hand, the look on her damaged face positively triumphant. It made Aris raise her own chin with pride. "Today marks an enormous victory for those who oppose the unsanctioned and, frankly, evil leadership of Ward Balias."

The audience burst into applause.

"Let's not forget," Ward Vadim continued. "This blow would not have been possible without the brave men *and* women of our Military. While our two dominions have been squabbling over whether women should be allowed to stand in line beside their brothers, three of our female soldiers played instrumental roles in Elom's capture."

Ward Nekos stepped up beside her at the podium. Together, a united front.

"Today we honor the brave soldiers involved in my rescue," Ward Vadim said, "as well as in Elom's capture. But these triumphs did not come without a price. Four soldiers lost their lives during these missions. Lieutenants Wolfe and Daakon, of Ruslana, as well as Lieutenant Talon and Specialist Galec, of Atalanta. They made the final sacrifice to uphold the values and laws of our great dominions. Please join me in a moment of silence to honor their contributions and their memories."

As silence stretched throughout the room, Aris bent her head in remembrance. Beside her, without a sound, Dysis cried.

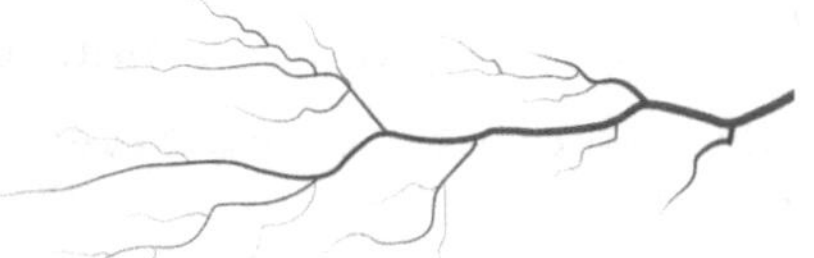

CHAPTER FORTY-TWO

THE MUSIC MOVED ALONG ARIS'S SKIN, SINUOUS AS ocean currents drawing her out to sea. The ceremony attendees pressed close in the center of the room, swaying and spinning in a dizzying procession of color as dresses caught the light.

The musicians broke into a new song, fast and sensual. All around Aris, couples were pairing off, twisting closer and closer to each other in the insulating light. In the center of the floor, she saw a streak of green as Pallas twirled by in Baksen's arms.

Dysis leaned closer to her. "Do you think we should—"

Before she could finish her thought, Calix appeared out of the crowd. His face was still splotchy with bruises, but his leg didn't seem to bother him anymore.

"May I?" he murmured. Not to Aris, but to Dysis. Without waiting for an answer, he took her hand. They spun deep into the crowd, their bodies pressed against each other, Dysis tall and sparkling, Calix a steady presence in his uniform.

Aris watched, open mouthed. *Didn't expect that.* From the flash of wide eyes she saw as Dysis spun away, her friend hadn't either.

"I guess that leaves us?" Jax said, offering his hand and a friendly smile.

Aris's stomach jolted. She hadn't noticed him approach. When she turned to smile at him, it sent another shock through her. Every time she looked at Jax, she saw Dysis. She couldn't help it. Disguised as a man, Dysis had looked almost exactly like her brother.

"Uh, sure." Aris took Jax's hand. The music was her favorite kind: throbbing and rich, enticing. It reminded her of The Toad, the bar back home in Lux.

Jax was a handsome man with mischievous eyes, hard muscles, and a full-lipped smile that turned most girls to mush in his hands. Aris was less accommodating. It took all her strength not to glance around the room for Milek. But they'd agreed it was best to keep their distance in public.

"He's standing just at the edge of the dancers." Jax swayed his hips, drawing her with him into a tight turn. He didn't lose the beat or falter, but his gaze was knowing.

"Excuse me? I don't . . . I mean—" Aris blustered.

"I'm a spy, Aris." Jax grinned. "Although my training isn't entirely necessary in your case."

Warmth flooded Aris's cheeks. "I don't know what you're talking about."

"Of course you do." He spun her, tracing his hand along her waist as she twisted and turned back to him. "And so does Major Vadim. Incoming."

A hand touched her arm. "Lieutenant Haan, I need to speak with you," Milek said. "It's urgent."

Every part of her wanted to reach for him, fall into him. She focused on his words. The beat of the music still pounded in her chest, but she fought its hold on her. "Of course, sir," she said, careful to keep her voice blank and casual, as always.

Jax dropped his hand from her waist. "Anything I can help with, sir?"

"Thank you, no, Lieutenant Latza. This is a highly sensitive matter, for which Lieutenant Haan's expertise is invaluable. Please excuse us." Without removing his hand from her arm, Milek drew her away from Jax.

It wasn't until they reached the edge of the dancers that Aris picked up on the true urgency in Milek's movements. His hand on her arm was clenched so tight it was almost painful, and he walked quickly, without his usual grace. *Something is terribly wrong.*

Automatically, her eyes swept the gathering, looking for her parents. *No. They already went to bed.* She'd seen them off herself less than an hour ago. And they were staying in a room here in the capitol. Lots of security. They were safe.

"What's going on?" she asked quietly, as they wove through the thinning crowd of revelers. "Is your mother alright?"

The main hall was flanked by two sprawling wings. The western wing held offices and smaller meeting rooms for official dominion business; the eastern one held rows of bedrooms for traveling dignitaries, security, and honored guests. Milek slowed as he approached the tall doorway that led to the eastern wing. A giant man with two solaguns strapped to his waist waited with a scanner.

"Good evening, sir," the guard said, nodding placidly to them.

Milek placed his hand on the scanner, and with a high-pitched beep it identified him as an overnight guest. Next it was Aris's turn. Her heart pounded. What was going on? Had something happened back in Spiro?

When a second beep sounded, the two frosted glass doors slid apart in silence.

"Please, Milek," she whispered as they passed by the guard into the long, echoing hallway, their shoes clicking loudly on the marble. "What's so urgent?"

He turned and backed her up against the wall, his hands snaking around her waist before the door had finished sliding close. "This. You," he answered, and kissed her in that soft, insistent way she loved.

Even as her hands found their way to the back of his neck, drawing him closer, her eyes flashed to the doorway. The frosted glass wasn't entirely opaque. "What if someone sees?"

"Let them." He kissed her harder. He tasted of pineapple and dark, red wine. Her fingers dug into the skin at the base of his skull and a soft moan escaped her lips.

Not for the first time today, she wished she was wearing her uniform. If she was, she could slide her leg up his, he could pick her up so she straddled him, he could press her harder against the wall. But her dress's full skirt caught between them.

Still, Milek's heat filled her. His lips singed hers. He made her ache.

A voice. "Good evening, sir." It was the guard on the other side of the door speaking to another guest.

Milek pulled away, grinning. "Come on."

By the time the door slid open, they were running hand in hand down the hall.

Aris was slowed by the heavy skirts and high heels, but she could still run fast enough to feel a cool breeze against her cheeks. They skidded around a corner, giggling like children. Milek punched the panel for the lift, and once inside they kissed breathlessly, still laughing, until they reached their floor.

"Come with me," Milek murmured, drawing her past her own door.

Aris's heart danced a crazy rhythm. They hadn't found a single moment to be alone since she'd returned from Safara. But here they were, alone in this long, dim, richly carpeted hallway. With their own rooms. With privacy. *Oh Gods.*

Outside Milek's door, he paused before opening it and took a deep breath. Like he was steadying himself. Aris looked at him curiously. He swept his passcard over the panel, and the glossy faux-wood door slid into the wall.

"Aris." The way he said her name raised goosebumps along her arms. He stepped over the threshold first and turned to her, reaching for her hands, drawing her into the room.

It was dim, flickering. Lit by candlelight. Aris's breath caught. On every flat surface, candles burned. The light bent and moved, a golden dance against the walls. Soft, sinuous shadows flowed across the ivory bed.

And there, on a small table just beside the bed, clean and white, with a faceted ice-blue crystal embedded in it . . .

A Promise candle, unlit.

Aris's eyes flew to Milek's face. "Is that . . . I mean . . ." The words wouldn't come.

He led her to the table, taking a place across from her, the candle and its two smaller, lit brothers between them. For the first time, maybe ever, Aris noticed nervousness in the crease between Milek's brows, the restless way he rubbed his palms back and forth against each other and cracked his knuckles. Inside, her own nerves stretched taut as a fishing line.

"I . . . I had this all planned out before you were shot down." He cleared his throat, his usual gruffness fading. "You don't know how happy I am to have you here. To have a second chance." Another pause, a little smile. "I have a speech." Aris couldn't breathe.

"Ever since that day in the cave, when your veil broke and I discovered who you really were, my life has been completely different. It was like a door opened. You were so beautiful, with your real face and your real body right there next to me. I couldn't believe how brave you were. And now, after these past few months together, I am even more in awe. You give *me* strength, a support I never realized I needed." He grinned, looking oddly boyish despite his scar. "I don't know if you've noticed, but I'm a *little* happier now than when we first met."

Aris gave him a sardonic look, though inside she was glowing brighter than a million candles. "When we first met, your mother had been kidnapped. You had plenty to be unhappy about."

"True. But it's more than that and you know it." He continued, more quickly. "I'm happy with what we have.

But I . . . well, I'm scared that we won't be able to *have* it anymore if we don't act now. Military will establish rules against relationships like ours eventually. Maybe soon. And I don't want us to have to choose between being who we are and being together."

As she stared into Milek's eyes, Aris felt hot and cold at once. So much they hadn't said and there it all was, plain as day.

He reached for her hands. "I know this is fast and you may not be ready. But I love you, and I don't want you to have to choose between being a flyer and being with me."

Something shifted inside her, deep in her soul where her greatest insecurities and strengths lived side by side.

I don't want you to have to choose.

No one had ever wanted her to be *everything* that she was, everything she could be.

But *could* she really be everything?

"How would it work back on point?" She stared at their joined hands. It felt so good to touch him, to know they had the whole night together, no interruptions. "This . . . you're talking about an official agreement. How would we keep that a secret?"

He squeezed her fingers tighter. "We wouldn't. We would be open about our relationship. No more sneaking around. No more pretending distance. We could even share a room, if you wanted."

A happy shiver ran through her at the thought. Every night, coming back to her bunk with him waiting . . . being able to touch, to lie in bed together, while they talked about the day. . . .

"And Military will allow it?" She knew he was hoping for

an answer, that her questions probably made him impatient, but she couldn't move forward without understanding what she was gaining—and what she might be giving up. The days of her blind need for love over everything else were long gone.

"Right now there are no rules in place to forbid it. We're officers. . . . If we were Promised to civilians we'd be allowed to live with them near the stationpoint, if we chose."

"Still. You said you want to do this now in case the rules change. Won't they just change for us later?"

"The sector doesn't work like that. Rules are made for future cases only; if we have an agreement before the rule is in place, they can't enforce it for us, or for any soldiers who do the same."

"And . . . and what about our unit? How will they react?" The racing heart, the breathlessness . . . it was all fading as reality set in. Aris gently disengaged her hands from Milek's.

He rocked back on his heels and stuffed his hands into his pockets. "Aris, none of this was meant to make you uncomfortable or . . . or put upon. If you're not ready, it's okay. You can just say—"

"No!" Aris hurried around the table so she could be closer to him. "It's not that. I just . . . I want to talk about it first. I want to know what this really means for us, you know? I'm sorry. It's not very romantic."

He smiled down at her. "Talking about our future? It blighting *is*." He drew her to him, pulling until they both fell back on the bed. Milek stuffed a pillow underneath his head, and Aris cuddled close on her side, using his chest for her pillow. Once they were comfortable, wrapped in each other's arms and her voluminous skirts, Milek said, "Alright, let's talk this through. How it'll work, what we both want. Then you can decide. Okay?"

Aris nodded, rubbing her cheek against his fancy jacket. It felt good to have this conversation so close to him, with so much of their bodies touching. In her silky dress and thick makeup, in this enormous bed, she felt like some kind of ancient queen, lying with her handsome, battle-scarred paramour. For a moment, Aris lost track of all of her important questions.

"So, you want to know how it'll be on point, if we show up Promised?" Milek asked, reeling her back in.

"Your mother's wonderful speech notwithstanding, they already give me so much grief for being a woman. If I'm Promised to you, won't that make things worse?"

Milek smoothed his hand over her hair and along her jaw. "Honestly? Maybe at first. Then again, being open about our relationship means anyone who disrespects you is disrespecting *me*, too. That could make things easier for you."

She leaned up to look him in the eye. "I don't want to be some fragile sparrow protected under your wing. I want to prove myself worthy of respect on my own merits."

"That's the thing. You do already. I mean, look at everything you've accomplished. Aris, you have *earned* your place," he replied earnestly. "The men on point are just stuck on their own prejudices. I'm not asking you to Promise to protect you or elevate your standing or something. All I'm saying is that it might *not* be worse . . . it *could* be better, with us presenting a unified front."

She relaxed back onto his chest, smiling a little. "Well,

okay then. As long as this isn't some misguided 'protect the girl' scheme."

He growled playfully and rolled her onto her back, shifting his weight onto her. "I wouldn't dare. You never struck me as the damsel in distress type, anyway."

Aris couldn't help but laugh. "Oh, I was. Believe me. But I'm not any longer and you better not forget it." She stretched up to him, using her hands to draw him down for a kiss. His weight and her skirts pinned her legs against the bed, even when she arched against him. He deepened the kiss. Right now, in this unfamiliar place, in this strange, beautiful dress, she did feel a little like a damsel, fragile and feminine. But definitely not in distress.

After a few breathless moments, she pulled away from the kiss. "What will you do if I disobey orders? The guys'll expect you to give me special treatment."

"Special treatment like this?" His lips descended on hers again, stealing her breath.

She fought the warmth in her belly and pushed at his chest. "I don't think *that* would be the best strategy."

Milek let the amusement slip from his face, suddenly serious. His eyes became dark pools in the low light. "I haven't let this relationship affect my ability to lead my soldiers into combat, and I won't in the future either, no matter what you decide. My responsibility is to my unit, above all, and if that means disciplining you, I will. As I will discipline any other soldier. I can't . . . I won't pretend otherwise. Whether we're Promised or not, we're still soldiers first and foremost. I hope you can understand that."

She snaked her arms around him and drew him into a

demanding kiss. He responded in kind, sowing heat everywhere he touched.

"That was exactly the right answer, Milek," she murmured against his mouth. "I haven't come this far"—her words slipped out around his lips as he kept kissing her—"to let you . . . or anyone . . . hold me back."

For a while they let their mouths speak without words. Aris's dress twisted against her legs, holding them still in a silky, thrilling cage, as Milek traced her throat, her collarbone, her exposed shoulders with his lips and hands, igniting fireferns beneath her skin with every touch. At some point, she found her dress hitched up around her thighs. Her legs free, she slid them against his, up across his hips, as he pressed his full weight into her. Their breath came faster.

"Aris?" Milek's lips brushed the sensitive skin just above the low neckline of her dress.

"Hmm?" Her attention was caught on the sensations unfolding deep within her. Her limbs felt weighted, heavy with desire.

"Does this mean you want to?"

She arched into him, more aware of his body than she'd ever been before. Her hands slid up his chest, seeking the buttons of his jacket. "*Yes . . . yes . . .*" she breathed. It didn't matter if he was asking her to Promise, or asking her if she wanted to make love. To both questions, her answer was *yes*.

She popped the last button and shoved his jacket off his shoulders. With a hurried twist, he extricated his arms and threw it on the floor, narrowly missing the tables of candles. Urgency filled the space between them. Aris ran her hands down his muscled arms, loving their strength, as he dispensed with the rest of his uniform. His hands found her thighs, sliding up the smooth skin, taking the silky dress with them. Everywhere he touched her, blood pulsed under her skin, contrasting with the cool air that followed his fingers. He didn't remove her dress, just pushed it out of the way, letting its silky fabric become part of the seduction, whispering against all the shivering skin between them.

Weeks of stolen moments cut short, embraces interrupted, the forced separation. . . . They had longing packed tight into every muscle, every pore. Their want spilled into impatience: frantic, breathless need. And then they were together, as close as two people can ever be. It was everything Aris had hoped for: the slaking of a thirst she couldn't name, and the beginning of a journey she was eager to take.

She lay against Milek afterward, sleepy and sated, their skin sticking together as if glued. As if nothing could ever tear them apart.

At some point, before they made love again, before they slept curled against each other, they lit the Promise candle and said the formal words, binding them to each other in a two-year trial partnership that would help them decide whether to make the ultimate, irrevocable decision to marry.

Milek gave her a ring. "I know it's not the latest style, but it's been in my family for generations." It was made of burnished gold, with a large oval stone in the center. "It reminded me of you. See?" He rubbed a finger over the stone's luminescent blue surface. "It looks like the sky."

Aris's heart fluttered, as if she were soaring far overhead, full of sunlight. Everything felt good and right. And the war felt very, very far away.

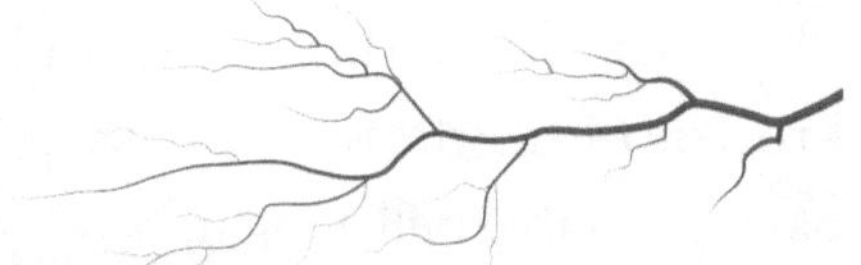

CHAPTER FORTY-THREE

AFTER THEIR OFFICIAL DUTIES WERE COMPLETE, Galena and Pyralis removed themselves to Galena's room for a few moments of quiet.

Each suite was fitted with a small washroom, separate office area, and expansive living space, complete with several comfortable chairs and an oversized bed. The first thing Galena did as she entered was retract the shade completely from the window, letting in the sparkling evening lights of Sibetza.

"You spoke beautifully," Pyralis said as he sank into one of the chairs.

Galena leaned against the cool glass and regarded him. "It's the first time in months that I've given a hopeful speech and actually meant it."

"I know what you mean." Maybe it was the clear emerald tones of his tunic, but he looked less tired tonight. Fewer shadows lurking behind his eyes. "Lieutenant Haan has returned to us, and Elom is locked in Atalanta's highest security prison, awaiting what is sure to be a prolonged and painful interrogation. Today is a good day."

Galena smoothed her hands over the heavy crimson brocade of her dress as her face relaxed into a smile. "I'm still having trouble believing it."

Pyralis smiled back at her. "I am, as well."

She wanted to ask him about his visit to Bett. He had told her only that he'd gone and Bett hadn't given any useful information, but she could tell there was more to it. What had the woman said? And how could Galena comfort him?

As she studied him, an unreadable expression stole over his features. Slowly, he stood and approached her, as he would a skittish dog. "You look lovely tonight." He took her hands, his skin sliding against her sensitive fingertips. Then, when she didn't draw away, he leaned close.

All thoughts of Bett flew from her mind.

She held her breath as his lips touched hers. And, with a great sense of inevitability, she let herself melt into his embrace.

Someone knocked quietly on the door. They sprang apart.

"Did you order food?" Pyralis asked.

Galena shook her head. He left her side to open the door.

Lieutenant Jax Latza stood in the hallway. At Pyralis's nod, he strode into the room. His short dark hair stuck up in tufts, as if he'd been running his hands through it. "I'm sorry to disturb you during the festivities," he began, seemingly unconcerned to have found them both in Galena's bedroom.

"We have a serious problem," Latza continued, without waiting for a response. "After speaking with the Safaran refugees, I had my suspicions, but I've just received unequivocal confirmation." He held up a red, high-security digitablet.

"Of what? What's happened?" Pyralis asked.

"I finally figured out where Ward Balias has been diverting resources to." Galena did *not* like the expression in Lieutenant Latza's eyes. "He's building a bomb."

Pyralis looked skeptical. "A bomb? Worse than the firebombs they already use?"

"This is much, much worse." The furrows in Lieutenant Latza's brow deepened. "In recent weeks a strange glow has lit the night skies near Pakan. The children of the village called it 'the flaming scorpion'."

Galena glanced at Pyralis; his confusion matched her own, and yet a growing sense of horror slowly filled her gut.

"I've just received confirmation that those lights mark a testing site for a weapon that kills instantly, over a vast area. If Balias releases it on Atalanta, the destruction will be worse than anything this world has ever seen."

Galena could not find the words to reply.

Pyralis asked a few more questions, his voice an ominous rumble. Then he thanked Lieutenant Latza and released him back into the hall. The spy had a long night ahead of him, gathering more information.

Galena and Pyralis sat in the two softly padded chairs and stared at each other. All the hopefulness and joy of the evening had slithered from the room on Latza's heels.

At last, when she'd given herself some time to process, Galena stood. They'd have to call in their top Military commanders. Tech experts. Spies. They'd have to sit down with Lieutenant Latza again, all the people of Pakan, get as much information as they possibly could.

"We have to stop him," she said aloud. "Balias cannot be allowed to destroy Atalanta."

Pyralis bent his head over his clasped hands, almost as if he were praying. "If this bomb is as lethal as Lieutenant Latza thinks," he said, "Ward Balias could destroy the whole world."

ACKNOWLEDGMENTS

This series has been a true labor of love, spanning ten-plus years now. From submitting to publishers, to self-publishing, to selling it to a digital-first imprint, to going out of print, to bringing it back to the world with Snowy Wings Publishing, it has been a JOURNEY. There have been countless people at all the different stages of this book's life who have helped, encouraged, supported, and inspired me.

I want to thank Regina Wamba for the beautiful cover, Intisar Khanani for teaching me the Kickstarter ropes and being a sweet and supportive friend, Victoria Alessandri for the incredible character art, Virginia McClain for the graphics, and Jessica Khoury for the incredible map and stormy endpapers. Pam Gruber, my agent, for helping me get the rights to this series back. And all of my incredible Kickstarter backers, who made the special edition possible.

But, of course, this book had a life before. So I'm going to share my previous acknowledgements as well, because we would never have gotten to this point without the following people:

I'm here to tell you that writing the second book in a series is HARD. I've heard author friends say it before, but I didn't quite understand until I sat down to write *Storm Fall*.

Thankfully, I had a ton of support, encouragement, and fabulous feedback to get me through.

Thank you to Lanie Davis and Eliza Swift, who read this book over and over from the very first draft to the last. Who offered incredible insight and feedback, sent me awesome pep talks, and kept their faith in me and my writing throughout the process. You guys are amazing.

Thanks to all the folks at Alloy, especially Les Morgenstein, Josh Bank, Sara Shandler, Heather David, Romy Golan, Natalie Sousa, and Elaine Damasco, and Caroline Carr and Philip Patrick at Amazon, for giving this series such incredible support.

As a work-from-home mom, I am only as productive as my child's naps are long. Special thanks to Meema, PopPop, Nana, Grandpa, BiJo, Grana, Daddy, and Adriana for doing such a good job distracting Ollie while I snuck in a little more work time. And a big fat extra thank you to my family for always believing in me.

To Aimee L. Salter, Rachel L. Hamm, Jax Abbey, J.D. Robinson, and Paige Elizabeth Nguyen: You guys have kept me sane and laughing over the past few months, and I couldn't be more grateful. Here's to new friendships becoming lifelong ones (and continued bonding over *Jane the Virgin*, *Austenland*, and hot fictional boys).

And to the rest of my wonderful writing community—Shari Arnold, Jennifer Walkup, Susanne Winnacker, Ali Cross, Autumn Kalquist, Heather Hildenbrand, Morgan Michael, the Critters, S3G, Indelibles, YA Binders, and so many more—you are inspiring. Thank you so much for letting me share this lovely playground with you.

Jody Escaravage, you're awesome and I value your

friendship so much I may someday commission a (tasteful, of course) painting of us to hang above my mantel.

To all of my readers, your response to *Rebel Wing* has been incredible. I wish I could give each and every one of you a huge smooshy hug, but since I can't, I will do the only thing I can: I'll say thank you from the bottom of my heart, and I will keep on writing books for you.

Ollie, yesterday at lunch you reached your small arms out to me and demanded a hug. When I obliged, you said, "I love you, Mommy," for the very first time without prompting. In that instant, all of the stress of the past few months disappeared. Thank you, my sweet boy. You are magic.

Andy, the list of reasons I love you keeps getting longer and longer, but one thing always stays at the top: how supportive and encouraging you are of my writing career. Thank you for making me feel lucky and loved every single day.

And last but not least, thank you so much to all of the brave women and men who are serving or have served in the Armed Forces. We owe so much to you.

ABOUT THE AUTHOR

Tracy Banghart is the author of many young adult books, including the Grace and Fury series, *A Season of Sinister Dreams*, and *Perfect Girl*. She also writes picture books, including *Love Like Chocolate*. She has a BA in English from Davidson College and an MA in Publishing from Oxford Brookes University. She is an enthusiastic journal writer, traveler, Girl Scout leader, Army wife, stained-glass artist, and mom to two kiddos and three pets. Follow @tracythewriter on Instagram or visit her at www.tracybanghart.com.

www.ingramcontent.com/pod-product-compliance
Lightning Source LLC
Chambersburg PA
CBHW061651190726
48289CB00006B/1824